U0063259

PREFACE

A Brand-New Guidebook for History

During the recent revival of interest in the local history of Taiwan, research specialists and interested laymen alike faced recurring problems while attempting to capture facets of early Taiwan : the anecdotes left by past personalities were so numerous that it was difficult to portray the entire picture from existent literature and documents alone. In the past, even the senior historian Lien Ya-tung was perplexed.

In the preface of Lien's monumental work, the 《General History of Taiwan》, the author laments that historical data on Taiwan was fragmented and scattered, making the collection of material of formidable task; a plethora of accounts and versions contributed to the suspense. We fully empathize with the difficulty and confusion encountered, even when a learned scholar embarks on such an undertaking.

Mr. Dean T. Chou, the founder of the Rainbow Sign Publishing Co.,has profound insights about the literary and historical materials on Taiwan. He is also very enthusiastic in searching for aspects of cultural significance in the modern history of Taiwan. Over the past decade, Chou has engaged at great expense in the collection of authentic pictures of Taiwan both at home and abroad, especially the collection of images and records during the 50 years of occupation by Japan when Taiwan was ceded under the Treaty of Shimonoseki in 1895. This rich compendium of rare historical data is ultimately due to Chou's unswerving perseverance and dedication in the quest to document Taiwan's past. We are pleased and congratulate Chou for his significant contribution.

The publication of this book was based on a new and unconventional concept that first of all abandons earlier conservative presentations in which the content of writing was largely devoid of meaningful relevance to illustrations. Much attention has been devoted in the planning of the themes, while passages are imbued with a lucid and lively rhythm. Historical highlights and items of related interest are interlaced accurately in an organization resembling the veins and arteries of the circulatory system. With stunning visual quality achieved through art editing, the overall image design retains a elegant style befitting illustrated historical compilations. The planning of the pubilcation is certainly worthy of utmost admiration.

The content of this book series covers a wide range of fields, including historical information dealing with the society, economy and culture of Taiwan during Japanese occupation. The complementary use of words and pictures creates a sense of realism that heightens the interest of readers and leaves a rewarding impression.

This is a book to be cherished and collected because it is also an indispensable reference work. From the prespective of journalism, yesterday's news becomes today's history. In contrast, this narrative of historical events dating back a century can be viewed as news that was never before disclosed in any contemporary publication. I am honored to write the preface to 《A Collection of the Visual History of Taiwan》 on the occasion of its publication.

Gertrude Lu

President
Taiwan Shin Sheng Daily News

代　序

1995 年 6 月立虹出版社負責人周鼎先生及其同事們來到我畫室，談及周先生所收藏的一些日治時代的手繪明信片，當時，他們將資料也帶來了，我看過之後，覺得這些明信片相當珍貴，想不到間隔五、六十年，居然還能找到這麼這麼豐盛的收藏，令我十分驚訝，當時心想，像這一批完整的資料可以說是可遇不可求，除了有心搜集之外，還得靠機緣配合。

這些卡片反映出當時中上流社會的生活片斷，那時的生活較有人情味和文人氣息，不像現在有事就打電話或者傳真，只要求把意思傳達給對方就算達到目的了。對於現在生活很少動筆寫信，即使談戀愛時也不像以前的人得藉由書信來傳達情意的現代人，透過這些信件反而能夠流露內心的感情，可謂信中有深情綿綿的文字，至於賀年卡也常是手製的，若是擅於繪畫者，有時也會提筆畫點簡單的揷圖，有的是水墨，有的用水彩甚至其他各種技法，更能藉此傳達深厚的友誼。

例如，大文學家夏目漱石的作品「三四郎」裡就有一段提及在美禰子寄給三四郎的明信片上畫了兩隻小綿羊和惡魔的情節，由此可見手繪明信片在當時的上流社會是頗爲盛行的事，如同早年洪瑞麟老師在年終寄給我賀年卡時，也常以新一年的生肖做爲題裁畫水墨的揷畫。當我接到這些賀年卡時，更容易體會到洪老師眞切的心意。

此次，立虹出版社周社長在多方搜購之下，能收藏到百餘張此類的作品，彌爲珍貴。其中亦有不少出於名家手筆的作品：例如木下靜

PREFACE

At the beginning of 1995, Mr. Dean T. Chou, President of the Rainbow Sign Publishing Company, came to my studio along with his colleagues. We talked about some hand- painted postcards from the Japanese Occupation Period in Mr. Chou's collection, which they brought with them. After I looked at these postcards, I felt that they were quite precious. I was surprised that after an interval of some 50 to 60 years, there could be such a rich collection. In my opinion, such a complete set of materials was to be acquired almost only by chance. Beside collecting them with intent, luck is also very important.

These postcards are remnants of the lives of the middle- and upper-classes societies during that period. Life back then was, so to speak, warmer and more refined. Nowadays, whenever we need to contact others, we can just telephone or fax them, and as long as the message is passed onto the other party, the objective has been achieved. We rarely write letters now. Even when we fall in love, we do not write love letters like people in the past used to. Inner feelings, however, could be expressed more clearly through these letters. We could say the words in these letters carry much more affection with them. Even New Year greeting cards were often hand-made. Simple illustrations were often added by those adept at painting. Some with ink and wash, some with watercolor, and still others with other kinds of techniques, these paintings expressed profound friendships more explicitly.

For instance, in the novel Samshiro by the great literary writer Matsume Soseki, one paragraph mentions that two lambs and a devil were drawn on a postcard mailed to Mineko. From this, we can learn that hand-painted postcards were quite fashionable in upper-class society. On the postcards that prof. Rai Lin Hong, sent me at the end of the year, he often painted some illustrations using as a topic the animal sign used to symbolize that year. When I received these greeting cards, I could more easily understand Mr. Hong's genuine feelings.

At this time, it is all the more precious that the Rainbow Sign Publishing Company procured from many different sources over one hundred such works, a number of which were created by famous painters. For instance, Kinoshita Seqai was a renown artist during 1895-1945. In addition, some were put together using Ukiyoe

代　序

涯便是日治時代的名畫家，此外還有一些以浮世繪或印刷品剪貼的，也能表達出製作者的誠意；更有不少能提供給民俗學家參考的資料。

由此可見，這些明信片是以做爲研究當時的民俗、社會生活及人際關係的一種難得的資料，我大致了解之後，本來周社長打算請我寫上解說予以出版，但礙於我自己忙於作畫、教書，生活已十分忙碌，湊不出時間，因此考慮半天才極力推薦陳淑華來從事此工作。

陳淑華於師大畢業後至巴黎留學五年餘，獲得西洋藝術史的博士學位及繪畫修護的專業知識。學習期間接受了考古、文獻整理及美術史分析訓練，再加上她在繪畫材料方面的深入了解，對於從事這些明信片的分析工作應頗爲適合，因此極力推薦，幸而能勝任完成此項艱難的工作。

當陳淑華接下此項工作之後，日文的部分就求教於余女士，對她在文字內容的了解上幫助頗大。加上任教於東吳大學的中日文化史教授高橋正己先生的鼎力相助，方能在半年的努力之下完成解說的工作。

際此付梓之前，覺得立虹出版社能在現今注重功利的社會中，不計成本，出版這本有學術性、且較爲冷門的資料，實爲難得，令我殊感欽佩，僅此寥寥數語以祝福此書的出版，不僅因爲它讓我們回憶起昔日的生活，對於想要了解日治時代的另一個生活層面來說，更是相當難得的資料。

國立台灣師範大學美術系　教授

陳景容

or printed materials and also show the maker's sincerity. There are also some data that folklorists can use for reference.

From this, we know that these postcards can provide invaluable data for research on the folk customs, social life and interpersonal relationships back then. After familiarizing me with the postcards, Mr. Chou was originally going to ask me to annotate and then publish them. However, as I was occupied by painting and teaching and already have a very busy life, I could set aside no time for this work. After careful consideration, I highly recommended Ms. Shu-hua Chen to undertake this work.

After her graduation from National Taiwan Normal University, Ms. Chen furthered her studies in Paris for another five years. There she earned a Ph. D. in Western art history and also acquired professional knowledge in painting maintenance. When she studied the history of Western art in France, she was trained in archaelogy, document filing, and the correct analysis of art history. With her indepth knowledge in painting materials, she is very suitable for the analysis of these postcards. Therefore, I highly recommended her for this work. I am glad to see that she has finished this difficult task.

After Ms. Chen undertook this work, she consulted Ms. Yu when she encountered problems in Japanese. Ms. Yu helped her a great deal in understanding the meanings of the words. With the help from the folklorist Taka Hashi Masami who currently teaches at Soochow University, she was able to finish the work within six months.

As the book is about to go to print, I feel that it is really great for the Rainbow Sign Publishing Company to publish such a scholarly work with relatively little popular appeal in this materialistic society. I admire the company for their endeavor, and with these few words wish all the best for the publication of the book not only because it brings back to our memory the life of the past, but also because it contains quite precious data for understanding another aspect of life during the Japanese occupation.

Chen, Ching-Jung

Professor

Department Of Fine Arts National Taiwan Normal University

出 版 序

爲台灣歷史留下見證

對於《台灣影像歷史》系列叢書的出版，是我們經歷了長時間縝密思考與規劃所精心製作的。有關台灣400年的歷史，從早年原住民時期，16世紀歐洲殖民勢力的介入，至大清納入版圖(1717)，漢民族大量遷徙來台，有關台灣文獻的記載頗爲欠缺。而日人據台（1895－1945）所留下的有關台灣的紀錄，又難以擺脱帝國殖民的觀點。 1945年國民政府遷台，台灣被殖民統治的陰影及在民族主義思想教育矯枉過正的影響下，亦未能以台灣人的眼光去正視台灣的歷史，致使飽經世界文化衝擊，擁有豐富族群土地發展史的台灣先民所留下的史料文物，大都陸續散失湮没；殊爲可惜！

歷史教育是爲文化紮根，史料文物可爲歷史作忠實的見證。鑑此，本社秉持對史料的保存及闡揚，不遺餘力的將蒐藏台灣早期影像史料及文物眞跡約萬餘件，並將之做有系統的規劃與整理，付諸文化出版事業，訂名爲《台灣影像歷史》系列叢書，本套書共分十冊：《見証——台灣總督府》上、下冊、《典藏手繪封》、《斯土繪影》、《高砂春秋》、《蓬萊舊庄》、《海國圖索》、《開台尋跡》、《台灣古書契》、《殖產方略》。

《台灣影像歷史》系列叢書，是一部集體創作的結晶，匯集了台灣各大學術研究機構及民間文化藝術社團人士，共同參與編纂。本叢書以台灣的影像史料文物爲主軸，參考已有的文獻論著，賦予相關圖像、背景說明，並承蒙有關歷史、地理、美術、人類學、社會學、古物鑑定家等多位著名學者，透過專精的學術功力審訂，終使本書得以順利出版。

《台灣影像歷史》系列叢書的出版，本社摒除預設立場，力求超然、詳實，希望藉由影像歷史的表述，來塡補文字紀錄的空白，帶給讀者更眞實、貼切的閱讀方式，進而領略台灣歷史文化的内涵。

立虹出版社　社長

FROM THE PUBLISHER

Attesting to Taiwan's History

The publication of 《A Collection of the Visual History of Taiwan》 Series embodies the prolonged efforts in discreet thinking and planning of this publisher. Taiwan's four hundred years of history, dating from the early times of aboriginal settlers, through the intervention of European colonial power in the 16th century, the enclosure into the domain of Ching Dynasty (1717), followed by large settlement of the Han people, has been scarce in documentation. The records of Taiwan documented during Japanese occupation (1895 - 1945) were hard pressed to shake off the notion of imperial colonialism. The post-1945 era after the Nationalist Government moved to Taiwan was also subject to the shadow of the colonial reign and characterized by over-ratification in ideological education. Taiwan's history has never been examined square and fair from the vantage point of the people inhabiting the land. Lacking any focus in our own heritage, Taiwan is more impacted by outside cultures and a lot of Taiwan's own historical records and relics dissipate in the progression of time.

Culture takes root in the education of history and historical data and relics provide truthful witness to history. As such, under the precept of preserving and promoting historical relics, this publisher has vigorously collected tens of thousands pieces of early Taiwan photo-documentary records in authentic form, sorted them out systematically and put to publication titled 《A Collection of the Visual History of Taiwan》 Series. The series contain a total of ten volumes: 《Witness —— The Colonial Taiwan (1895-1945)》 Volume I & II*, 《Postcard Drawings —— The Rare Collection (1895-1945)》, 《The Drawings of That Land —— The Interpretation of Taiwan(1895-1945)》, 《The Exquisite Heritage —— The Culture and Arts of Taiwan Aborigines》, 《The Abodes in the Bygone Era —— Taiwan's Town and Country Settlements(1895-1945)》, 《The Landscape of the Island Country —— The Development of the Natural Geography of Taiwan (1895-1945)》, 《Strolling the old Trails》, 《Archaic Land Documents of Taiwan (1717-1895)》, 《The Schemes of Production ——Taiwan's Industrial Development (1895-1945)》.*

A compilation of collective creation, 《A Collection of the Visual History of Taiwan》 Series assembled the participation of various university research institutes and people from cultural and arts organizations in private sector. Centered around Taiwan's illustrated historical records, this series refer to extant literatures and documents to provide background information to relevant pictures. Thanks to the expertise of many scholars in history, geology, fine arts and painting, anthropology, sociology and antiquities assessment, this book is finally put to print.

Determined to be free of any predisposition and endeavoring toward impartiality and authenticity, the publication of 《A Collection of the Visual History of Taiwan》 Series hopes to make up for the voids of written characters and offer to the readers a clearer picture of Taiwan's history and culture through the illustration of historical images.

Dean T. Chou

President
Rainbow Sign Publishing Company

作者序

在傳播電訊高度發展的今天，透過機器，例如一部電話或者傳眞機，便可以使兩個相隔千里之遠的人立刻獲得聯繫，信件的往來已逐漸成爲一種奢侈、費時的行爲，更遑論再多費些心思寫首小詩或畫點挿圖來代替文字傳達情誼了。這樣的改變，使得原本就是別具心裁的手繪明信片，成爲珍貴的歷史產物，即使對於一向重視民俗文化承傳的日本人而言亦是如此。

然而，就在多方用心蒐集的努力之下，立虹出版社社長周鼎先生匯集了數百張日治時代所留下來的手繪明信片，這些作品本身確實頗值得費心研究。但由於其取材及製作手法十分複雜，涉及範圍甚廣，欲作一完備詳盡的介紹誠屬不易。首先，在歸納分類的問題方面便難做到盡善盡美；例如，某些作品本身因兼具美學及民俗研究價値，而僅能擇一方予以歸類，實屬憾事。其次，仍有部分佳作，因難以納入我們的分類之中，而不得不忍痛予以擱置。

在研究的過程中，由於筆者對於日本文化的涉獵薄淺，除了得不斷求助於一些書本知識的輔助之外，還端賴各方熱心人士的鼎力相助，不吝予以筆者指導者不在少數，實難一一列舉，在此得特別感謝師母余佳蓉女士爲我解讀了大部分的日文，而諸多關於民俗方面的認知則幸有東吳大學日文系教授高橋正己先生的指引，若非這些友人予以後學的指導，本書便難以在短期間内完成，感激之心，實非筆墨所能形容。

至於取捨的標準，自然可以有千百個不同的方案，除了著眼於其創作品質之外，我們亦考慮其獨特性，希望儘量做到不重覆、不遺漏的要求。介紹的方式則儘可能地以精簡的篇幅，對每一件作品的材質、製作的手法、畫面的構成、以及其寓意、民俗背景做介紹。

由於本書乃《台灣影像歷史系列》叢書中的一本，有其預期出版的壓力，使得筆者在教學及繪畫工作之餘，除了需積極閱讀相關書籍並走訪某些可能對此類作品有所認知的人之外，還承受了不少時間的壓力。然而，在整個過程當中，乃至結束，筆者從未後悔接下此項挑戰性的工作。因爲，除了看著一切從無至有，對其認知從誨暗至逐漸明朗的知識面的收獲之外；在訪談的過程中，結識了一些好友，深深感受到學者那種率眞、不藏私的一面。表面上，此項工作即將在完稿印刷之日告一段落，然而，本書仍留有許多研究的空間，筆者對其研究之心並未因此稍減，期盼各方專家能慷慨指教。

國立台灣師範大學美術系　副教授

陳　淑　華

AUTHOR'S FOREWORD

Today, with the development of advanced communications technology, two persons thousands of miles apart can get in touch instantly with each other via such electronic devices as telephones or fax machines. Correspondence by mail has gradually become a time-consuming luxury; making a little more effort to write a short poem or draw a little picture in place of words to convey friendly sentiments is even rarer. Such change has made already unique hand-painted postcards truly precious historical relics, even for the Japanese who have always placed great emphasis on the preservation of their culture.

Nevertheless, through concentrated efforts to collect these postcards by all possible means, Mr. Dean T. Chou, President of the Rainbow Sign Publishing Company, has gathered hundreds of hand-painted postcards left behind from the Japanese Occupation Period. The works themselves are quite worthy of careful research. However, due to the complexity and wide scope of the materials and techniques, it is truly difficult to make a complete and detailed introduction. To begin with, it is rather difficult to be perfect in the classification of some works. For instance, it is truly a pity that some works with value both in terms of aesthetics and research into folk customs can only be classified according to one aspect. Secondly, because some wonderful works are difficult to bring into our classification, we cannot help but reluctantly lay them aside.

In the process of research, due to my shallow understanding of the Japanese culture, not only did I consult many books for information, but also depended on the kind assistance of different enthusiastic people, many of whom gave me guidance generously. It is truly hard to enumerate them one by one. Special thanks are due to Ms. Chia-jung Yu, my teacher's spouse, who explained most of the Japanese to me. As for knowledge of folk culture, I am indebted to Prof. Taka Hashi Masami of the Japanese department at Soochow University for his guidance. But for the assistance of these friends, this book would not have been finished in a short time. Words can hardly describe my gratitude.

As for the criteria of selection, there can be of course hundreds, even thousands of proposals. Apart from the emphasis on the quality of creation, I also put its uniqueness into consideration, in the hope that there would be neither repetition nor omission. As for the way of introduction, I have fried to be as concise as possible to give an introduction to the materials, techniques, composition, implication and cultural backgrounds of each piece.

As this is one volume of a series of books and therefore there is some pressure to publish it by a certain date, not only did I have to actively read books related to this topic and visit some people who might know about these works in my spare time apart from teaching and painting, but also I was under some time pressure. However, during the whole process till the end, I never regretted undertaking such a challenging task. This is because I benefited in terms of knowledge, as everything started from square one and as my understanding of these works moved from total darkness to gradual clearness, and in addition I made some good friends during my visits and interviews, and I experienced deeply the forthright and unselfish aspect of these scholars. On the surface, this task seems to be coming to an end, as this book is about to go to print. However, in my view, my desire to research these works will not end with the publication of the book. It is my sincere hope that experts in different fields will be generous with their comments.

Chen, Shu-Hwa

Vice-Professor

Department Of Fine Arts National Taiwan Normal University

作者簡介 ABOUT THE AUTHOR

陳淑華，1963年生於彰化縣，台中女中畢業後就讀於輔大圖書館系期間，因畫家洪敬雲先生的啓蒙與鼓勵，遂重新選擇志向，考入師範大學美術系，並以油畫第一名的優異表現，負笈法國巴黎第一大學攻讀西洋藝術史，以五年九個月學得了極專業的知識；不但順利取得博士學位；更成爲法國「科學與技術學院」油畫修護系歷年來第三位獲准入學且畢業的東方人。

回國後曾任教於輔大應用美術系、織品服裝系副教授，現任職於師大美術系副教授，教授繪畫材料學、西洋藝術史、素描等課程。課餘從事油畫創作甚勤，專作研究及從事繪畫創作是其職志。

本書即爲陳敎授以宏觀的西洋藝術史理論基礎、個人從事畫作多年的美感心得及在美術材料鑑定的專業素養下首度著墨的藝術鑑賞專著。作者不受拘束的個人風格，不強調畫派分門，亦不限制研究的範圍，不但表現在其畫風上，更主導了全書在專業之餘，兼具感性、活潑、瀟灑的風格。

Born in Changhua County in 1963, Shu-hua Chen majored in library management at Fu Jen Catholic University after her graduation from the Taichung Girls' Senior High School. With the initiation and encouragement of the painter Hong Ching-ming, she re-selected her goal, was admitted to the Department of Fine Arts at National Taiwan Normal University from which she graduated with the top score in oil painting. She furthered her study in Western art history at the First University of Paris, France. During the five years and nine months of her study, she acquired considerable professional knowledge. She not only earned a Ph.D. in Western art history, but also became the third Asian admitted and graduated from the Department of Oil Painting Maintenance of the Academy of Science and Technology, France.

After her return to Taiwan in 1994, she taught at the Department of Applied Arts at Fu-Jen Catholic University. She also taught as an assistant professor at the Department of Art Education of National Taipei Teacher's College. She now serves as an assistant professor at the Department of Fine Arts of National Taiwan Normal University and also teaches courses such as paint materials, Western design history, and sketch at the Department of Fabrics and Clothing at Fu Jen Catholic University. Beside teaching, she is diligent at creating oil paintings in her leisure. Her goals are to focus solely on research and to create oil paintings.

This book is her first work devoted solely to the appreciation of art. It is based on Professor Chen's macroscopic theoretical foundation in Western art history, the aesthetic experience accumulated during her many years of devotion to painting, and her professional accomplishment at the appraisal of art materials. The author's unbounded personal style, with no emphasis on the different schools of artistic style and no limitation in the scope of her research, not only is reflected in her painting style, but also adds a sensible, cheerful, and unrestrained style throughout this professional-standard book.

目錄
Contents

前言

近年來，隨著台灣政經文化的蓬勃發展，掀起了對本土藝術的關懷熱潮，同時也引發了對台灣早期美術西洋化影響甚深的日本美術的再探討。談到日本美術，最容易讓人聯想到的，恐怕就屬傳入西歐而激起印象派漣漪的「浮世繪」了。浮世繪泛指以眼見耳聞之社會百態爲題材的作品，早期浮世繪的製作方式是以彩繪肉筆畫爲主，逐漸才演變成衆所悉知的木刻版畫，乃至於多色套印的錦繪。這些作品當屬浮世繪的一種，俗稱「摺物」，是私人往來時可做爲賀卡或明信片之用的小型浮世繪。此類作品有別於今日市面上的卡片，亦不同於一般的浮世繪，它們多半是出自於一些文人雅士之手，親自製作用來寄予友人的作品，反面可貼郵票並書寫簡單的問候祝賀之語，以傳達眞切的友誼。由於並非爲了滿足市民階層的需要，不具商業用途，因而所使用的素材，通常亦十分考究，製造手法亦分外精巧，其中只有極少數是屬於可以複製的木刻版畫，其餘均是珍貴的肉筆畫，也就是紙或絹本的彩繪原作。其製作手法多樣化而複雜，雖然僅是方寸的小明信片，卻頗能展現日本文化的海綿性質。

除了有日本自 7 世紀以來自中國美術所吸納而來的技法及面貌之外，尚顯示了西洋繪畫中的寫實風格的深刻影響。由於本收藏的作品，除極少數完成年代較早之外，多半介於 19 世紀中葉至二次大戰日軍自台撤退前的期間，正是日本史上經歷一場前所未有的大變革的時代，雖然日本早於 16 世紀中葉，由於基督教的傳入，已奠定日本西洋畫的根基，但明治維新(西元 1868 年)所帶來的新訊息、新風潮以及新的藝術手法及觀念，正沖擊著舊繪畫模式，這一代的藝術家在西方藝術的感染和啓迪之下，有著新的表現手法和技術，並以更開闊的視野，放眼予自然界和社會生活本身，使客觀世界以更豐富的眞實面貌，充分地展示出來。

此外，自然亦不乏保留日本民族文化獨特風格的題材及表現手法的作品，例如，自 20 世紀初，立體派開始，成爲西方藝術創作手法之一的「拼貼」，一直被誤認爲是西方人的創新，其實早在 10 世紀，拼貼技法便爲日本人普遍使用（△），並在本書的收藏品中大量出現，可能是受西潮的喚醒吧！除了融合了傳統及外來的技巧之外，廣泛的創作題材，更是這類作品的特色，自神話傳說、歷史事件，以至於自然景物、風俗民情、日常生活和肖像等，揉合了東西方的哲學意念，表現出日本繪畫多彩多姿的藝術風格。

由於純粹是爲了鑑賞而作，並無任何商業考量或主宰日本藝壇的政治壓力，這些手繪明信片，通常除了極盡日本藝術所特有的裝飾本色之外，往往亦能締造出有個性、匠心獨具的作品，比一般純爲創作的藝術品或衆所周知的浮世繪更能反映出畫家的創作理念及其個人對社會的實際感受，流露出製作者自現實生活中所體驗出來的情感痕跡。雖然均非宏篇巨幅的大作，亦無驚心動魄的題材，仍不減其藝術價值，加上均屬手繪孤本，非市井小民的經濟能力所能蒐購典藏的，故而特爲浮世繪收藏家所珍視。

(△)：Dictionnuire le la peinture, sow la direction de Michel Laclotte et Jean-Pierre Cuzin arouse, Paris, 1987, P.165

Foreword

Along with the thriving development of the political and economic cultures in Taiwan in recent years, a great mass fervor for indigenous art has been aroused. In the meantime, a new probe into Japanese art, which had a rather profound impact on the westernization of early Taiwanese art, has also been launched. When one thinks of Japanese art, what comes into one's mind most readily is perhaps the Ukiyoe or "pictures of the floating world" style of painting, which spread into western Europe and inspired the Impressionist movement.

Ukiyoe refers to works which use the life of the common people as their motif. The earlier Ukiyoe were for the most part color paintings done by hand. Gradually, another technique, the well-known woodblock print, was brought into use, and later it even evolved into Nishikie, or polychrome print using numerous color blocks. These works, known as "Surimono", constitute a genre of the Ukiyoe, and are actually small Ukiyoe that can be used as greeting cards or postcards for personal correspondence. Different from the cards for sale nowadays and from other ordinary Ukiyoe, they were mostly personally made by the literati for personal correspondence with their friends. On the back, stamps could be attached and simple greetings written to express sincere friendship. Because they were intended neither to meet the needs of Ordinary people nor for commercial purposes, the materials used were usually quite exquisite and the technique very delicate. Only a small portion of these works are woodblock prints that can be duplicated, and the rest are all precious paintings done by hand, i.e. color originals on silk or paper. The techniques used to make these works were versatile and complex.

Small as these postcards may be, they demonstrate quite sufficiently the assimilative nature of the Japanese culture. In addition to the techniques and features that Japan has absorbed from China since the 7th century, they also reflect the profound influence of the realist style from the West. Except for a very small number that were done earlier, most of the works in this collection were finished between the mid-19th century and Japan's retreat from Taiwan after the Second World War, a period of unprecedented change in the history of Japan. As early as the middle of the 16th century, the foundation of Western fine art was laid in Japan along with the introduction of Christianity, yet the new information, trends, artistic techniques and perspectives that came along with the Meiji Restoration (1868), however, churned away at the old mode of painting. Under the influence and inspiration of Western art, this generation of artists had new ways of expression and techniques. With wider views, they looked at nature and social life itself and fully illustrated the objective world in its richer, genuine aspect. In addition, there are naturally also works which preserve the unique style, motifs and ways of expression of the Japanese culture. For instance, collage, which became one of the techniques of Western art along with the rise of cubism in the early twentieth century, has always been mistaken as an innovation of the West. In reality, however, the technique of collage was used commonly by the Japanese as early as the tenth century. It also appears in many of the works in this collection. Perhaps it has been reawakened by the rise of Western cultural influence!

In addition to the fusion of traditional and foreign techniques, another feature of these works is the extensiveness of their motifs, ranging from legends, folklore, and historical events, to natural scenery, customs, daily life of the commoners, as well as portraits. The philosophical thoughts of the East and the West are merged to illustrate the colorful artistic style of Japan.

Done purely for the purpose of enjoyment and without any commercial consideration or political pressure that dominated Japanese art circles, these hand-painted postcards are usually not only the apotheosis of the decorative nature of the Japanese art, but also works that show personality and ingenuity. They can reflect the painters' ideas of creation and their actual feelings about the society more than ordinary works that were created for the sole purpose of creation or other well-known Ukiyoe. The traces of emotions experienced by the artists in the real world are shown in these works. They are not large-scale grand works, nor do they contain soul-stirring themes, yet the artistic value of these works is not at all diminished. On the contrary, because these are unique originals done by hand, and were not affordable for the average man, they are valued all the more by Ukiyoe collectors.

岩繪之美
The Beauty of Paintings in Mineral Pigments

岩彩畫是一種利用礦物質研磨成粉的顏料，大都用在日本畫，不退色、不起變化，有它的永恆特質。日本畫是今天我們所稱的膠彩畫，就繪畫分類來說，水彩用水，油畫用油，膠彩用膠，均能使之顏料稀釋，以利著色。

在唐朝有所謂「青綠山水」者，就是以金碧艷麗的色彩作畫，此藝後來被奪於「水墨山水」，唐朝著色畫流傳到日本後，貫穿一千年未曾衰竭，反而確立了日本美術的風土之美。

今天正式的日本畫，塗色都相當濃，小品的日本畫則隨興而發，所以筆觸比較樸拙，塗起來也較薄。

岩繪可以畫在絹布上，也可以畫在紙上，但今天的日本畫大都是敷在板面，或用木條撐平，與畫油畫的方法一樣，不像水墨畫仍然是攤一張宣紙在桌上，畫成之後再裱背。

總之，岩繪是一種賦彩的日本畫，雖然早期自中國傳入，但自中國失傳，反而成爲日本特有的畫種，外國人直呼賦彩岩繪爲「NIHONGA」，就是「日本畫」的音譯。

Mineral pigments are made of pulverized minerals. It is mostly used in Japanese-style painting. It does not fade and remains constant. Japanese-style painting is actually what is referred to as glue-solution paintings. In terms of painting classification, watercolor paintings use water, oil-paintings use oil, and glue-solution paintings use glue. These three materials are used to dilute the pigments, so that coloring can be facilitated.

During the T'ang Dynasty, the so-called "blue and green landscapes" paintings were made in bright colors of green and gold. This kind of paintings was replaced later by ink-and-wash landscapes. However, after these colored paintings of the T'ang Dynasty spread to Japan, they remained popular for a good thousand years, establishing the status of landscape painting in Japanese art.

Nowadays conventional Japanese-style painting uses richer colors, while ad-lib miniature paintings use simpler strokes and thinner colors. Paintings in mineral pigments can be done on silk or paper. Unlike ink-and-wash, which is done on a sheet of painting paper and framed after finished, today's Japanese-style paintings are mostly done on a wood plate, or propped up with wooden sticks, in the same manner as oil paintings are made. In a word, paintings in mineral pigments are colored Japanese-style painting. Though this kind of paintings had been introduced from China to Japan in early times, they were lost in China, but became a unique painting style in Japan. Westerners call colored paintings in mineral pigments "Nihongo," which is a transliteration of "Japanese-style painting."

日本女子 Japanese Woman

這幅描繪日本女子背影的作品是運用橙色顏料描繪在深灰色的卡紙上，形成強烈的色調對比，人物在整個畫面上所佔之比例雖然十分渺小，畫面效果卻顯得十分醒目。畫者以清新、明晰的繪畫語言把極爲平凡的日本婦女的背影詩意化。人物的整體造形和明暗處理，渾然天成。畫面上並沒有用任何線條勾勒輪廓或做細節的描寫，只是簡要數筆，便處理出微妙的明暗色調，成功地表現了人物概括渾圓的體積感及光線明暗的變化。畫中日本女子被簡化的造形，並沒有任何非本質的多餘細節，但卻那麼富和耐人尋味，充份展現了作者敏銳的觀察力及其形體造形的功力。

然而，此作品成功之處在於它不僅描繪了生動的外在形態，還巧妙地觸及了人物內心靈魂的刻劃。少女動人的側影和略微低垂的神態，使人感受到她那天眞、純潔，甚至有點兒羞澀的可愛。自然毫不作做作的姿態中，流露出一種質樸恬靜、溫文典雅的美感及高貴端莊的情操，給予觀者安詳優美的慰藉。

This piece portrays the back of a Japanese woman created in orange pigment on dark gray card paper, presenting a strong contrast in color. Although the figure is relatively small in proportion to the entire frame, the visual effect of the figure is nevertheless eye-catching. The artist employed fresh and clear language of painting to add poetic quality to the back of a common Japanese woman. The overall shape of the figure and the handling of brightness are natural; and the contour is not created by any lines, nor is there any detailed depiction in the picture. With just a few simple brushstrokes, the artist presented distinctions between brightness and darkness, and successfully brought out the generally round solidity of the figure, as well as variations of lighting. The simplified configuration of the Japanese woman in the picture is not accompanied by any excessive details irrelevant to the substance of this picture. Yet, the contour of the figure is exuberant and pithy which attest to the sharp observation of the artist as well as his skills in the creation of shapes.

However, the success of this piece lies not so much in its lively depiction of external forms as in its subtle portrayal of the inner self of the figure. The engaging profile and the somewhat droopy pose of the young lady make her innocent, pure and even bashful loveliness directly discernible. Her natural and unpretentious pose lends tranquillity and delicacy to the aesthetic and noble quality of the woman, bringing peace and comfort to viewers.

RD-001

風雨中的決鬥 Duel in the Rain

此張卡片是以在風雨交加的夜裡互決生死的日本武士爲主題。整幅畫面採用強烈的明暗對比，以突顯在風雨中對峙的兩位武士軒昂的氣勢及誓死不辭的決心。畫面上，灰綠色的背景適切地傳達了夜晚幽暗的氣氛。作者以逆光的效果處理前景人物的背影，使其在紅色火炬的映照烘托之下，有如雕像般突出有力，同時也予人一種深感不安的存在感；而其對面武士的身影，則以若隱若現的手法表達，以呈現風雨中煙水迷濛的感覺，並強調遠近空間的距離。斜風中強而有力的雨絲及火把誇張的動勢，則強化了畫面中高張的戲劇性氣氛。作者還刻意用金銀兩色勾勒火焰及武士刀的刀刃，以製造火光騰閃的效果。

全畫以強烈的明暗對比的處理方式，來呈現生死之間對立的象徵意義，成功地烘托出武士冒雨前進的步伐，宏偉雄壯的氣勢及面對戰鬥時的生死決心。

This card employs as its theme Japanese sumurai facing off for a duel on a rainy and stormy night. A strong contrast between darkness and brightness is utilized to delineate the vigorous power and the determination of the two sumurai facing each other in the rain. The background of the picture in sage green aptly conveys the gruesome and dark atmosphere of the night. The artist deals with the backs of the foreground figures through a back-light effect, so that the figures when relieved by red torches stand out conspicuously and forcibly like statues. This arrangement also evokes a sense of uneasiness. The subtle presentation of the sumarai's backs is intended to create an aura of fogginess typical of a rainy and stormy scene, and to highlight the space between the foreground and the background. The ferocious and powerful raindrops flying slantingly in strong gusts of wind, as well as the exaggerated dynamism of the torches, strengthen the tense and dramatic atmosphere of the frame. The artist also intentionally employs golden and silver colors to brush the fires and the blades of the katanas to create a flickering effect of fire.

The strong contrast between darkness and brightness throughout the painting is intended to convey the symbolism of life and death. In doing so, the artist succeeds in portraying the stances of the sumurai in the rain, their majestic and magnificent vigor, and their determination in fighting a battle.

RD-002

枯骨執扇圖 Fan Held by Skeleton

這幅枯骨執扇圖是以不透明水彩在絹本之明信片上厚塗而成的。偏右的構圖，加上骷髏身體和足部朝右（走出畫面）的動勢，使得作品充滿動感。然而，作者巧妙的運用枯骨的手勢及回眸的姿態，取得觀者視覺上的平衡，亦使得構圖不致流於平板。簡潔洗鍊、提頓有致的筆法與枯骨生動活潑的造形，賦予主題新的生命，觀者似乎可以透過畫面聽到其骨骼擺動所發出來的咔咔聲響。至於用以描繪枯骨的灰色調子變化唯妙唯肖。枯骨手上所握的彩色扇子，更在以灰色爲主調的畫面上增添了豐富的色彩。至於片片飄零的花瓣，非但加強了畫面的空間結構，更予人一種虛幻、蒼茫的感受。這些精心的安排，讓單純的主題，不致流於單調、並獲得最大的變化。

明顯地，這是一幅暗喻著生與死的作品。這個題材，自古以來，便一直是藝術家所關懷、描繪的主題，或許是因爲這與人世間毫無關連的死亡，能帶走人生所有，而在無可避免的死亡之中，藏有人類對現世繁華的虛幻與無常感。畫面上，枯骨空洞的雙眼及其嘴角上，似乎帶著譏笑的表情，加上其執扇回眸觀望落花的姿態，似乎正傳達著人世間的榮華富貴，遲早會因死亡而結束的無常觀。

This "Fan Held by Skeleton" is created by means of a thick coating of watercolor on a silk postcard. This is a dynamic piece, with a right-leaning composition as well as a dynamic posture demonstrated by the skeleton's body and feet which point to the right (as if to walk off the edge of the picture). However, the artist's tactful use of the skeleton's hand gesture and its backward-glancing pose create a visual balance for viewers and save the composition from insipidity. This motif is given new life, thanks to the simple, economical, sophisticated and varied brush strokes and the lively contour of the skeleton. The viewers might even be able to hear the rattling sound of the bones from the picture. The gray tincture of the skeleton is great for its lively variations. The color fan held in the skeleton's hand, against its gray background, is intended to add color variations to the picture. As for the withering and scattering petals, they serve to reinforce the spatial structure of the picture, and more importantly to create a sense of illusion and vicissitude. This masterly arrangement prevents the simple motif from degenerating into monotony and creates maximum variety.

It is evident that this piece touches upon life and death, a time-honored motif of paintings for artists concerned about this subject. This is probably because death, which has nothing to do with our living existence, is bound to take away everything we have; and there is no escape for anyone. Thus this motif leads us to the awareness of impermanence and illusion of human life. In the picture, the skeleton's hollow eyes and mouth, its facial expression with a seemingly sarcastic smile, and the posture of the skeleton looking back at the withering flowers while holding a fan in its hand seem to hone a message of impermanence where prosperity and wealth in human existence will eventually be brought to an end by death.

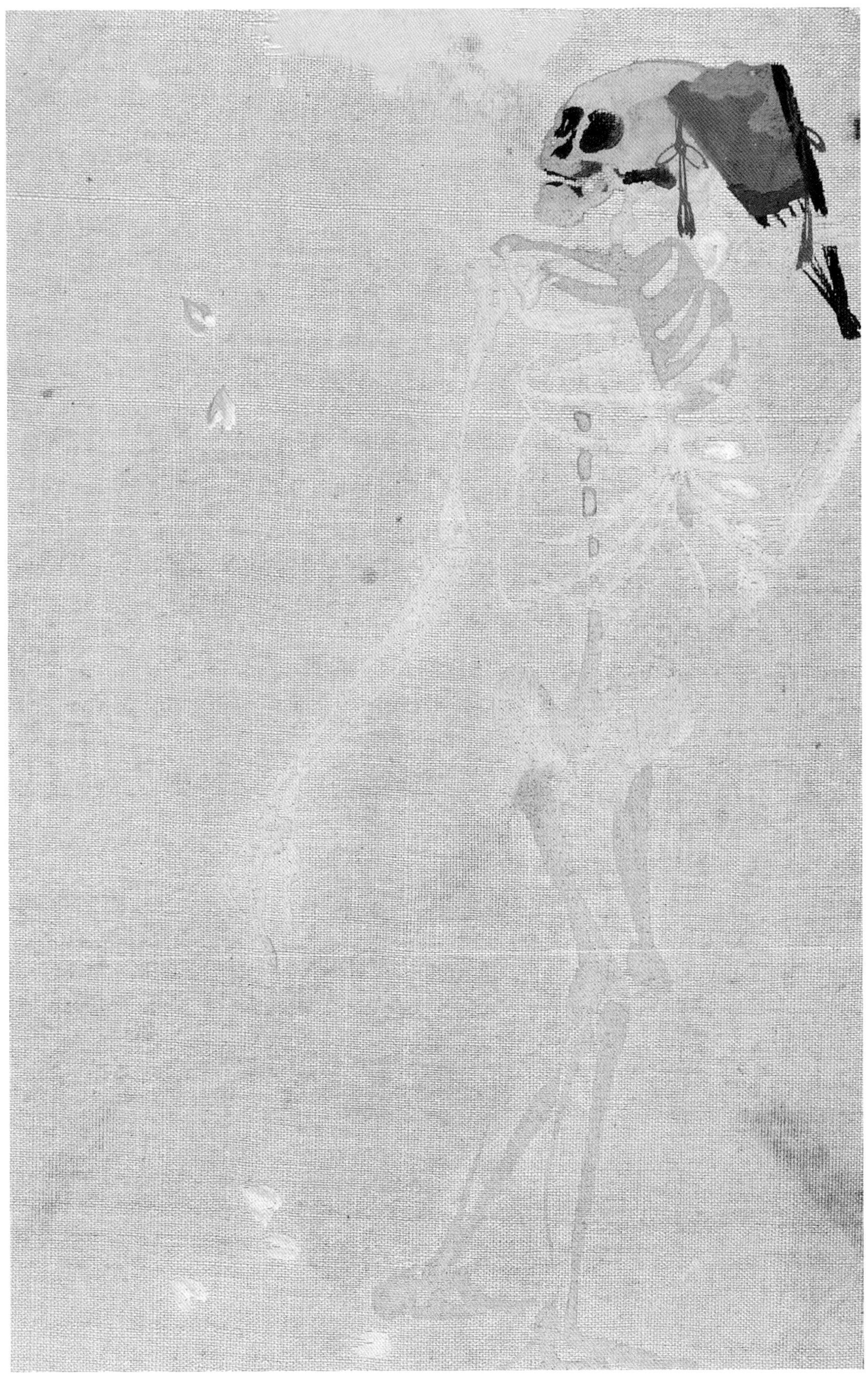

（絹本 Silken Card） RD-003

遮面女像 Woman with Covered Face

這件作品是直接在絹本卡片上以淡墨勾勒人物的輪廓造形，再以平面圖案的繪畫方式賦予色彩。線條自然流暢，用色炫麗明快又不失和諧。女子所穿著的小袖（和服之總稱），藍底上有著淡雅的粉紅色花朵及綠葉的圖案，紋飾精美，並呈現如絲綢般的質感，其腰帶更有銀色顏料所繪的花紋。整體造形、紋飾的描繪，細緻華美，呈現豪華、貴族化的氣息，加上風格平面化，極富裝飾意趣。

畫中女子的造型深具典型的日本風味。其頸部髮際所修的髮脚爲兩條，是京都的習俗（江户，也就是明治維新之前的東京，則爲一條）；而其腰帶係以整片寬度、二重回繞的「柳結法」，留下過長部分打成兩折垂下來，結在背後，顯示其身份可能仍是待字閨中。她執扇掩面的嬌羞姿態，有如一株玉樹般搖曳動人，端莊典雅的氣質、溫柔婉約的姿勢，充分表現日本女子特有的含蓄美。

This piece portrays figures and objects first shaped via light ink brushes directly on a silk card and then colored with graphic art techniques. The lines of this art work are smooth and natural; the coloring, though gorgeous and resolute, is harmonious nevertheless. The Kosode (collective term for a kimono) worn by the woman has quiet pink flowers and green leaves, with beautiful patterns and markings. The apparel is also characterized by a silk-like quality. The girl's sash contains markings drawn by means of silver paint. Projecting a luxurious and autocratic aura, the overall configuration of the piece as well as its portrayal of markings are delicate and aesthetically appealing. Also thanks to its graphic style, this piece is permeated with decorativeness and fascination.

The woman in this picture is shaped in a classical Japanese style. The woman's hair is braided in two tresses along her neck, the traditional style of Kyoto. (In Edo--Tokyo as it was called prior to the Meiji Restoration--women braided their hair in a single tress.) Her sash wraps around her waist in two laps without any folds, a knotting method known as Ryuketsu-Hō (willow-knot method). The excess portion of the sash is then folded twice and tied on her back. This probably indicates that she is not married. Her timid mannerism of covering her face with a fan is lively and attractive. The majestic and classic aroma emanating from this picture, as well as the tender and gentle posture of the woman, amply projects the conservative beauty that is characteristic of a Japanese woman.

（絹本 Silken Card）

RD-004

RD-005～RD-008

日本歌舞伎臉譜

歌舞伎是日本傳統舞劇之一，興起於 17 世紀，最初流行於京都，後來傳至江户，是日本庶民戲劇的代表。

歌舞伎融合了能樂及文樂（玩偶劇）的特點，因此兼具舞蹈劇及音樂劇的性格，無論台詞、動作都充滿節奏感，俳優（演員）的肢體語言誇張且形式化。爲迎合庶民的需求，歌舞伎逐漸演變成爲上演由章回小説改編的連續劇目，主題則以描寫昔日的貴族及武士社會或平民生活爲主。

此系列四張絹本卡片便是分別以歌舞伎中扮演朝比奈、弁慶、暮仙人（蟾蜍仙人）以及嬲（奸臣、小人）等角色的臉譜爲設計主題，造形簡潔，卻深具優雅、沈靜的特性，畫者以嫻熟的技巧、純淨的用色，加上明快俐落、不拘泥的筆法，微妙微肖地表現出每一個角色獨特的性格。抽象化的曲線造形及色彩成了象徵的符號，含義深奥又富有魅力，整個系列的作品充滿一種象徵性的神祕氣氛。

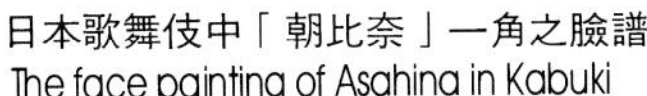

日本歌舞伎中「朝比奈」一角之臉譜
The face painting of Asahina in Kabuki

（絹本 Silken Card）

RD-005

RD-005～RD-008

Face Paintings of Japanese Kabuki

Dating back to the 17th century, Kabuki is one of the traditional forms of opera in Japan. Kabuki, which was popular at first in Kyoto and later found its way to Edo, represents plebeian drama of Japan.

Incorporating the characteristics of No and Bunraku (puppet shows), Kabuki carries the characteristics of both operas and musicals. The scripts and body language are rhythmic, and the body language of the actors is formal and exaggerated. To cater to the need of the common people, Kabuki gradually evolved into episodic drama through the adaptation of serial novels. The themes of the drama deal mainly with aristocrats, the world of the samurai and the life of the common people in the past.

This series of four silken cards centers around the face paintings of Asahina, Benkei, Bosennin (Sengyo-sennin) and Naburu(wicket retainers or villains) in Kabuki. The forms are simple, graceful and quiet. The artist succeeded in his accurate and lively rendition of the unique personality of each character through his sophisticated techniques, immaculate coloring and decisive, untrammeled brush-strokes. The abstracted curvy lines and coloring become meaningful and attractive symbols, and this series of works is filled with symbolic mystery.

日本歌舞伎中「弁慶」一角的臉譜
The face painting of Benkei in Kabuki

（絹本 Silken Card）

RD-006

日本歌舞伎中「暮仙人」（蟾蜍仙人）
The face painting of Bosennin (Sengyo-sennin) in Kabuki

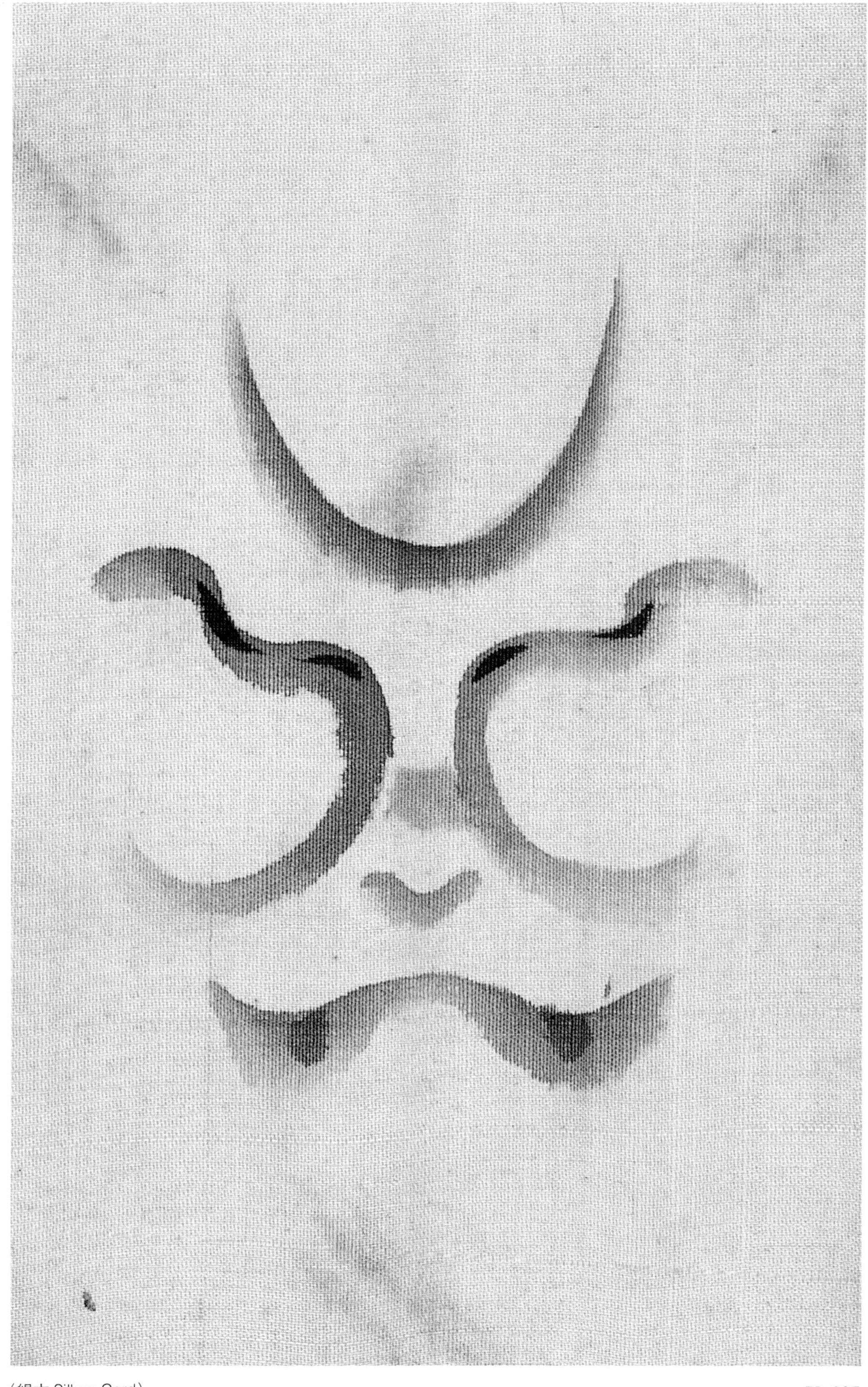

（絹本 Silken Card）

RD-007

日本歌舞伎中「嬲」(奸臣、小人)一角的臉譜
The face painting of Naburu (wicked retainers or villains) in Kabuki

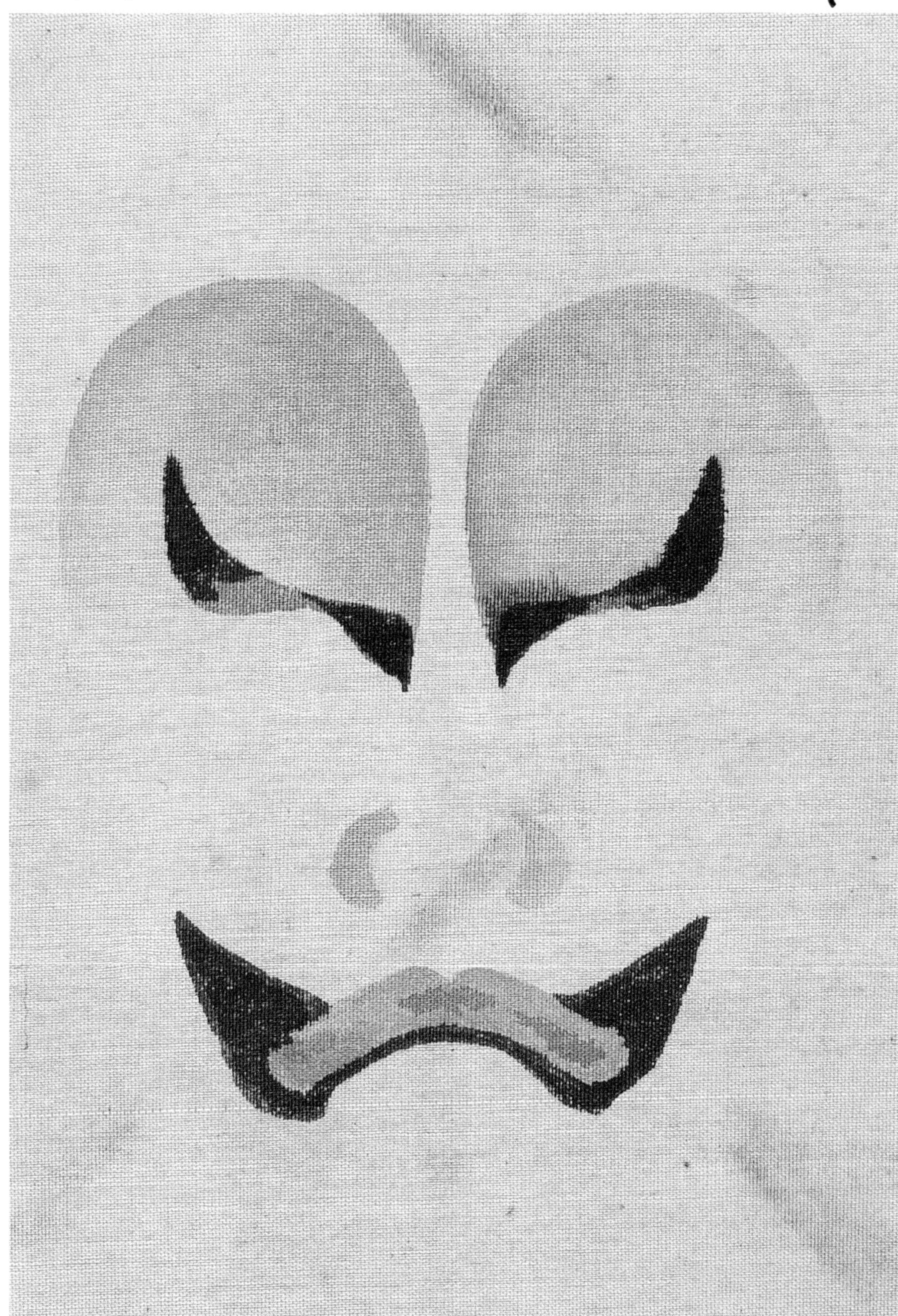

(絹本 Silken Card)

RD-008

RD-009～RD-011

南極探險之片吟鳥圖

Portrait of Birds during Expedition to the Antarctic

日本早在本世紀初便由白瀨矗中尉帶領探險隊抵達南極，這組卡片之一便是以白瀨矗中尉於1910年帶領之南極探險隊所拍攝的活動寫眞（記錄影片）的壹等券（頭等座位的入場券）做爲主題，配合宮嶋氏所畫的南極特產片吟鳥（企鵝）和白瀨矗隊長的簽字及蓋章；另一張則繪有四隻圍成一團的企鵝及白瀨矗於台北的題款。畫面構圖富趣味性，筆法帶著天眞、純稚的特質，流露出樸素、簡明的原始風味，具有素人藝術的特徵。然其所描繪之企鵝造形生動，誠如白瀨矗所提詞句「宮嶋氏畫筆逼眞」，巧妙地傳達了質樸、親切的一面。

As early as the beginning of this century, a Japanese expedition team headed by Lieutenant Naoshi Shirose reached the Antarctic. One of this series of cards employs as its theme a first-class admission ticket to the showing of the film (documentary) about the expedition undertaken by an expedition team led by Shirose in 1910. This card also features Antarctic penguins painted by Miyagima shi as well as the signature and seal of Naoshi Shirose. Another card features four penguins flocking together and the epigraph written by Naoshi Shirose in Taipei. These cards are characterized by interesting composition and innocent brush techniques, emanating an original flavor of simplicity and brevity, as if rendered by an untutored artist. Like what Naoshi Shirose said in his epigraph: Miyagima Shi's depiction is realistic, the penguins are lively shaped, giving the cards an aspect of purity and affability.

爲紀念白瀬中尉南極探險50週年所發行的信封套

It's an envelope in commemoration of the 50th anniversary of the antarctic expedition by Lieutenant Naoshi Shiroe.

RD-009

RD-010

RD-011

京都一隅 A Corner of Kyoto

京都是日本西部的文教中心。西元 794 年，桓武天皇將皇都遷移至此，而其營建完全仿照唐朝首都長安。直至西元 1868 年的一千餘年之間，京都便一直是日本首都所在地，其境內所擁有的豐富文化遺產，實非其他都市所能比擬，光是寺院宮幃便有兩千餘座，因而整個城市一直保有濃厚的宮廷色彩，洋溢著古典的風貌。

此張卡片便是以京都極具歷史風味的一隅爲題材。絹本的卡片上還特別先遍塗金色做爲底色（需知在當時金粉仍是極爲昂貴奢侈的畫材），再以社寺町高貴、優雅的建築及庭園設計爲主題。此作品當有別於一般的地圖，雖然畫面上亦用文字標示著每一個古蹟名勝，且其地理相對位置頗爲精確，然從其流暢的運筆及鮮明的設色，足見該作者必曾領受過古典文化的滋養，咀嚼過京都宮廷文化的精華。彷彿沉澱著歷史的畫面上，有著貴族藝術華麗洗鍊的彩衣，優雅與濃艷相得益彰。可見作者旨在融合日本古典傳統的色彩與圖案化的造型來詮釋京都的詩情。

Kyoto is the cultural and educational center of west Japan. In 794, Emperor Kanmu relocated the capital to Kyoto, whose construction emulates the configuration of Chang'an, the capital of the Tang Dynasty of China. Kyoto remained the capital of Japan throughout the ensuing millennium until 1868. The abundant cultural heritage of Kyoto is without parallel in any other city in Japan. Kyoto has more than 2000 temples and palaces alone; therefore, the city has always been unique for its characteristics of court culture and classical flavor.

This card employs as its setting a corner of Kyoto which is quite unique in its historical flavor. Golden color is first applied as the background of this silk card. (It should be noted that golden pigment was very expensive and extravagant at that time.) The noble and delicate structures and court designs of the city's Syagi-cho district were used as the subject of this card. This piece is different from a typical map. Although the picture also specifies the name of each historic resort, whose relative geographic location is quite accurate vis-a-vis other resorts, the smooth brush strokes and bright coloring of this piece attest to the artist's upbringing in classical culture and his extensive experience in digesting the essence of Kyoto's court culture. This painting, characterized by a considerable historical flavor and a harmonious combination of elegance and brightness, seems to be a refined and sophisticated product of noble art. Hence, the artist intended to utilize the classical color schemes of Japan and various patterns to interpret the poetic lyricism of Kyoto.

（絹本 Silken Card）

RD-012

燈籠圖 Lantern

這幅〝燈籠圖〞所呈現的是一般夜行照明用的提燈(可掛在腰上或手提)，紅色的燈罩上所繪的乃商店或家族的徽章，通幅畫面是以明亮的色彩和簡單樸素的形態組合而成的。構圖簡明嚴謹、平穩莊重，卻又不失變化。前前後後交錯排列的紅色燈籠，在微妙的色彩變化之下，隱約露著燭光的躍動，加上其上的符號變化，使得畫面在單純之中，有一種細膩的感覺，而零落飄散的花瓣，更爲畫面增添了寧靜的氣氛。

紅、白、黑三色構成的主題，在淡黃色的仿布紋卡紙上，顯得十分顯目。純淨鮮明的色彩和平舖的構圖所造成的裝飾風格引人注目，讓觀者很容易便忽略了畫面中間偏右的兩個燈籠之間不合理的空間關係。作者巧妙地運用了單純的色彩及穩定的造型，在反覆運用的技法之中，加上微妙的變化，成功地賦予了這件作品秩序、節奏感，使得原本平凡的日常事物，搖身一變而成爲純粹的美感表達。

This "Lantern" depicts a typical lantern carried by pedestrians for illumination in the darkness. The lantern can be hung around the waist or carried in one's hand. On the shades of the lanterns are store or clan logos. This picture was created through the combination of bright colors and simple shapes,with a composition that is sparse, meticulous, smooth and solemn, yet does not lacking variety. In subtle and varied colors, the lanterns placed on the foreground and background in a random fashion seem to exhibit the flickering candle light within. In addition, the variations of the marks on the lantern add delicacy to the simplicity of this piece. The falling petals create an atmosphere of tranquillity.

The motif created in red, white and black is quite conspicuous on a buff-colored card, which is similar to cloth in texture. The pure and fresh coloring, along with its decorative style created through a graphic composition, is so eye-catching that the viewer is likely to ignore the unreasonable spatial arrangement between the two lanterns located in the center towards the right. The artist succeeds in creating a sense of order and rhythm out of this piece, through his skillful use of simple colors and substantial shapes, in conjunction with subtle variations to the technique of repetition. As a result, what would otherwise have been commonplace daily objects are transformed into pure aesthetic expression.

RD-013

賞楓圖 Admiring Maples

這件背面簽有〝田代生〞之名的作品，是作者手繪寄予京都友人的絹本卡片。畫中人物所穿戴之黑色高帽及服飾，乃日本平安時代（794-1192）的士人特有的裝扮。人物的頭部五官是以極爲纖細的筆觸一筆筆勾勒而成的。其身上所穿著之長袍則以匀細流暢、不作粗細轉折變化的線條描繪。衣衫褶痕雖不見暈染，而純粹以線條表現，卻仍能展現人物身軀的實體感及背風飄動的衣袖動態。鮮紅的朱砂所繪成的楓葉和人物所穿著的石綠色長袍，在泛黃的背景襯托之下，形成強烈的色彩效果。畫面上方有田代生所題的和歌歌詞，歌詞上則有鼠灰色礦物顏料舖點的痕跡，其效果恰與地面上星星點點的跳躍筆觸相呼應。作者巧妙地運用了各個不同明度、不同形狀的色塊，造成相互照應、對比、襯托的效果。這些單純又富變化的色彩，配合剛勁的線條，使全幅畫面帶有強烈的裝飾風味。

This piece bearing the signature of Tashirosei is a silken postcard hand-rendered and sent by the artist to his friend in Kyoto. The black high hat and the costume worn by the figures in the picture are typical of the Heian Period of Japan (794-1192). The features on the face of the figure are depicted with detail by fine brushstrokes. The robe worn by the figure is rendered by even and smooth lines which do not vary in thickness. Although the creases on the robe are not color-shaded and are simply represented by lines, they are nevertheless effective in presenting the solidity of a human body and the motion of the costume flapping in the wind. The vermilion maple leaves and the green robe of the figure present a sharp contrast of color against the yellowish background. On the top section of the picture are lyrics of a Japanese responsive poem (*waka*) written by Tashirosei. The lyrics are covered with dots in gray mineral pigment, which correspond to the jumpy strokes for the spots on the ground. The artist skillfully employed a variety of brightness and shades to create an effect of correspondence, contrast and relief. The simple and varied coloring, along with forcible lines, contributes to the strong flavor of decorativeness permeating the entire picture.

（絹本 Silken Card）

RD-014

和歌紙牌

Japanese Music Cards

圖上的兩張黑框和歌紙牌，是作爲和歌接伩遊戲之用，左爲一首完整之和歌，右爲和歌之後段，用來銜接參與遊戲者先前所唸之前段，全副紙牌共有兩百張，一百首和歌。

背景之楓葉藉由不同底色而勾勒出富層次感的楓葉。

The two black-framed cards were used when playing relay games of traditional Japanese Music. On the left one is a complete song, and on the right is only the second half of the same song, intended to link up the first half read by another player. There are two hundred cards in a complete deck, containing one hundred songs. The maple leaves in the background are distinctly layered by different background colors of the mountain.

RD-015

冬鹿 Winter Deer

圖中的鹿是日本春日大社和嚴島神社之特產,兀立在冬日曠野,遍地的落楓,以及烘爐的背景,由於用色的濃郁、彩度與明度的合宜搭配,少卻了幾份寂寥與蕭瑟。

The deer seen in the picture are only found in Kasuga Shrine and Itsukushima Shrine in Japan. They were seen standing alone in the wildness of winter, with fallen maple leaves all over the ground against a backdrop like that of a hearth. Because the richness of the colors and the appropriate combination of color and brightness, the loneliness and bleakness of the picture were lessened.

RD-016

新撰八雲琴指南

New Yakuno Goto Study Book

此張絹本卡片是以「錦繪」(西元 1765 年後所採用的多色套印的浮世繪)斜貼在畫面上方以充當「八雲琴指南」的教本封面，然而作者並不滿足於錦繪本身既有的效果，還自行在其上以銀筆畫出層層的波浪，以強化樂音如波濤起伏的意境。畫面的前景則繪有狀似古箏的八雲琴及彈琴用的拔子。實際上，日本音樂深受中國影響，尤其是日本傳統音樂，無論形式或精神，多半都是由中國本土學習而來的，圖中的八雲琴便是最佳的例證之一。

This silken card features Nishikie (chromatographic Ukiyoe, which debuted in 1765), attached slantwise to the picture as the cover of the textbook titled *Yakuno Goto Study Book*. However, the artist was not content with the existing Nishikie effect; therefore, he depicted layers of waves with a silver pen to strengthen the impression that the waves fluctuate just like musical notes. On the foreground are an antique-looking Yakuno Goto and a pick used for playing the instrument. In fact, Japanese music, especially traditional music, is deeply affected by China and was mostly acquired from mainland China both in terms of format and essence. The Yakuno Goto depicted in the center of the picture offers a good example.

(絹本 Silken Card)

RD-017

蛇蛙圖 Python and Frog

這幅水彩繪製的蛇蛙圖，意圖藉由兩個對比顯明的個體，去捕捉大自然循環不息的生態。全畫著重在運用構圖曲線的安排，製造畫面的動態生趣；再加上懸空的背景，更襯托出主題的明顯性。畫面上方，張口吐信的大蟒蛇扭轉的身軀已延伸至畫頁之外，足見其身軀之龐大。而它所設定之目標是一隻翻肚跳躍的青蛙；後者翻躺的姿態，似乎顯露出一種認命或因驚嚇過度而昏眩的意味，造型雖略嫌誇張，不盡符合眞實的生態，卻能深刻地傳達這一刻緊張的氣氛。

畫中單純的取景所形成的虛實張力，賦予了這件作品紮實的空間凝聚感。畫面上生動傳神的造型，不但具有逼眞的光影立體效果，更成功地傳達了蛙驚蛇囂的刹那動勢。蛇乃蛙之天敵，青蛙面對著對它吐信的大蟒蛇，就等於面對生死關頭，畫中所隱藏的不安，正象徵著自然世界中，乃至於生命中所潛伏的危機。

This "Python and Frog" picture in watercolor intends to depict the perennial ecology of nature through the two contrasting objects. The focus of this picture is creating a sense of the dynamic pleasure of life through the arrangement of its composition and lines. Its empty background makes the motif all the more conspicuous. On the upper section of this picture is a hissing python whose wriggling body extends beyond the edge of the picture, indicating the enormity of the python, which sets its eyes on the belly-up frog on the ground. The posture of the frog lying on the ground seems to suggest fatalism or the feeling of having fainted due to extreme terror. Although such a creation is somewhat exaggerated and not exactly in conformity with realistic ecology, it aptly and accurately conveys the moment of tension.

The ethereal tension created through the simplistic selection of scenes gives solid spatial coherence to this piece are portrayed with realistic lighting and a three-dimensional effect. The picture also succeeds in creating the dynamism of a scared frog and an aggressive python. So far as the frog is concerned, facing a hissing python, which is one of its nemesises, is tantamount to facing a critical moment of life and death. The uneasiness permeating this picture symbolizes the potential danger in the natural world, or even in our lives.

RD-025

RD-026

RD-027

RD-028

RD-029～RD-032

旅遊指南圖 Travel Guide

此四張地圖裱褙作品，圖一爲草山地區的路線指示圖，左下蓋有草山地方的戳章。圖二爲東北地區的產業分布圖，並蓋有蘇澳圖案的地方戳章。圖三爲台北四個著名的株式會社的相關方位圖。圖四爲台灣南部與外島的航路圖，可惜僅取局部無法窺其全貌。

The first one of the four framed maps shows the routes within the Grass Mountain area. In the lower left corner of the map is stamp of the Grass Mountain area. Map Two, upon which a local souvenir stamp of Suao, shows the distribution of industries. Map Three shows the relative positions of four famous companies in Taipei. Map Four shows the sea routes between the southern part of Taiwan and its outlying islets. It is a shame that only part of the map is available.

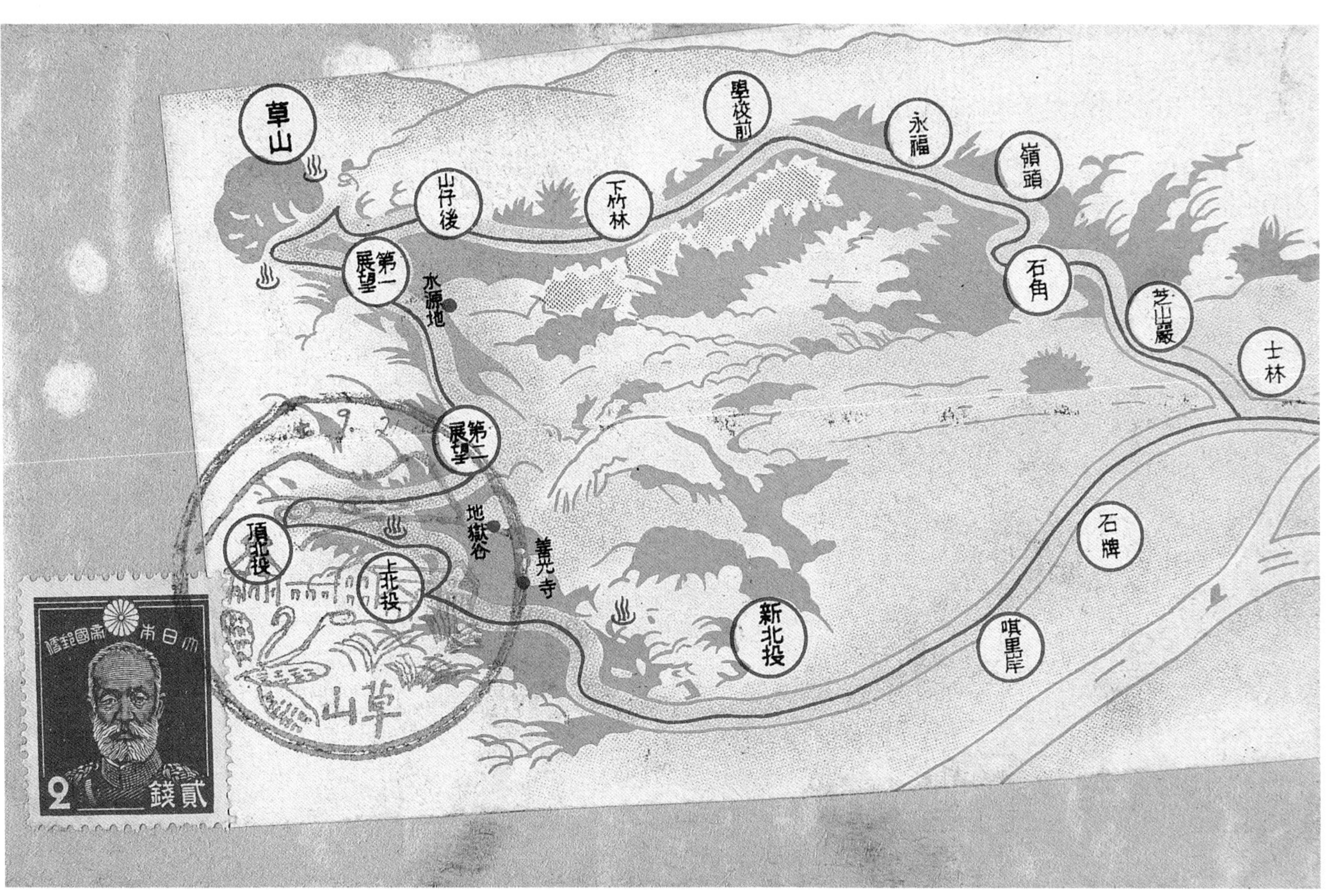

(圖一)圖左下角爲手刻草山地方風景戳 RD-029

(Map First)Grass Moutain landscape of the postmark named Mt. Yang-Ming today.

(圖二)明信片空白處蓋有二枚手刻蘇澳地方風景戳
(Map Two)There are two hand-carving postmarks of Suao sealed on the postcard.

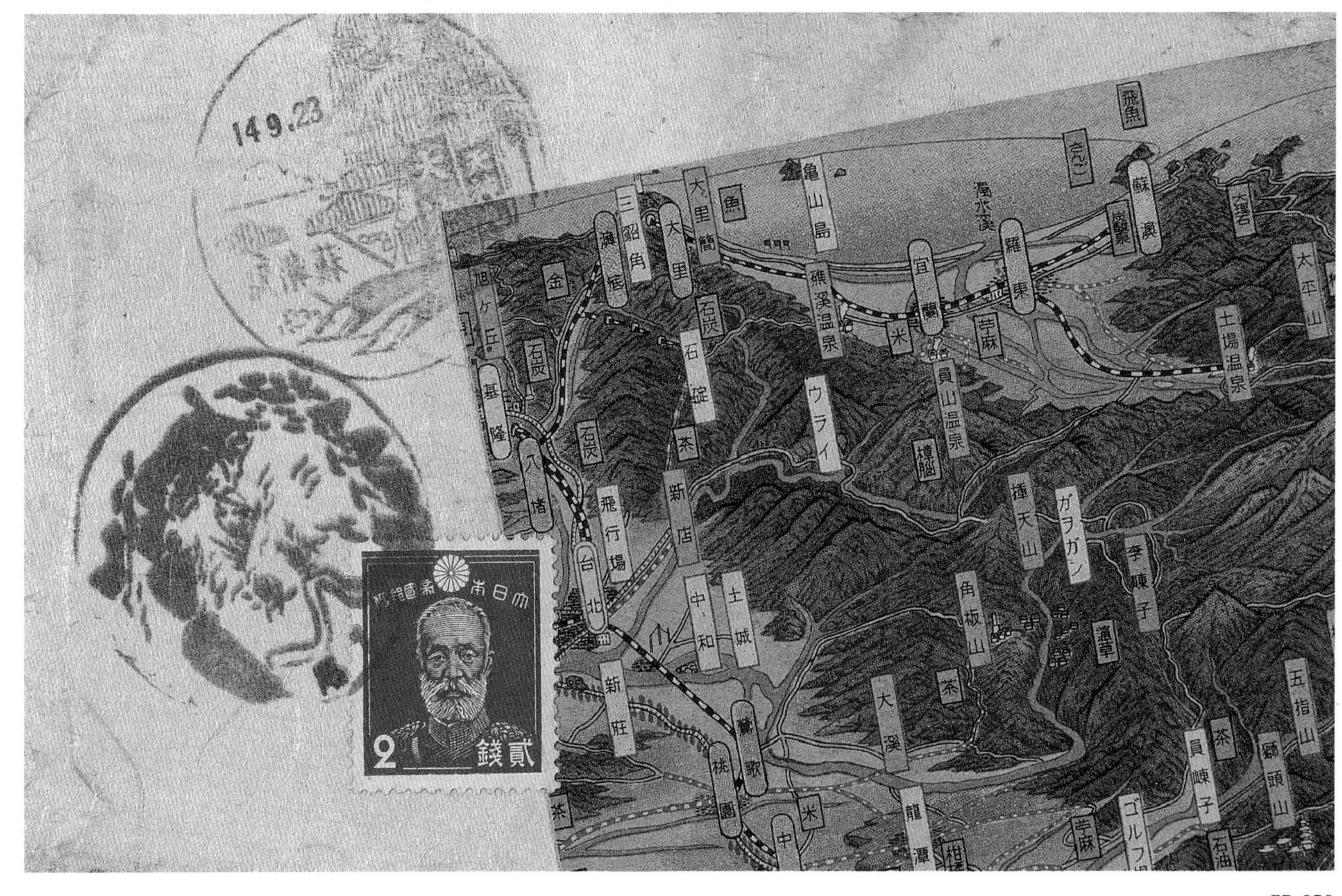

RD-030

RD-036

格言美術 Art of Sayings

畫面上躍然出現的四個大字「嚴而眞嚴」想必是創作者心中的格言或祖傳之家訓，此一作品顯然又是一幅書法與彩繪結合之作，書法的空間排列方式與其旁兩隻飛鳥的組合關係，增加了畫面的跳躍感，擺脫了嚴肅、刻板而厚重的書法格言之寓意。

The four large characters in the picture "strict, but sincerely strict" must have been a personal adage or a proverb passed down in the family. This work is obviously another combination of calligraphy and color painting. The space arrangement of the calligraphy and its combined relationship with the two flying birds add to the vividness of the picture, getting rid of the strictness, stiffness and heaviness of the proverb in calligraphy.

RD-037

曲本與書架

Scores and Shelves

依左列長幅的書目提字看來，推斷應爲各謠曲段落的集錦；左下角應爲一置放謠曲本的書架。

From the inscription of the bibliography on the left, this could be a melange of various stanzas of songs. There might be a book shelf full of scores in the lower left corner.

（絹本 Silken Card）

RD-038

千鳥之曲

Song of the Plover

這件作品是先以兩張已印有紋路的紙裱貼在鑲有金邊的卡片上，再在空白之處做適當的構圖變化。裱紙上寫著「琴唄」及「千鳥之曲」的墨字（『唄』：小曲；『千鳥』：一種沿海生存的小飛鳥），文字旁邊繪有琴弦的角，以加強畫面與音樂的關連性。畫面構圖疏落有致，以率真寫意的筆觸描繪而成的千鳥，姿態生動可愛，並且有遠近大小的變化；而以藍、白及銀色顏料所勾勒的海中波浪及浪花，翻騰的造形變化多趣。畫面右方則有以尖嘴筆描繪裝釘線裝書頁用的繩索，效果生動逼眞。由整體設計上看來，作者意圖製造線裝樂譜的封面效果，畫面意趣横生、清新宜人，予人抒情愉悦的感受。

For this piece, two sheets of paper which had been printed with markings were mounted on a postcard with a golden border. And then, fitting compositional variations were added to the blank spaces of the picture. On the mounted paper are the characters for "melody of the lyre" and "Song of the plover." (The plover is a type a small bird whose habitat lies in coastal areas.) The corners of a Japanese musical instrument are painted alongside the text to emphasize the relationship between the picture and music. This piece has properly spaced composition; and the plovers depicted through direct and realistic strokes are engaging and lovely with variations of distance. The sea waves and white water in blue, white and silver pigments feature an interesting variety of shapes. On the right of the picture are cords used for the binding of a book which are depicted in a lifelike and lively manner by means of a stylograph. Judging from the overall design of this piece, the artist intended to create an effect similar to the cover of a musical score bound by cords. The fun and pleasure pervading the picture as well as its quality of freshness create an aura of lyrical zest.

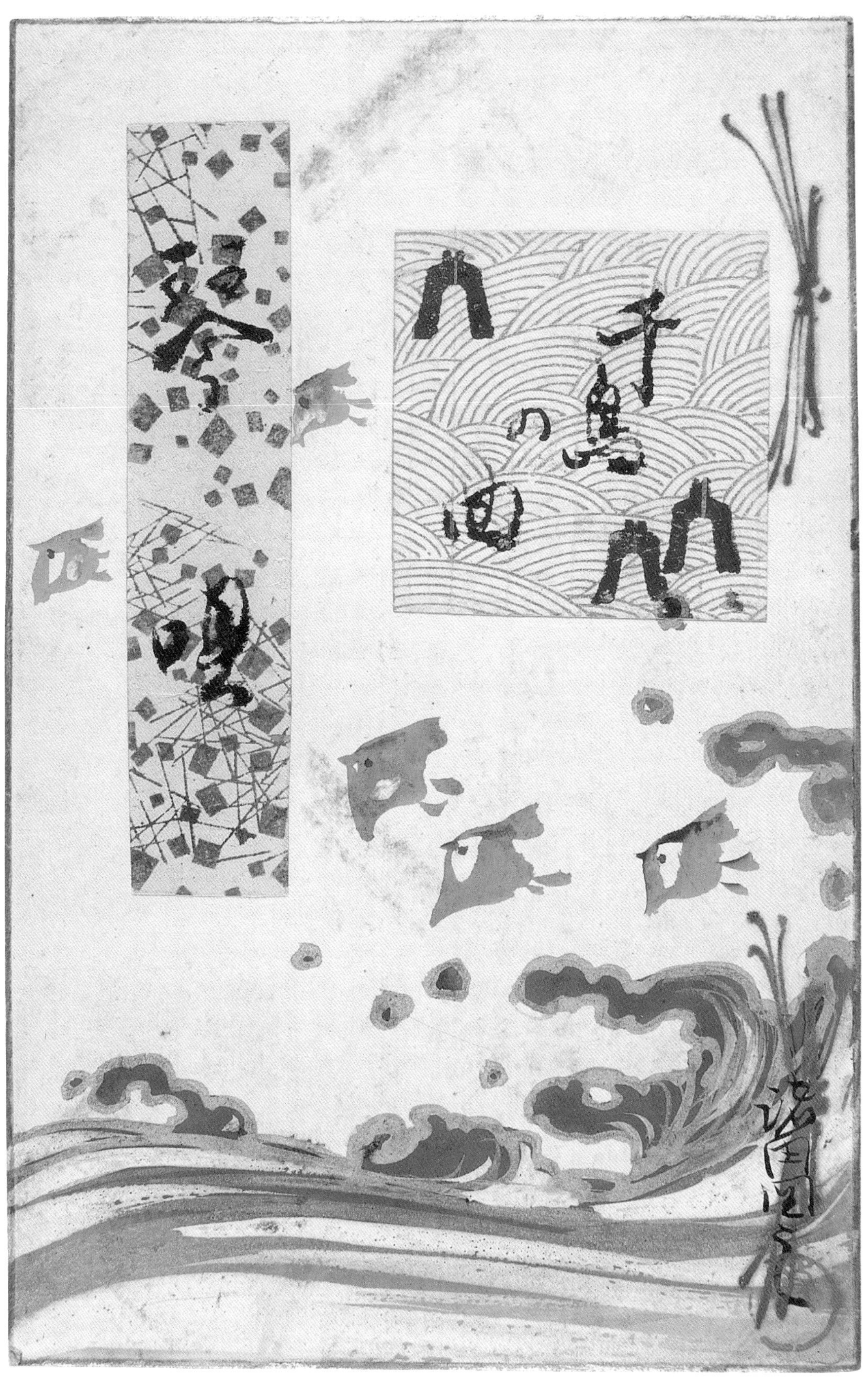

RD-039

愛宕山紀念

Memory of Atago-Yama

此張卡片是以洛西（京都西北）愛宕山的名物（名產）包裝紙做爲表現的主題，作者將包裝紙斜裱在卡片上，並以平塗的手法描繪愛宕山做爲背景，前景則以橋面欄杆來陪襯，圖案化的畫面上，色彩鮮明對比、簡潔清新。此類作品的紀念價值勝於美感的追求，足見日本文化對周遭細微事物之關心。

Wrappings for specialties of Atago-Yama, located in Rakusei (northwestern part of Kyoto), are chosen as the theme of this piece. The artist mounted the wrapping paper slantwise on a card and depicted Atago-Yama as its theme through flat painting. The rails of a bridge are put in the foreground to present a contrast. This picture features graphic-orientation, a sharp contrast of color, brevity and freshness. This type of work emphasizes commemorative value more than aesthetic appeal. This shows that in Japanese culture, attention may be directed toward even a trivial event in the surroundings.

（絹本 Silken Card）

RD-044

「平」、「源」氏之爭

Battle between Kagekiyo and Mioya-Juro

作者在裱貼著書頁的絹本卡片上，用連綿有致的筆觸，一筆筆的表現了水光波動的感覺，並以潑灑的方式，製造了波浪拍擊在岩石上所激起的浪花；筆法簡潔生動，使觀者彷彿可以聽到浪花拍打在岸上岩石的聲音。

數顆碎石子，暗示了前景的海岸；在岸上，棄置著日本武士的大刀和頭盔。波浪和刀刃特別用銀灰色的顏料描繪，以製造波光粼粼、刀刃鋒利的質感。

從畫面右邊傾斜裱貼的《日本外史》書頁中的文字，可以了解作者意欲藉著平家和源家爭霸的歷史故事中的一段情景，抒發其感慨。在平源雙雄勢力消長的過程當中，源氏獲得最終勝利；戰敗的平氏家族則棄兵卸甲、投海自盡。

波濤洶湧的岸邊，但見丟棄了的盔甲和兵器，呈現一幕〝大江東去浪淘盡〞的淒涼景況。

In this piece, the artist employs continuous and consistent strokes on a book leaf mounted on a silk card to create a sense of the motion of waves in water. The white water created by waves splashing against rocks demonstrates economical brush-stroke, through which the viewers are almost able to hear the sound of waves splashing against the rocks.

Tiny pebbles indicates the setting of a beach in the foreground. On the beach, there is a sumurai's spear and helmet. Silver-gray pigments are employed in the coloring of waves and knife blades to delineate the quality of waves and sharpness of the weapon.

From the words on the tilted leaf (of the *Unofficial History of Japan*) mounted on the right section of the picture, we learn that the artist intends to express his feeling through the historical episode of the rivalry between the Heike clan and the Genji clan. The Genji clan eventually prevailed at the end of the tug-of-war between the two clans. The Heike clan, who were defeated, committed suicide by drowning themselves in the sea.

On the beach touched by raging waves, the discarded helmet and weapon create a scene of desolation reminiscent of a bloody defeat.

（絹本 Silken Card）

RD-045

RD-046～RD-047

信貴山 Mount Shigi

此張卡片是以信貴山上三樂莊店鋪的感謝紙條自正面反摺至背面斜貼在絹本卡片上。金底卡片上有作者所描繪的風景小品，構圖取巧，用筆渾圓精簡，漸層暈染的斜坡上洋溢著綠意；坡上的樹叢濃淡交錯的枝葉輪廓，也有部分經過些微暈染，製造出逆光中煙霧迷濛的效果，使人感受到户外明朗的空氣氣息。畫面上的題款，則適度地予以單純的構圖更豐富的變化。卡片背面則說明了這是作者自信貴山寄予在台友人的親筆手繪作品。

On this card, the thank-you note used by the store of Sanraku-Sō in Mount Shigi is folded backward from its front side and then mounted slantwise on a silken card. Against the golden background of the card is the artist's scenic painting characterized by deft composition and round, simple brush-strokes. The slope painted in transitional color evokes a sense of greenness. The contours of intertwined twigs and leaves of the thickets on the slope as depicted in alternating shades have, in addition to the slight coloring of a portion of the contours, created a misty and smoky effect as if against the source of light and brought out the freshness and brightness of an outdoor environment. The epigraph on the frame aptly adds variation to the simple composition of the picture. The back of this card reveals that it was hand-rendered by the artist, who sent it to his friend in Taiwan from Mt. Shigi.

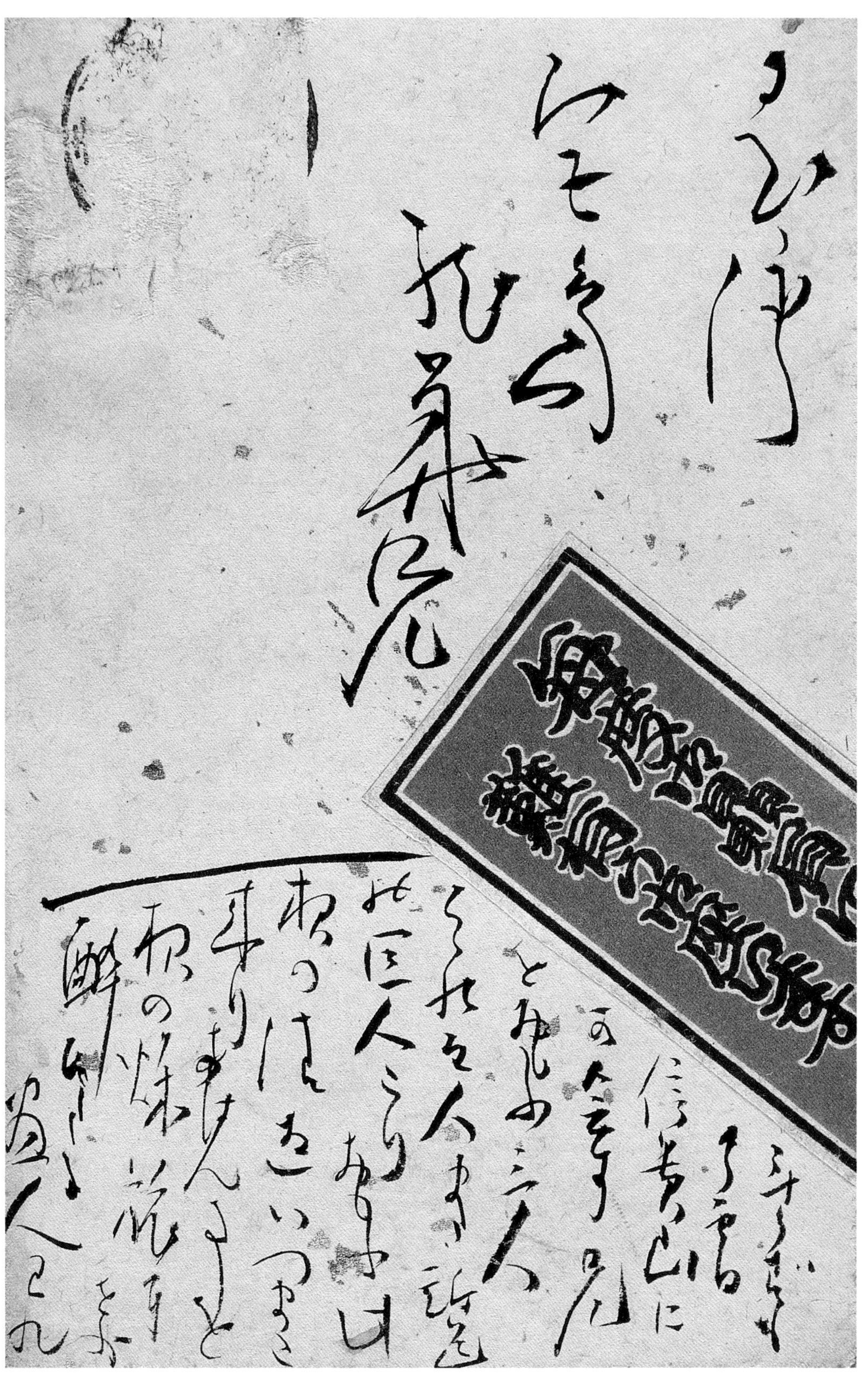

RD-046

（絹本 Silken Card）

RD-047

水墨小品
Ink and Wash Miniatures

日本水墨畫也是從中國傳去的，14世紀起初興於禪宗寺院，江戶年間轉爲儒學文士的遣興，至明治初年又成爲地方遺老擊鉢吟詩的墨戲，等於說日本水墨畫未曾在中央畫壇上呼風喚雨，卻老是存在於讀書人的雅興階段。

近代以還，日本水墨技法最常用於書籍報刊的插圖，草草幾筆，掌握了小說情節或地方紀遊。至於四君子（梅、蘭、竹、菊）等一類的花卉畫，由於日本水墨畫未能成爲主流，創作者又都是業餘興趣，要求不嚴，反而走出了中國水墨畫一切以擬摹爲本的框框。作者很自由地取竹節的一段、梅花的一枝、蘭葉的一片，自己再加上不必按章法的一隻小蟲，一幅趣味性的水墨，自娛而娛人。

日本還有一種水墨畫是題上俳句的，筆法很簡單，什麼都可以入畫，稱之爲「俳畫」。水墨小品多少有與之相類似的意境。看多了中國正宗水墨，再看日本水墨小品，也有一種嚴肅中求灑脫的輕鬆感。

The Japanese ink and wash was imported from China. It originated in Zen temples in the early 14th century. During the Edo Era it became a hobby of the literati. In the beginning of the Meiji Era, it then turned into a pastime for the old educated class to express their poetic feelings. It was never, so to speak, the center stage of the Japanese art world, but yet it lingered on as a hobby among the literati.

In recent times, Japanese ink and wash has been mostly found in illustrations of books and magazines. With just a few strokes, the gist of the novel's plot or a local journey was captured. Because ink and wash was never the mainstream of Japanese art, and because most of the painters were amateurs, pictures depicting blossoms such as the "four men of noble character," i.e. plum blossom, orchid, bamboo and chrysanthemum, broke the convention of imitation upon which Chinese ink and wash was based. The painter might freely choose a section of a bamboo stick, a branch of plum blossoms, or a leave of an orchid, and add a little insect without following the conventional composition. An interesting and amusing ink and wash both to the painter and the viewers was thus created.

There is another genre of Japanese ink and wash on which a haiku or a short poem could be added. With simple strokes, anything could be the subject matter of the painting. It is generally referred to as a haiku painting. Ink-and-wash miniatures have a somewhat similar artistic conception. If you have seen enough orthodox Chinese ink-and-wash, Japanese ink-and-wash will give you a feeling of relief and freedom.

甲蟲圖 Portrait of Beetles

這幅甲蟲圖，構圖簡潔、墨色淨潤、筆法自由奔放。畫面上並不強調寫實的描繪，而偏重以筆墨意趣的表現和構圖的創新，去捕捉寫生花蟲鳥獸的生命神韻。淡墨簡筆處理的竹身，顯得格外的清淨含蓄；與重墨敷彩的甲蟲形成鮮明的對比。簡潔的畫面上充滿一種靜謐穩定的氣氛，没有強烈的運動感受，像夢幻中的景象，散發出細膩的藝術韻味，雖然只是簡要的數筆，卻也蘊含著畫家掌握自然生意神韻的能力，及其對筆墨效果的深切了解和傑出的創意。

This single portrait of beetles is characterized by its simple composition, clear and pure ink, and untrammeled brush-strokes. Instead of focusing on the delineation of reality, the artist strove to capture the verve of flowers, insects, birds and animals through the impressionistic representation of brush and ink and the innovation of composition. The bamboo depicted in light ink and by simple strokes appear all the more immaculate and enigmatic in stark contrast with the garish coloring of the beetles, to which heavy ink is applied. An atmosphere of tranquillity and stability permeates the simplistic painting which does not evoke a strong sense of movement even though a dream-like scene emanating a delicate artistic flavor is discernible. Though created with simple strokes, this piece demonstrates the artist's ability to capture the verve of natural life, his in-depth knowledge of brush and ink effects, as well as his unrivaled creativity.

RD-048

雙貓圖 Twin Cats

這件作品著重在利用雙貓的神態，製造畫面的生趣。兩隻黑背白肚的幼貓，蜷縮成圓球狀，蹲坐於樂器之上，其中一隻，低頭俯視；另一隻則昂著頭，其睥睨仰窺的雙眼，巧妙地將觀者的視線延伸至畫外。雙貓一上一下的眼神，不但擴展了畫面上的視覺空間，同時也爲這寧靜的景象，帶來了微妙的動態變化。這種裝飾性的動態，使畫面充滿了一種象徵性的神祕氣氛。

雙貓的形象是以纖細的筆觸精工刻劃而成的。樂器則是先以細線勾勒輪廓，再用渲染的方式處理立體明暗，其形體結實，結構肯定，明暗交界面毫不含糊。大筆勾劃的粉紅色牡丹，則爲畫面增添了抒情的韻味和愉快的氣氛。畫中的樂器乃日本最通俗的傳統樂器之一，名爲「三味線」，是從中國傳入的「三弦」，唯獨演奏的方式有所改變，至今，三味線仍是日本各地的樂坊、劇場和舞台表演的主要伴奏樂器之一。據説三味線的音箱是以貓皮製成的，如此一來，此「雙貓圖」在裝飾的表面之下，當蘊含更深沈的意念。

象徵「富貴」的牡丹，與貓、樂器的配合，成爲畫家精心選擇的優雅母題，共同組成這幅精美、富裝飾意念的作品。

This art work creates an aura of fun through the verve emanating from the eyes of the two cats. The two kittens, with black backs and white bellies, curl on a musical instrument, with one looking down and the other raising its head. The eyes of the kitten looking upward subtly extend the viewer's line of sight outside the picture. The light in the eyes of the cats looking up and down not only contributes to the extension of the visual space of the picture, but also brings subtle yet dynamic alteration. This decorative dynamic adds symbolic mystique to the frame.

The shapes of the twin cats are depicted through fine and delicate brush strokes. As for the musical instrument, fine lines are first scribed for the creation of its contour. Then the light colors are applied to create a three-dimensional contrast between brightness and darkness. This piece is characterized by solid shapes, firm structures and a clear-cut demarcation between brightness and darkness. The musical instrument depicted in this piece, is a *syami sen*, one of the most conventional musical instruments of Japan which in fact is derived from the Chinese tricord, with a different method of performance. Up to today, the *syami sen* has remained one of the major musical instruments for musical workshops, theaters and stages in Japan. The cats and the instrument, in conjunction with peonies, which symbolize "wealth," are an elegant motif favored by the artist and embodied in this delicate and decorative art work.

Note: It is said that the music box of *syami sen* is made of cat skin. If that is the case, the decoration of the Twin Cat conveys a deeper message.

（絹本 Silken Card）

RD-049

大象與藝妓

Elephant and Courtesan

這幅大象與藝妓的取材詭異、構圖新奇，畫面上，運用正面取景及灰色調子的明暗變化所描繪的大象形體，顯得壯碩而笨拙，與其脚旁的弱小藝妓相映成趣。幾乎塡滿整個畫面的大象，予人一種沈重的壓迫感，但嬌小的藝妓閒散柔和的姿態及其所穿著的粉紅衣裙，巧妙地緩和了上述的氣氛，同時也給畫面增添了溫和的感受及無限的意趣。

This piece is characterized by the selection of a strange theme, "Elephant and Courtesan," and exotic composition. In the picture, the elephant, depicted from a frontal perspective and with the light-and-shade contrast of gray coloring, appears to be gross and clumsy, presenting an interesting contrast with the feminine courtesan. The oppression created by the elephant, which almost fills the entire frame, is subtly mitigated by the tender posture and the pink costume of the petite courtesan. The depiction of the courtesan also lends considerably to its tender feeling and infinite fascination.

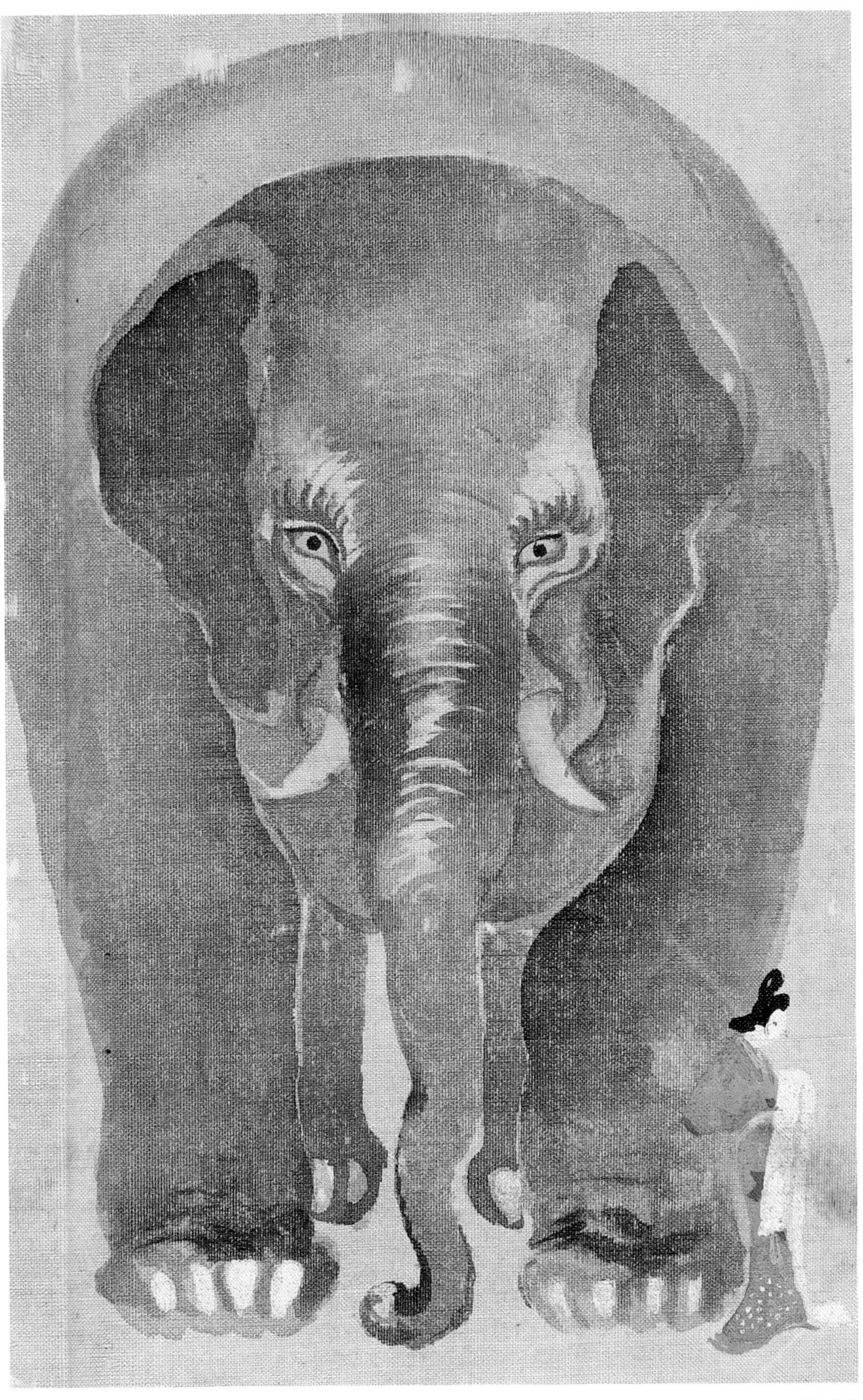

(絹本 Silken Card)

RD-050

雪山雲 Clouds Over Snowy Mountains

此張款署「靜涯」的作品係日治時代，「台展」中「東洋畫部」審查員木下靜涯的手筆。由其背面的郵戳和文字資料證明這是畫家於明治13年元月1日(西元1937年)用來寄給台北友人的新年賀卡。

這是一幅刻意處理得很單純但卻充滿了細膩情感的作品。輕快瀟灑的筆觸、簡潔古樸的構圖、均勻和諧的灰藍色調，呈現出明朗爽目的高雅氣質，扼要的勾畫出一幅孤寂的冬日美景，畫面意境清幽、生意盎然。

木下靜涯重視寫生，就連所繪之深山大川亦非幻想的山水畫。而其筆墨上較抽象的表現，則是來自對具體事物之觀察所產生之感受。儘管這幅作品裡所描繪的不是神仙樂園，而是現實風光，但畫面上所呈現的亦不是自然的再現，而是比自然更美的抒情詩篇。畫面上，首先吸引我們注意的是一片灰藍色彩的山峯和點點的群雁，然後才是隱約可辨的飄雲及雲層中半隱半露的山脊。在這裡，形已不重要，重要的是呈現在畫面上的那種山嵐迷濛的氣氛，而那些模糊的形是那麼恰到好處地扮演了這種氣氛。在畫面上，我們似乎可以感受到雲氣的溫潤、嗅到空氣的清新、以及靜謐閒適的氣息。

此卡可能是靜涯爲準備「中央山脈的雲海風景寫生圖」的同時所繪之小品，並將之自關仔嶺溫泉旅館寄給友人做爲祝賀的卡片。

This artistic work bearing the signature of Seigai was created by Kinoshita Seigai, a reviewer of the Japanese Painting Division of the Taiwan Art Exhibition when Taiwan was under Japan's rule. The postmark and wordage on the back of the piece testify that this piece dated January 1 of the 13th year of the Meiji Era (1937) was a greeting card for his friend in Taipei.

As a work of art handled with simple techniques, it is both delicate and touching. Its brisk and dashing strokes, simple and classic composition, and an even and harmonious grayish blue tint all help create an aura of elegance which is bright and pleasant-looking. Also pithily depicted is a desolate winter scene, with an aroma of tranquillity and vitality.

Kinoshita Seigai frequenthy went into the field to paint real scenes first-hand, so that his sweeping wilderness paintings were not merely products of the imagination. His abstract presentation of strokes and ink was derived from his experience through his observation of concrete objects. This painting portrays not a fairy land, but realistic scenery, yet what comes out of the art work is not a reproduction of nature but a lyric superior to nature. Looking at the painting, we are first fascinated by a patch of grayish blue mountains and sporadic waterfowl, followed by fuzzy clouds and ridges emerging halfway from the clouds. At this juncture, shape does not matter any more. What comes in its place is the misty atmosphere in the mountain, and the blurry shape incidentally brings out this atmosphere. Looking at the painting, we seem to be brought in touch with the tenderness and softness of clouds, to smell the freshness of air, and enjoy the aura of tranquillity and ease.

It is likely that Seigai created this greeting card when he was getting ready to work on the "Sketch of the Cloud Sea in the Central Mountains," and sent it from a hot spring hotel in Kuan Tze Ridge to greet a friend.

RD-051

一枝春光 A Spring Twig

這張在右下方有「一枝春光、靜涯試筆」題字的作品係木下靜涯親手筆繪用來寄予台北友人的賀卡。木下靜涯（西元1889～1992年，享年103歲）本名源重郎，是日治時期「台展」（西元1927年首展）中「東洋畫部」的審查員，對台灣早期東洋畫之發展有重大的貢獻。

木下靜涯早期師事竹內栖鳳，屬京都派畫家，擅長於山水花卉。其繪畫題材都是來自日常生活周遭與之切身相關的事物，並且均以寫生的方式作畫，不繪製憑空想像的作品。

此幅作品結構精練，挺拔高傲的樹枝，孤零零地出現在畫面上；淒冷的枝頭，稀疏地掛著幾朵含苞待放的花朵，令人有孤單寂寥之感。然而，寥落數筆，卻呈現出豐富的生命內涵。花朵和枝葉的姿態，彷若有微風吹動的感覺。典雅特殊的造型中，蘊含著優美自然的氣質，配合狹長的畫面，使整幅作品在落漠孤寂的氣氛之中，流露出高雅、端莊、素淨、和諧的視覺內涵。

這一幅看似極其普通的作品，不但充分表現了作者對自然生態的深刻體會，亦表現出東方文人「孤傲自賞」的氣節，實爲畫家深下功夫、潛心營造之結晶。

This artistic work, with the inscription "A spring twig by Seigai" on the lower right of the picture, was personally painted by Kinoshita Seigai as a greeting card for his friend in Taipei. Originally named Hara Sigero, Kinoshita Seigai (who lived to the age of 103, from 1889 to 1992). During the period of Japanese rule, he was a reviewer of the Japanese Painting Division of the Taiwan Art Exhibition (first established in 1927). Seigai made great contribution to early Japanese-style painting in Taiwan.

A disciple of Takeuchi Seiho early on, Kinoshita Seigai belonged to the Kyoto School and excelled at landscape painting and flower pieces. The motifs of his works were derived entirely from the immediate events of everyday life or things to which Segai could easily relate. His paintings were also based upon genuine scenes, not conjured from his imagination.

With a refined and sophisticated structure, this piece depicts erect and majestic twigs, scattered sporadically across the painting. Desolate twigs juxtaposed with a few budding flowers give a sense of isolation and solitude. Nevertheless, the simple strokes are able to bring out the richness of life. The posture of flowers, twigs and leaves create an illusion that they seem to be touched by a breeze. The elegant and unique configuration of this piece is permeated with an aesthetic and natural quality. In combination with the long, narrow shape of this piece, the visual effect of delicacy, decorum, purity, and harmony is able to stand out amid the atmosphere of solitude and desolation emanating from the piece.

Although this piece looks very common, it fully demonstrates the artist's in-depth insight into the natural world. Also exhibited is the disposition of oriental literateurs characterized by their pride and self-admiration. Indeed, this piece was created through the dedication of a conscientious artist.

RD-052

櫻花 Cherry Blossoms

每年春天，無論在山傍、水湄、城鎮……，幾乎全日本，都可覓得櫻花的蹤跡。作者以日本人最鍾愛的櫻花爲主題，畫面布局疏落有致，雖然右下角的枝椏末端造型稍嫌笨重，但花朵、枝幹交錯生長的姿態生動雅緻。花葉繁盛茂密及枝椏低垂的取景，傳達了朝氣蓬勃的氣息，通幅畫面充滿了自然的生機與生命之喜悅。這裡，寒冬過去了，春的倩影來到了，四處洋溢著生氣勃勃的盎然春意。

Each spring, cherry blossoms can be found on the mountainside, riverside, in cities and townships virtually all over Japan. The artist employs cherry blossoms, the favorite of the Japanese, as the motif of this picture, with a well-paced and properly arranged composition. Although the shapes of the twigs on the lower right corner of the frame are somewhat bulky, the postures of the intertwined flowers and twigs are nevertheless lively and graceful. The blooming flowers and leaves, as well as the dangling twigs, create an atmosphere of exuberance and vitality. The entire picture is permeated with natural vitality and the joy of life. This picture demonstrates the exuberance of spring as the cold winter is driven away by vernal beauty.

RD-053

山水圖 Landscape

這張以水墨畫在絹本上的作品，構圖樸實簡潔，巨大的岩石之上，有隱士草堂孤立於山林之中，山下的流水和山後隱約可見的小船，使得畫面上透露出一種脱離現實鬥爭、遺世而立的寂寥感。然而，畫者重視筆墨的情趣，則甚於模仿自然的寫實。畫面上，揮灑自如的筆法，顯得蒼勁有力，縱橫奔放。在這兒，山石林木的特質，並不是以傳統慣用的線條描繪而成的。作者以明朗簡練的筆觸勾勒岩石的輪廓，並將其上的皴筆和墨色渲染融合成一體。如此一來，既能表達出岩石的立體感，亦使得畫面的效果更和諧。而淡墨暈染的雲霧，則成功地烘托出煙潤虛淡的遠山和天空，造成一種溼氣迷濛的感覺，巧妙地顯現出大氣中陰沈的雨意。重墨粗筆的岩石樹林與淡墨渲染的山嵐煙水及蒼茫的大氣之間，形成強烈的節奏感，墨色雅澹，趣味引人入勝。

此作品雖無複雜的空間結構，然其遠近之推移都十分的成功。從前景的樹木岩石到遠方的山巒之間，我們可以很明確地感受到那種深遠的距離。這種距離既非完全眞實，亦非虛擬的，而是一種以眞實的感受爲基礎，經過過濾加強，最後僅剩下用來表達這種感受的詞彙之筆觸和墨色顯示在畫面上。氣勢雄偉的空間距離，除了充份地顯現出大自然的幽深感之外，也醞釀出一種如詩如夢，不屬於凡塵的虛幻仙境。景致古雅而寬闊，氣氛樸拙而恬適，使觀者油然興起歸隱的感慨。

Created by means of ink-painting on a silk scroll, this piece features simple and economical composition. A hermit's cottage stands desolately in the forest on a huge mountain rock. The water flowing down the mountain, along with the barely discernible little boat on the back of the mountain, evokes a sense of desolation as a result of detachment from earthly struggle and competition. However, the artist found more pleasure in the ink and brushstrokes than in the realistic imitation of nature. The picture's easy and unrestrained brushstrokes are solid, powerful and smooth. In the picture, the mountain, rock and forest are not shaped by conventional lines. Instead, the artist employed bright and refined brushstrokes to create the contour of the rock and integrate the axe-cuts with the coloring of the rock. In doing so, the three-dimensional quality of the rock is conveyed, and the harmony of the frame is created. The cloud and mist dyed in light ink successfully serve as contrast to the smoke-covered and ethereal mountain and sky in the distance, and evoke a sense of humidity and mistiness. Thus a gloomy atmosphere of rain is created with great subtlety. The rock and forest in heavy ink and rough stroke, as well as the mist, water and atmosphere colored in light ink, evoke a strong sense of rhythm, which, in conjunction with the elegant coloring of ink, transports the viewer into a different dimension.

Though devoid of a complex structure of space, this piece is a success in terms of its transition from the foreground to the background. The sense of depth between the trees and rock in the foreground and the mountain in the distance is directly discernible. The distance thus created is not entirely realistic; neither is it artificial. Rather, a realistic feeling is used as the foundation, which is then filtered an intensified, finally leaving only the brushstrokes and the shade of ink revealed in the picture, which are used to convey this vocablary of emotion. The majestic space and distance emanating from the picture not only display the intangibility of nature but also engender an ethereal fairyland, which is set apart from the earthly world for its dreamlike and poetic quality. The quaint and delicate scenery, together with its depth and its atmosphere of tranquillity and ease, causes deep sentiments of reclusiveness to well up inside the heart of the observer.

(絹本 Silken Card)

RD-054

船塢 Shipyard

這件作品的畫風豪爽、用筆率眞、造形簡化，從人物乃至於樹幹和低垂的柳葉等皆簡單幾筆以明朗的大筆觸來表現，水面却是以些微渲染及微薄的金色顏料製造波光粼粼、陽光閃爍的效果。畫中雖無古典派的面面俱到、精描細繪，然其誇張概括的形體、粗放大膽的線條和筆觸，則構成畫面獨特的風格，並反映出作者卓越的自信心。畫面上追求的並非物體可觸的眞實感，而是隱藏在物象背後的情感力量，作者爲求表現筆墨上的簡練，以「減筆」來誇張景物的「變形」與「動勢」，並省略了繁瑣的部分，其結果反而使得畫面更具生動的感染力和傳神的效果。

This piece is unique for its liberal painting style, its straightforward brush technique and the simple shapes of its objects. The figure, tree trunks and droopy willows are all reduced to several big, clear and bright strokes. As for the water, slight coloring and a thin layer of golden pigment are employed to create the glistening effect of waves as well as the radiating sunlight. Though devoid of the thoroughness and exquisite draftsmanship typical of the classical school of Japanese painting, this piece nevertheless represents a unique style and demonstrates the artist's extraordinary self-confidence, thanks to its exaggerated and generalized forms, and the rough and bold lines and brush strokes. The focus of this piece is not on tangible realism but rather on the emotional force behind the objects. To attain economy in the application of ink and brushstrokes, the artist sought to exaggerate the mutation and dynamism of the scene and objects by reducing the brushstrokes and omitting complicated elements of painting. As a result, the picture appears all the more lively and vivid.

（絹本 Silken Card）

RD-055

羅漢圖 Portrait of a Buddhist Monk

這幅山林中的羅漢圖是以傳統水墨描繪在絹本卡片上的，然而全畫深受西方繪畫觀念的影響，相當重視立體明暗效果及空間實體結構的掌握。作者以粗細濃淡多變化的線條及渲染的筆法賦予人物生動的情態。畫中羅漢的面容鬚髮是以細筆勾勒而成的，效果纖細逼真；淡墨描線渲染的衣衫深具立體感，作者還刻意以褐色處理羅漢暴露在日光底下的肌膚，全畫筆法趨近寫實；但羅漢濃眉大目、朶頤隆鼻的造型，則是經過典型化的處理；而其頭頂及手上的蟾蜍，除了顯示其修性高深乃至動物親之外，也説明了羅漢正教誨其手中的小蟾蜍當努力修行方能得道成長。全畫的用筆雖略嫌生澀，但對人物內在精神和氣質風度的刻劃則深刻入微，畫中的羅漢和蟾蜍似乎正在進行生命的交流及精神上的溝通，足見作者欲藉醜和怪的形象，引領觀者思尋其中的深刻意涵。

This portrait of a Buddhist monk standing in a forest is painted in traditional ink on a silken card. However, its creation is deeply affected by western paintings; therefore, the handling of light and shade, as well as the structure of space and body, is emphasized in this piece. The artist employed lines of varied thickness and shade and color-shading techniques to lend dynamism to the figure. The mustache and hair of the monk in this picture are created by fine strokes, contributing to its refined and realistic effect. The costume depicted in light-ink lines appears three-dimensional. The artist also intentionally depicted in tawny color the monk's skin which is exposed under the sun. The draftsmanship is nearly realistic. The portrayal of the monk's thick eyebrows, big eyes, droopy ears and protruding nose is typified. The toad resting on the head of the monk indicates his achievement in enlightenment whereby animals become congenial to the monk. In addition, the picture shows that the monk is teaching the toad how to achieve enlightenment through the practice of Buddhist rules. Although the brush technique is somewhat unsophisticated, the characterization of the inner spirit of the figure as well as his temperament is thorough and exhaustive. In this picture, the monk and the toad seem to be engaging in an exchange of life and communication. This shows that the artist intends to lead viewers to explore the deeper meaning behind the ugly and grotesque images.

（絹本 Silken Card） RD-056

（絹本 Silken Card）

RD-057

十二生肖圖

The 12 Animals of the Chinese Zodiac

這幅絹本墨色所繪的十二生肖圖，巧妙地運用了簡明而有秩序的圓形構圖，將簡化了的動物形象疏落有致地排列在畫面上。畫中的每一個個體的造形雖然簡約，卻都經過精心的安排，使其成爲整體結構的一部分；而濃黑的墨色和半透明的灰色交替運用，更突顯了每一個動物優雅的形態及作者精練的筆法運勢。全畫著重於「意」的表現，剪影的十二生肖的形體雖然概括而平板，卻各具各的動態生趣，成功地再創了自然生命的神韻。

A circular type of composition, which is brief and orderly, is deftly employed for the creation of the 12 animals painted on this silk scroll, and thus the images of the animals are properly spaced and arranged on the frame. In spite of the simplicity of the animals' shapes, they are nevertheless orchestrated to be integrated into the entire structure of the picture. Black ink is applied alternately with semi-transparent gray color to highlight the elegant form of each animal and demonstrate the refined brush technique of the artist. The focus of thc cntirc picture is on the impressionistic aspect of this piece. Although the forms of the 12 animals are generalized and flat, each animal exhibits its own animated fascination. The artist is quite successful in reproducing the verve of natural life.

圖章趣味

The Charm of Seals

圖章是漢朝時代由中國傳去日本的，後來變成一種印璽。大家熟悉的「漢倭奴國王」金印，是在九州考古發現的一只漢朝授予該地部落盟主的印信。

圖章再發展下去就變成印刷術，變成版畫。但在中國，圖章往往止於授信的功能，後來之視爲一種美，那是因爲歷史距離拉出了名跡價值。舉例來說，中國古畫總會蓋上好多印章，其實那是一再轉手的收藏家印記，久而久之好像沒有這些大小圖章，竟不能成爲名畫似的。

但是古畫上的印章總不會成爲要角，倒是在台灣，民間應用版刻技法拿來做銀紙、符咒，因爲用蓋章比畫的要快，可以大量生產，這時候印章的文字就在畫面中央。

近代日本所盛行的一種紀念戳，就是從印章藝術所延伸出來的，甚至店號商家自己會設計有趣味的招牌字體，刻成圖章，印在請帖上。當然這是指印刷品尚未普及前的宣傳手法，但今天看來，猶不失古樸手藝的精心與巧思。

Seals or stamps were introduced from China to Japan in the Han Dynasty. Later they developed into imperial seals. The well-known "Han King of the Wa people" gold seal, awarded to the chief of the local tribes by the Han Dynasty, was unearthed in Kyushu by archaeologists.

Seals, if developed onwards, evolved into the printing of wood block prints. In China, seals were often used for the sole purpose of authorization. Later they were viewed as an art, because history rendered them precious marks. For instance, it is not uncommon for an ancient Chinese painting to be stamped with many seals, all of which were personal stamps of collectors. As time went on, it seemed as if a famous painting could not do without these stamps.

But the seals on these ancient paintings were never the focal point. In Taiwan, however, the common people used the techniques of woodblock printing to make offering money and charm, because it is much faster to mass- produce with stamps than paintings. The characters of the stamps are then placed in the central part of the layout.

Commemorative stamps, which were quite popular in Japan in recent times, were developed from the art of seals. Some stores even designed fun-looking fonts for their signs by themselves. These fonts were then carved onto seals and stamped on invitations. They were of course a way of promotion before modern printing became popular. Nevertheless, they demonstrated ingenuity and skills even by today's standards.

嚴島神社 Itsukushima Shrine

此件在背面有「嚴島神社」戳印的卡片，是先用「妙法蓮華經」裱貼覆蓋住五分之三的卡紙表面，再於其上以較厚重的顏料繪製而成的。作者於全幅作品上充分運用曲線造形來表現物象在平面上的動勢及神韻。畫面構圖之用心巧妙，自右方飄入「佛經」世界的兩個人物，造形豐潤，衣飾雅緻，雖乏五官之描繪，然其雙手合掌跪拜之姿態，顯露其虔誠之心意。人物衣裾飄帶，皆用柔緩優美的動態曲線造形描繪之，展現極其柔軟的質感及迎風飄飛的動勢。雲彩的造形亦生動多變化，筆勢舒緩綿延，轉折皆成弧狀，在畫面上製造出波浪般的韻律感。作者的關心並不在於精確描繪物象實際的結構，而是在表現曲線造形自身的美感韻律。雲彩和人物彎延的造形，便使畫面充滿縹渺的動勢。

畫面用色工整細潤，展現作者以簡潔見豐富的高超造詣，背景的飄雲是以白色和金色顏料薄薄平塗而成的；人物的設色則較爲厚重飽和，對比強烈，俾使能自背景中突顯出來。全畫側重平面物象意韻之掌握，全無陰影烘染，不具三度空間立體感。顯見作者刻意經由平面性、圖案化的手法，製造出神奇、超脫自然的感受。

With the postmark Itsukushima Shrine stamped on its back, this postcard was mounted with the Myōhōrengekyō which covers three fifths of the entire surface of the card. Then a painting utilizing strong pigment was made on the card. The artist employed to a great extent curvy lines in this piece to portray the dynamism and poetic quality of physical phenomena in a two-dimensional setting. With conscientious effort to create intricate composition for the picture, the artist created two figures from the Buddhist world who seem to emerge from the right of the picture. The figures, with their rotund contours, are dressed in delicate costumes. Although the features of their faces are not depicted, their sincerity is nevertheless demonstrated through their genuflection with their palms put together on their chests. Soft, beautiful and dynamic curvy lines are employed for the depiction of their floating sashes to present the quality of softness of the costume and its floating motion. The configuration of the cloud also demonstrates great variation, and the slow and continuous brushstrokes create arcs during their transition, evoking a sense of wave-like rhythm in the painting. The artist's objective is not to attain an accurate depiction of the actual structures of the objects; instead, the artist intends to portray the aesthetic rhythm inherent in the curvy contours themselves. The curvy configuration of the cloud and figure contribute to the ethereal dynamism pervading the picture.

The picture is painstakingly colored and refined, demonstrating the artist's extraordinary technique of creating richness through simplicity. The floating cloud in the background is painted with white and golden pigment applied flatly and evenly to the picture. As for the coloring of figures, strong and solid shades are applied to create a sharp contrast to highlight the figures against the background. Without the use of shade and three-dimensional effect, the entire picture aims to demonstrate the spirit and essence of the two-dimensional objects. The artist intends to evoke a sense of splendor and the supernatural through a two-dimensional and graphic technique.

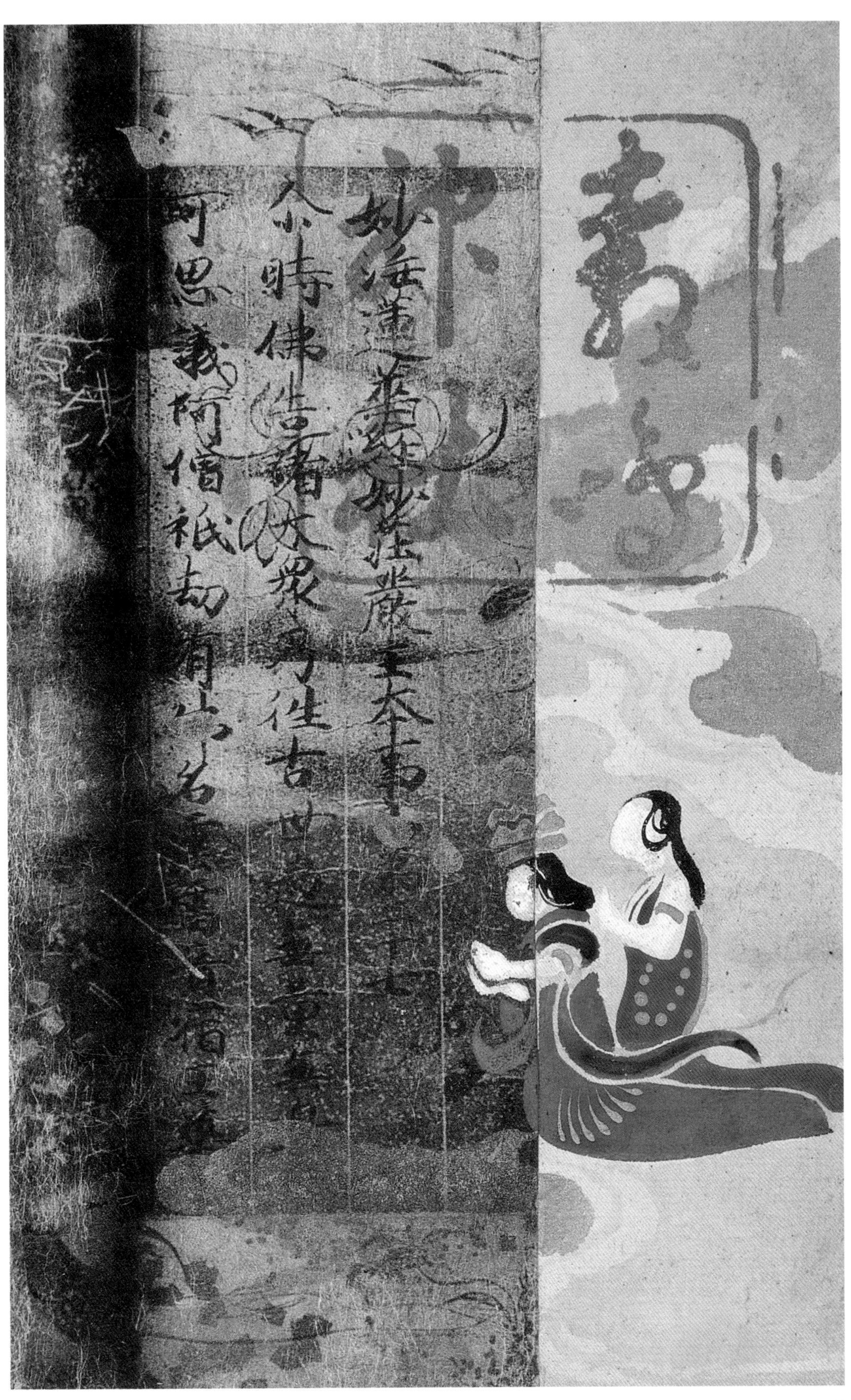

RD-058

春日社 Kasuga Temple

這件作品相當的古樸簡潔，褐綠色的卡紙上斜蓋著紅色的大戳印。畫面的右上方則垂掛著黑色的大燈籠。這個燈籠是先以纖細的黑線勾勒外形和鏤空的花紋，再將實體的部分塗黑，燈下的文字則是以白色顏料書寫而成的。由於年代古老，這張舊作新裱的卡片中的紅色戳印和其旁用白色顏料書寫的文字已逐漸變得模糊。但在仔細觀察之下，仍可辨認得出紅色戳印上有「春日社 (神社)、御水茶屋、火打燒、松田製」等字樣。至於白色文字則書寫著「鳴蟬、寬文 12 年(1672)5 月吉日、寄附……」等句子。春日神社位於日本奈良市境內，該神社因燈籠而馳名遠近，其燈籠爲數之多，達 3000 餘盞，且造型豐富，全日本無出其右。這張卡片便是選擇最足以代表春日神社特色的燈籠做爲裝飾主題，褐綠色的卡紙上，有著褪色的紅色印鑑和略顯模糊的白色題字，以及保存良好的黑色燈籠圖案，形成極爲柔和的色調，呈現出一種古樸之美。

這樣的一張卡片，經過如此漫長的歲月，仍能保存得相當完整，實屬難能可貴，但也由此可見類似這一類的〝摺物〞在收藏家心目中所佔的地位是何等重要了！

This simple and sparing work of art has a big red seal stamped on a piece of khaki green card paper. A big black lantern is placed in the upper right of the frame. Fine black lines are first employed to shape the contour of the lantern as well as its hollowed markings. Then black color is applied to fill the substantial portion of the lantern. The words under the lantern are written in white pigment. Due to its old age, the old piece was mounted anew, and its red seal and the writing in white paint have blurred. However, a closer observation will still reveal the content of the red seal: "Kasuga Temple, Royal Tea House, Firing, made by Matsuda". As for the writing in white, the inscription "Meisen, the auspicious date of May in the Second year of the Kambun Era (or 1672 A.D.), for..." can be deciphered. Located in Nara, Japan, the Kasuga Temple is known both locally and afar for its 3,000 lanterns, the stylish richness of which is unrivaled in Japan. This card makes use of lanterns as its decorative motif to demonstrate the spirit and characteristics of the Kasuga Temple. The khaki green card bears a red seal, somewhat fuzzy white writing, and a well-preserved pattern of a black lantern. The soft tone of this piece displays a type of classical aestheticism.

It is remarkable that such a Surimono card of this sort could be so wellpreserved, attesting to the unique place it has occupied in the heart of the collector.

RD-059

萬春樓 Bansyun Ró

這張蓋有「萬春樓」戳印的作品，構圖和空間組織相當新奇。人物分別散落在畫面的左上和右下角，其間卻空出一個極大的空間，前景的人物和遠景的組群還有著極明顯的大小比例的差異，如同使用著廣角透鏡的取景般，賦予畫面新鮮的變化。

This piece bearing the imprint "Bansyun Rō" features an exotic composition and a novel organization of space. The figures are scattered on the upper left and the lower right of the frame, separated by a huge space. There is a clear distinction between the figures in the foreground and those in the background in terms of their scales. It would seem that the scene is created through wide-angle lens, contributing to the multifarious variety of this art work.

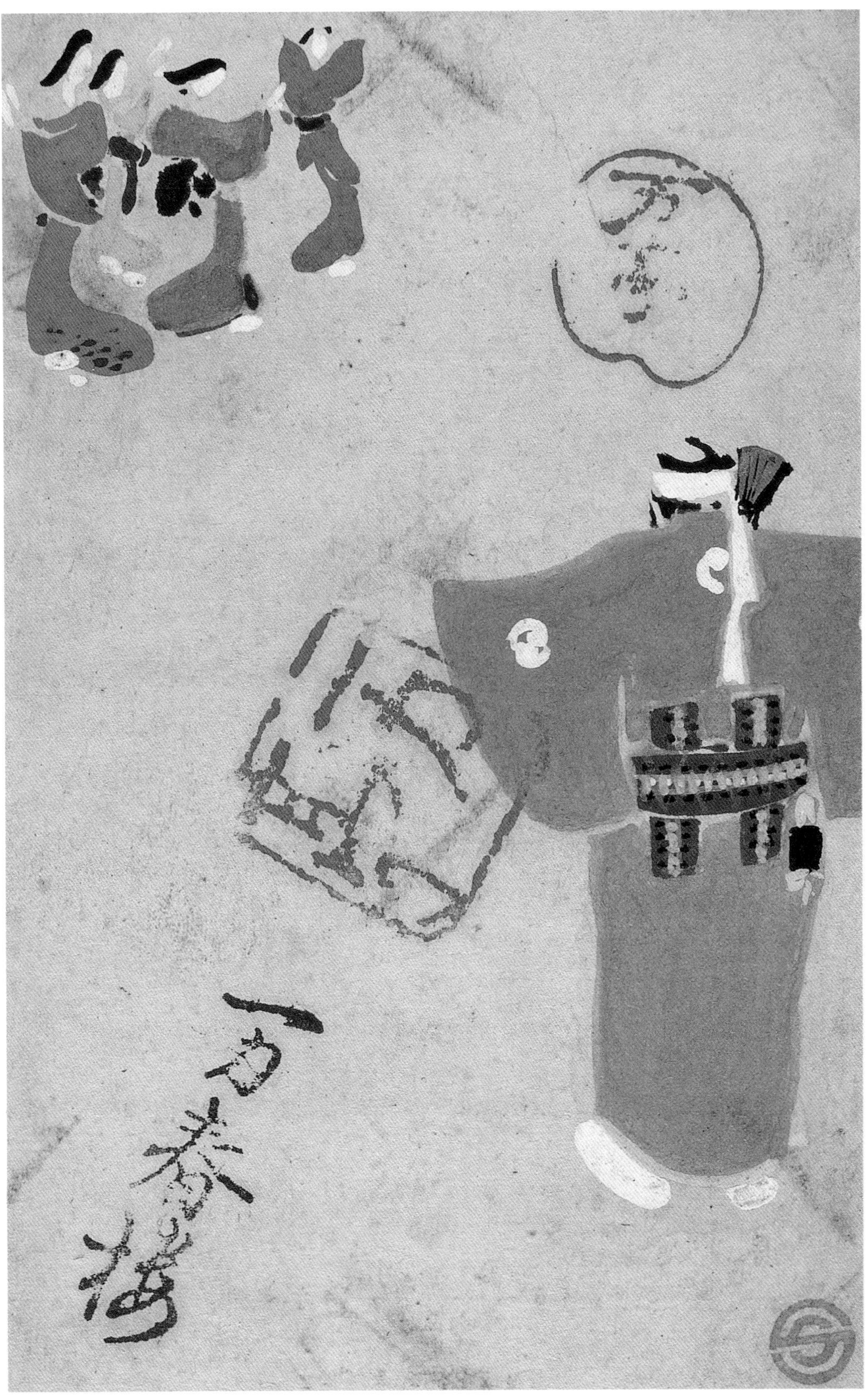

RD-060

不貳村 Hunimura

不貳村乃商店名，位於東京的本鄉境內，這張卡片是運用日本浮世繪木刻版畫的技法製作而成的。浮世繪是 17 世紀末至 19 世紀中，江戶（東京）普遍流行的一種玩賞版畫，其製作需經過三種專業工匠的參與，首先需經由「繪師」創作原稿，再由「雕師」刻版，「摺師」（印刷師）負責印刷，傳統浮世繪細緻的線條及精準的套色，反映出日本手工業的敬業態度。

此張作品簡潔瀟灑的構圖，不設陰影的平塗手法，以及取材於日常生活的作風，與傳統浮世繪相呼應。畫面的設計是以東京本鄉內的不貳村商店的店章爲主，再就其剩餘之空間發揮。枝葉彎延生動的紫藤軟枝蔓妙地穿梭在兩個店章之間，畫面簡潔有力，兼具裝飾性和藝術性的效果。

Hunimura is the name of a store located in Hongō, Tokyo. This card is created through an Ukiyoe-style block print technique. Ukiyoe was a popular category of block print for appreciation in Edo (Tokyo) between the end of the 17th century and the middle of the 19th century. The production process of an Ukiyoe print involves three professional craftsmen. First, the painter is responsible for the creation of the manuscript, for which an engraver creates a plate for a printer in charge of printing. The exquisite lines and accurate chromatography of traditional Ukiyoe prints reflect the dedication of the handicraft industry of Japan.

With simple and untrammeled composition, an even painting technique without application of shade, and a motif chosen from daily life, this print corresponds with the style of the traditional Ukiyoe. The design of this print centers around the store stamp of a store in Hunimura, Hongō, Tokyo. And then, the remaining space of the print is used to develop the draftsmanship of this print. The wisteria with winding leaves and twigs subtly extends its soft twigs across the two store stamps. The brevity and force permeating this picture are both decorative and artistic.

RD-061

RD-062〜RD-064

二軒茶屋 The Niken Gyaya Tea Hut

二軒茶屋原是京都八坂神社的鳥居（牌坊，即神社入口處）兩側的兩間茶屋，東面爲中村樓，西面爲藤屋。祇園建造的同時（足利將軍）改爲二軒茶屋。原本用來提供前來神社朝聖者休憩場所的茶屋，後改賣以阿蘭陀（荷蘭）的技術製造的豆腐及當地的名物（名產）田樂（黑輪）來吸引遊客。而茶屋的這兩項名產，因風味淡、脆，而遠近馳名，流傳時間亦相當長久，其廚師的現場製作工夫甚至被視爲一種藝術。關於這些，日本史書曾多方記載。而這一系列的卡片，便是以介紹茶屋及其特產的資料及插圖拼貼，加上戳印製成的。我們非但可以從其中文字了解茶屋的特色，還可以從其插圖一窺茶屋昔日的盛況。圖中顯示，竹屏圍繞的祇園有著寬廣的庭院，院内植有櫻花，宛若別莊，絡繹不絕的遊客，模樣悠然閒適。熟悉祇園茶屋者，見此卡片，必心生親切感，由此足見日本人將生活視爲一種文化的態度。

The Niken Gyaya Tea Hut was originally composed of the two tea buildings on both sides of the *torri* (the main gate) of the Yasaka Shinto Temple in Kyoto, with the Nakamura Building on the right, and the Vine House on the left. When Gion was being built, General Ashikaga changed its name to the Niken Gyaya Tea Hut. This tea house, which originally served as a resting place for pilgrims to the Shinto temple, later on turned to making tofu through a technique borrowed from the Dutch, as well as selling the local specialty *dengaku* (tempura), to attract temple vistiors. The two specialties offered by this tea hut became well-known far and wide for their thin and crispy flavors. Their popularity lasted for quite a long period of time, and the chefs' cooking skills, often demonstrated on the spot, were even regarded as an art. These have been extensively recorded in the history books of Japan. Incorporating illustrations, patchwork and seals, this series of cards is created as introductory material for the tea house and its specialties. These cards not only impart the unique features of the tea house to the viewers, but also the prosperity the tea house once enjoyed. In this picture, Gion, which was surrounded by a bamboo fence, has a large yard where cherry frees were planted, like an extension of a Japanese cottage. The visitors streaming into the tea house look relaxed and casual. This series evokes a sense of attachment among viewers familiar with Gion. Also demonstrated is the attitude by which Japanese treat life as a kind of culture.

RD-062

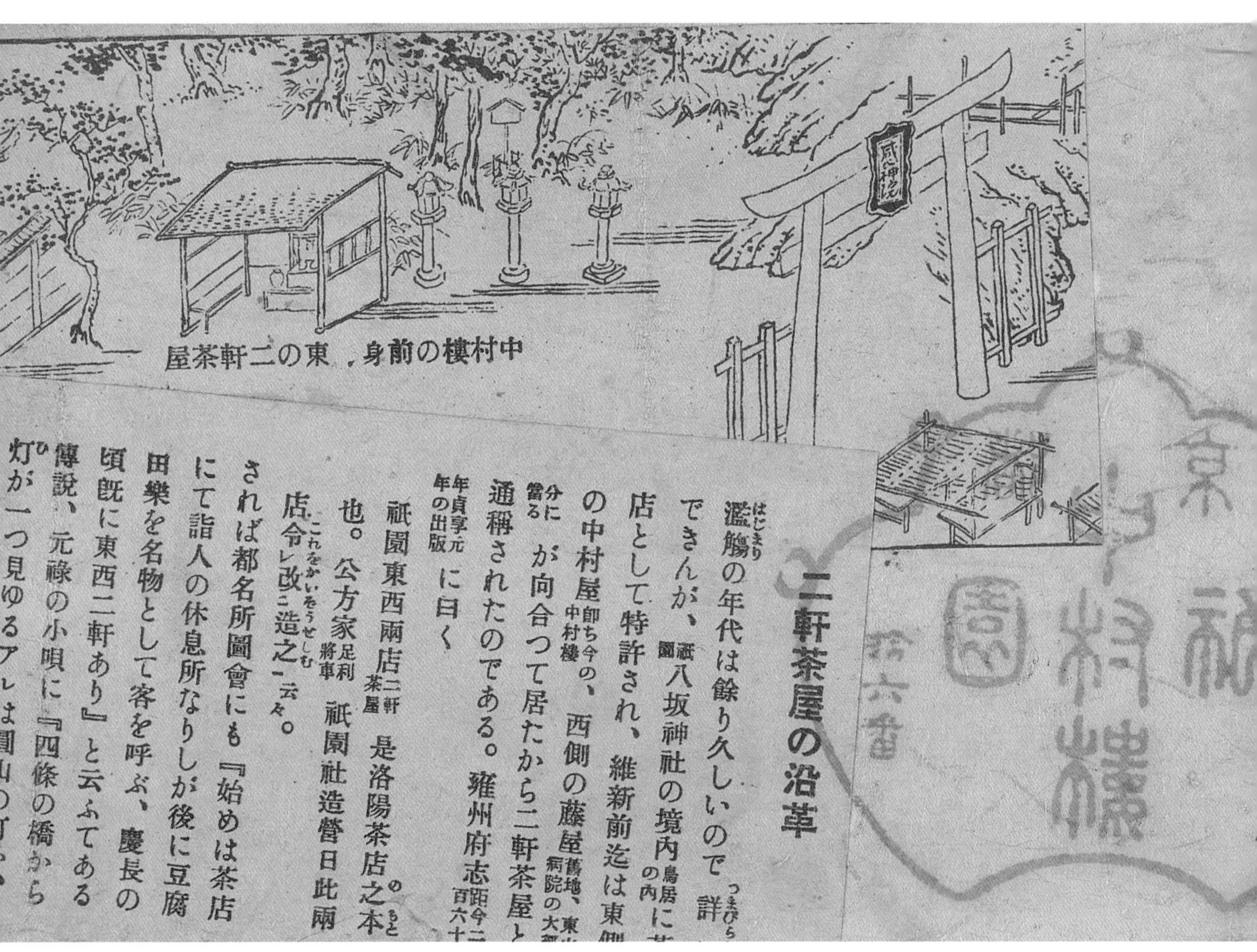

二軒茶屋の沿革

濫觴（はじまり）の年代は餘り久しいので詳（つまびら）
できんが、祇園八坂神社の境内（鳥居の内）に
店として特許され、維新前迄は東側
の中村屋（即ち今の中村樓）、西側の藤屋（舊地、東山病院の大部分に當る）が向合つて居たから二軒茶屋と
通稱されたのである。雍州府志（距今二百六十
年貞享元年の出版）に曰く

祇園東西兩店（二軒茶屋）是洛陽茶店之本（もと）也。公方家（足利將軍）祇園社造營日此兩店令レ改二造之一（これをかいぞうせしむ）云々。

されば都名所圖會にも『始めは茶店にて詣人の休息所なりしが後に豆腐田樂を名物として客を呼ぶ、慶長の頃既に東西二軒あり』と云ふてある
傳說、元祿の小唄に『四條の橋から
灯（ひ）が一つ見ゆるアレは圓山の丁、、

中村樓原爲二軒茶屋前身之一的茶屋
Nakamura building was originally one of the Niken Gyaya tea-hut.

RD-063

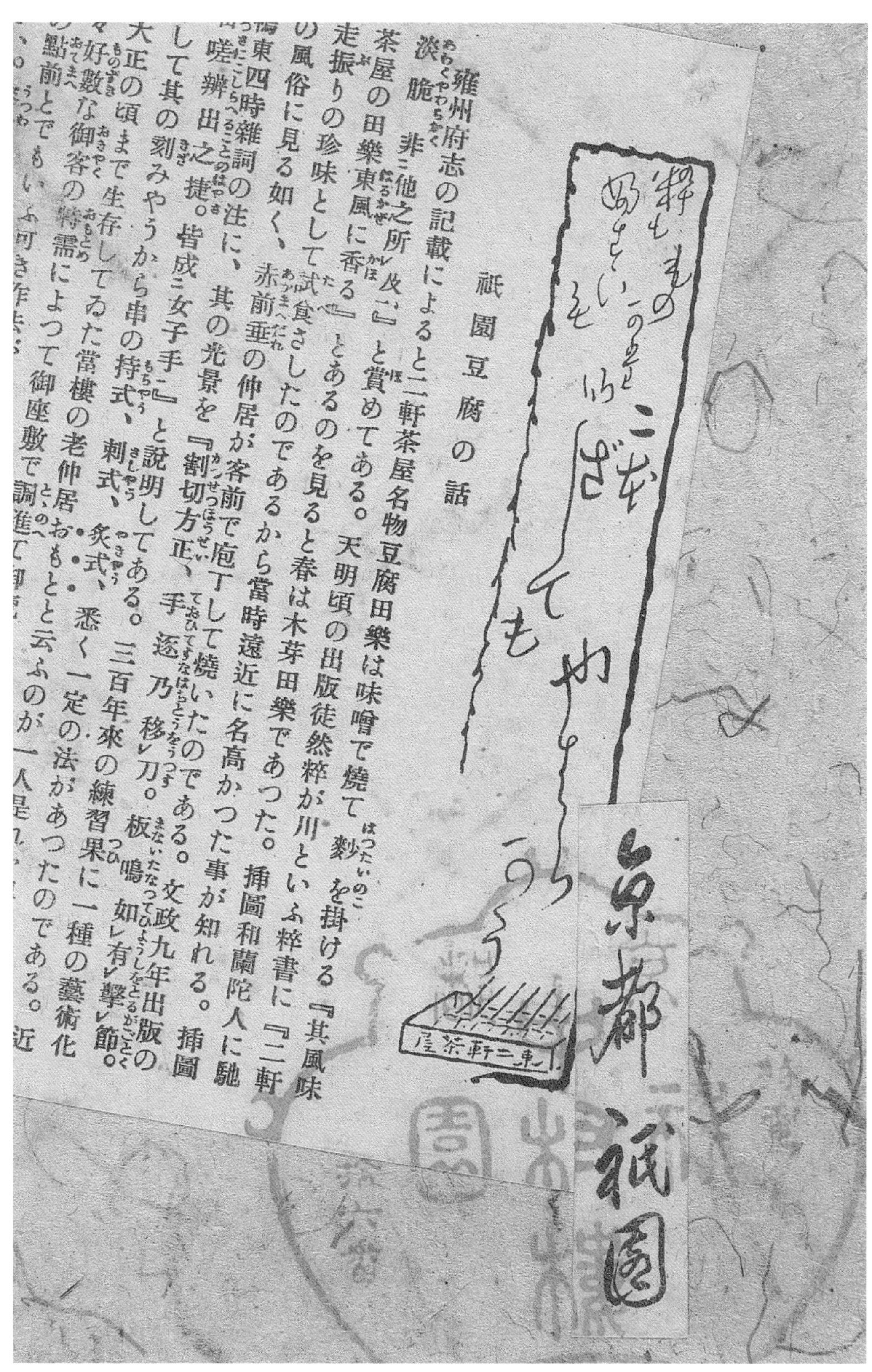

祇園豆腐の話

雍州府志の記載によると二軒茶屋名物豆腐田樂は味噌で燒て麨を掛ける『其風味淡脆非二他之所一レ及』と賞めてある。天明頃の出版徒然粋が川といふ粋書に『二軒茶屋の田樂東風に香る』とあるのを見ると春は木芽田樂であつた。挿圖和蘭陀人に馳走振りの珍味として試食さしたのであるから當時遠近に名高かつた事が知れる。挿圖の風俗に見る如く、赤前垂の仲居が客前で庖丁して燒いたのである。文政九年出版の鴨東四時雜詞の注に、其の光景を『割切方正、手逐乃移レ刀。板鳴如レ有レ撃レ節。嗟辨出之捷。皆成二女子手一』と説明してある。三百年來の練習果に一種の藝術化して其の刻みやうから串の持式、刺式、炙式、悉く一定の法があつたのである。近大正の頃まで生存してゐた當樓の老仲居おもとと云ふのが一人是れ……々好數な御客の特需によつて御座敷で調進して御……の點前とでもいふ可き作法……

有關祇園豆腐的歷史記載

RD-064

The story about Gion's tofu have been recorded in history book.

名物設計小品

Designer-Miniatures for Specialties

此幅岩繪的小品創作手法及風格，至今仍普遍見於目前日本特產品的包裝。隨興輕抹的幾筆彩墨，流露出日本特有典雅可人的韻味；圖中線條集大膽、簡潔、輕盈、溫潤、流暢之美感；書法之線條似又疏通了空間網絡，平衡了畫面塊狀的構圖。

The style and technique with which this miniature of painting in mineral pigments was created can still be easily found on packages of Japanese specialties. A few improvised strokes of color ink show the special pleasing and refined quality of Japan. The strokes of in the picture are a combination of aesthetic qualities such as boldness, simplicity, gracefulness, warmth, and smoothness. The strokes of calligraphy also seem to smooth the whole network of space, balancing the rectangular composition of the picture.

RD-065

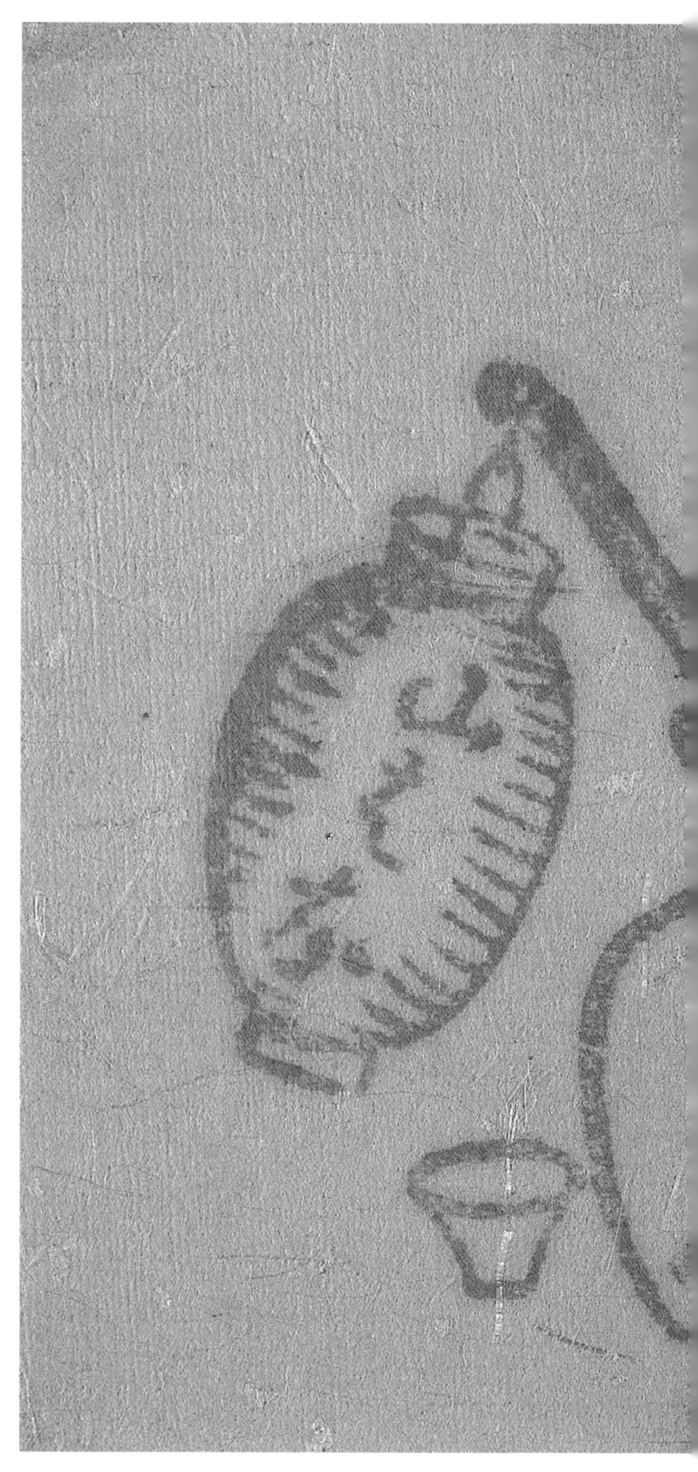

平八茶屋

Hirahachi Teahouse

圖中右邊之人物，實爲一茶壺所衍化賦彩而成的人形，「平八」可能是店名。提燈、茶壺與茶罐（或酒罐）、茶杯圖像成組的形象，將此店之性質表露無遺。

The figure on the right of the picture is actually derived from a colored teapot. The words "Hirahachi" can be the name of the store. The combination of images such as the lantern, teapot, tea or wine jar, and tea cups fully shows the qualities of the store.

RD-066

燈與劍

Light and Sword

圖中所蓋的印章爲東京某一區域之地名，而燈籠所提之字爲某一町（相當於里）之町名。燈籠與劍之搭配組合及其與印章、書法間之空間對應關係，正是此幅作品佈局的巧妙之處。

The stamp on the picture shows the name of a district in Tokyo. The words on the lantern are the name of a section of a city. The ingenuity of the picture in terms of layout lies in the combination of the lantern and the sword and its space interrelationship between the stamp and the calligraphy.

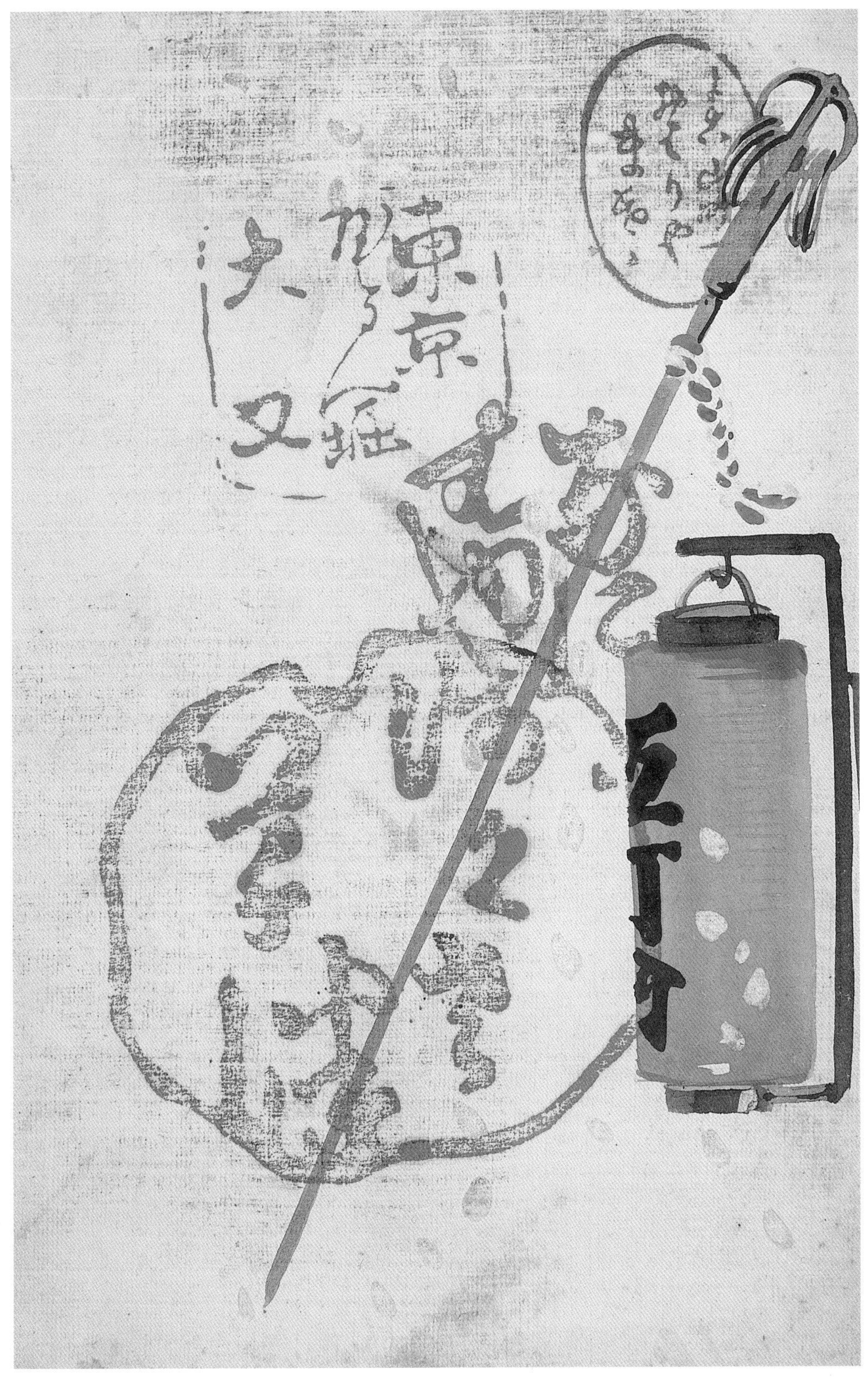

RD-067

美濃吉　Minokichi

這幅作品是以優美、恬靜、富有抒情詩意的自然景色為題材；畫面取景簡潔明快，畫風豪放洗鍊，技巧自然嫻熟，運筆走墨自由流暢。灰藍色為主調的設色，使整個畫面顯得十分和諧；隨意輕塗的數筆，便描繪出遼闊寧靜的水面及清晨中霧氣濛濛的氣氛。開闊的水面上則點綴著與人們生活息息相關的木樁及魚籠，呈現出清麗淡雅、樸素謙卑的氣息。

In this piece, a beautiful, quiet, lyrical and poetic scene of nature is employed as its theme. The selection of the scene is brief and decisive. Created in a dashing and refined style, this piece is characterized by natural and deft skills, with unrestrained and free ink-and-brush techniques. The color scheme of slate blue brings harmony to the entire frame. Expansive and quiet water and the misty atmosphere of a morning fog are created in a few simple and cursory strokes. The openness in the water sets off the wooden stakes and creels, which are closely related to the livelihood of people, and presents an aura of quietness, purity and humility.

RD-068

特殊材料與技法

Special Materials and Techniques

明信片或卡片是現代人利用郵政傳達訊息的媒介。日本明治時代，由於交通網路完備、郵政業上軌道，明信片之風最爲興盛。明信片文化亦於日本治台之後傳入台灣，那時候大批來台的日本人，需要與國內的親友通信、報平安，明信片可以說是最快捷、最方便的方式了。

往昔在台灣流傳的明信片，不限於台灣發行，因爲人來人往，只要是報信，那一國的明信片都可以用；但是只要在台灣發行的明信片，大都以本地風物爲圖案，這才是明信片文化最可貴的地方。

不過，還有人會花巧思，創造特殊材料的畫面效果，則更有別開生面的新意。有的是本片製成單張卡紙，畫上去的圖畫有自然暈開之效；有人以另種材料製成昆蟲直接黏在手繪的紅花綠葉間，更顯得有立體感；更有運用木片紋路，加強背景張力；或有作者以眞樹葉拼貼；或順著卡片原有紋路著上淡彩，造出下雨與倒影的氣氛。

這些畫都是作者的匠心獨運，是工藝與繪畫的結合，由於不可能量產，所以彌足珍貴。

Postcards or cards are a postal medium which people in a modern society use in order to convey messages. It was quite popular to communicate via postcards during the Japanese Meiji Era. This was made possible largely by an interconnected communications network and a sound postal service. The so-called "postcard culture" was brought to Taiwan shortly after Japan took over the island. For the large number of Japanese who came to Taiwan, the quickest and most convenient way to correspond with their friends and families back home was by postcards.

The postcards which circulated around Taiwan in the past were not all issued in Taiwan, because as long as the message was conveyed, it did not matter which country's postcard was used. The patterns on most of the postcards issued in Taiwan, however, were local scenery. Therein lies the preciousness of postcards.

There were some ingenious people, however, who spent time creating special effects on the layout with special materials, and a distinct novelty was achieved. Some used wood chips to make a single sheet of paper, and the paint applied onto it formed a natural halo. Some used an alternative material to make an insect and affixed it among the hand-painted red flowers and green leaves, making the picture look more 3-dimensional. Some reinforced their background tension by employing the grain of wood. Others joined real leaves together to form a collage. And still others applied a thin layer of paint along the fines lines of the card itself, creating a misty atmosphere of rain and reflections.

Manifesting the ingenuity and skills of the makers, these postcards are a combination of craftsmanship and painting. The impossibility to mass-produce these postcards makes them all the more precious.

牡丹 Peony

這件精緻典雅的小品，其製作方式相當的特殊。全幅畫面，包括花朵及葉片的舞姿，都是運用極爲纖細的櫻木薄片，精工嵌鑲在明信片上，嵌工細膩精確，乍看之下，猶如普通的印刷卡片。

畫面構圖取景簡潔，但並不致於單調貧乏。疏落有致的葉片，姿態靈巧鮮活，輪廓精細。以動勢曲線勾勒的花瓣外形，猶如波浪起伏，質感纖細柔軟。花瓣的輪廓線淡雅清晰，加上略微渲染過的效果，使得花朵的形象和立體感得以從柔和的調子中脱穎而出。含蓄淡雅的設色，賦予畫面素雅沉靜的感受，呈現古典的氣息。

這朵牡丹花的造型逼眞寫實，但其花葉健康豐美、自然舒展的體態，顯示了盎然生機，使人得以感受到生命的美好。可以窺出作者意圖藉由優雅的主題，及透過理想潤飾眞實的手法，抒發其精緻唯美的價值觀。

This piece of delicacy and craftsmanship is quite unique in terms of its methods of production. The entire picture, including the arrangement of the flowers and leaves, utilizes a slim sheet of cherry wood delicately embedded in a postcard. Characterized by fine craftsmanship, the embedding is precise and at first glance looks like an ordinarily printed postcard.

The picture's composition and selection of scenes are concise but not boring or flat. The contour of the leaves, which are properly spaced, are crafted with delicacy. The shapes of petals as lively and exuberantly depicted resemble the ups and downs of waves, rendering a sense of softness and exquisiteness. In addition to its slightly excessive exaggeration, the quiet and fresh contour of petals adequately projects the shapes and three-dimensional quality of the flowers from a soft color scheme. The conservative and quiet coloring add serenity and stillness to the picture, yielding a classical ambience.

This peony is shaped with accuracy and vividness. However, the rich and healthy leaves of the peony, together with its natural posture, demonstrate an exuberance through which the vitality of life becomes readily appreciable. Apparently, the artist attempts to express his delicate and aesthetic value through an elegant motif and his embellishment of reality.

木片鑲嵌 Marguetry

RD-069

蝸牛 Snail

此張木本明信片的木紋別具動勢，作者成功地運用木紋本身曲線的運動節奏及旋律變化，簡筆描繪上蝸牛及其身後所留下的軌跡，通幅畫面帶有一種誇張的幽默感。

The grains of this wooden postcard are full motion and infensity. the artist succeeded in utilizing the rhythm of movement and variation inherent in the curvy lines of the grainy texture of the postcard to draw in a few strokes a snail and the trail behind it. The entire picture is filled with an exaggerated atmosphere of humor.

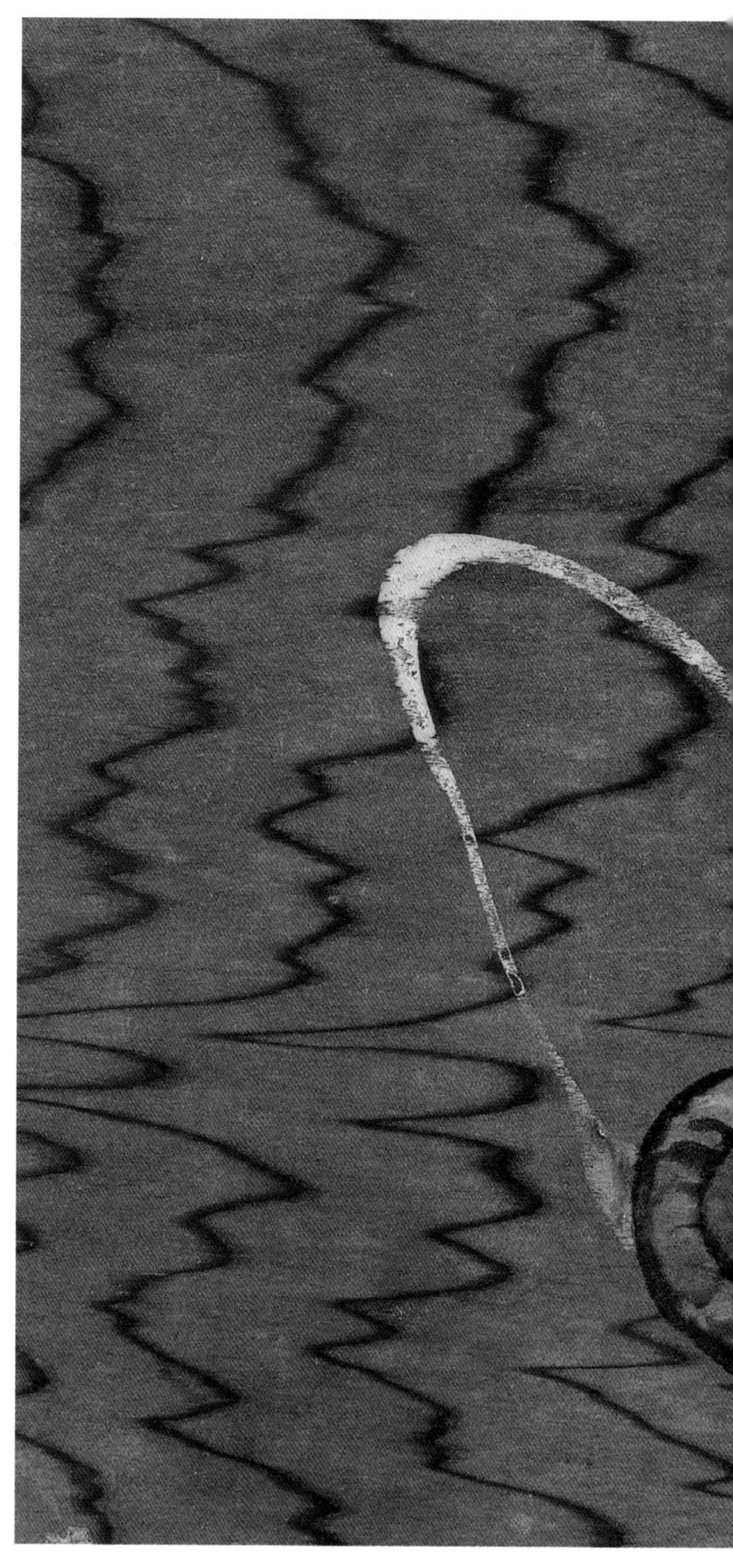

手繪木片 Wood shaving postcard

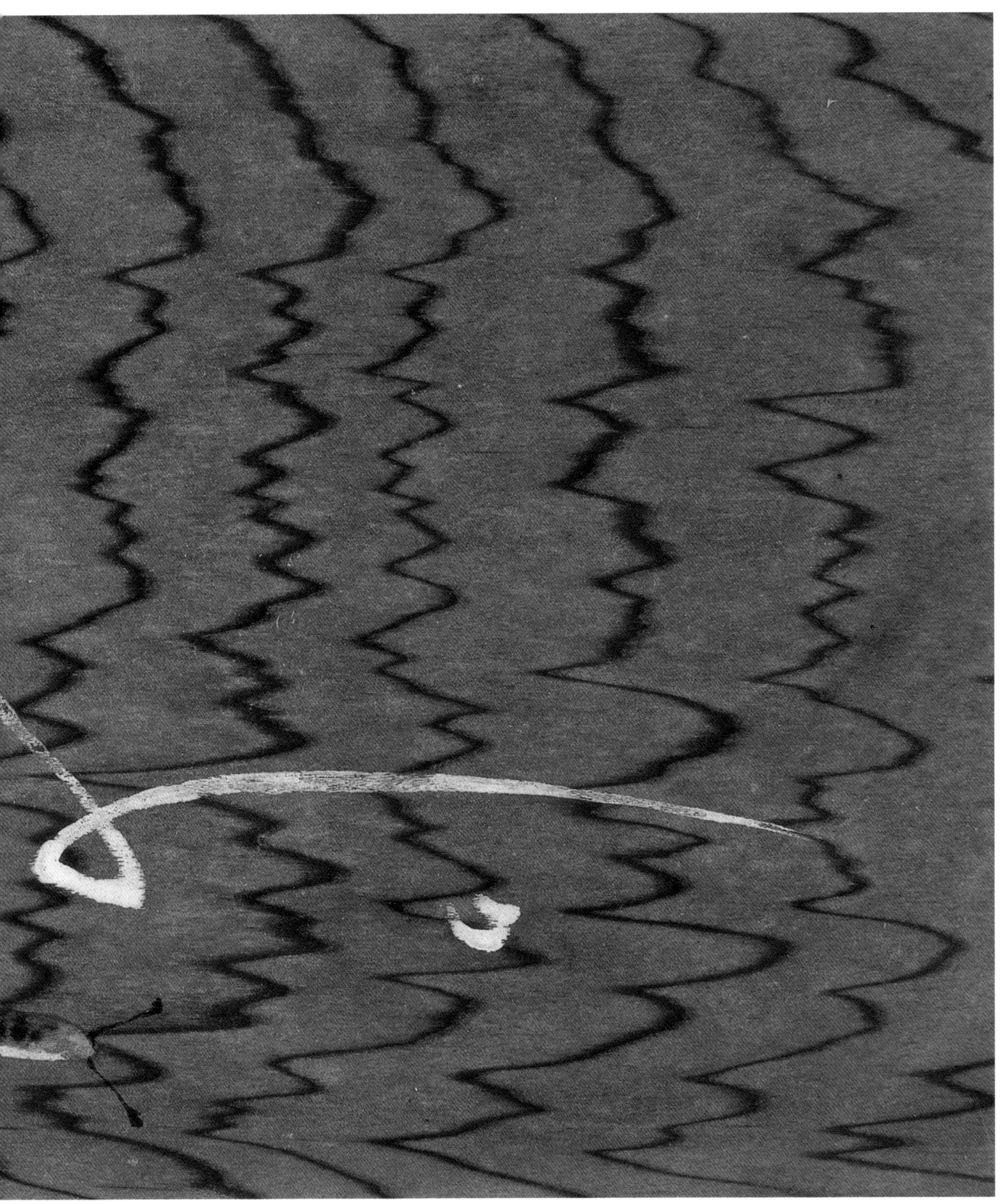

RD-070

採蜜圖 Collecting Honey

此作品與上一幅同以追求普遍和典型的題材爲訴求，畫面上也洋溢著牧歌式的清新氣息，但平穩的三角形構圖更加強了畫面靜謐的感受。花朵的設色柔和而含蓄，散發著沁人的溫馨，在深綠色的葉片陪襯烘托之下，更顯得清新嬌嫩。前來採蜜的蝶兒則豐富了主題，增添了畫面柔美浪漫的氣氛。這隻以精密刺繡的方式做成，再貼在畫面上的蝴蝶，逼眞寫實，但自然舒展的姿態，則顯露出清幽閒適的氣息。整幅作品像是一首優美抒情的樂曲，明朗歡娛的情調躍然紙上。

Employing the same commonplace and typical subject matter as in the previous piece, this picture is also permeated with an atmosphere of bucolic freshness. A stable triangular composition further intensifies the aura of tranquillity emanating from the frame. The soft and demure color scheme of flowers brings out radiant warmth. Juxtaposed with deep green leaves, the flowers appear to be increasingly fresh and supple. The honey-collecting butterflies enrich the theme of this picture and add a dimension of tenderness and romance. Created by means of detailed and precise embroidery and attached to the frame, the butterflies are extremely lifelike. The natural posture of the butterflies brings out a feeling of purity, peace and ease. This piece in its entirety resembles a beautiful lyric, with exuberant and happy notes leaping on the paper.

圖中的蝴蝶爲刺繡裱貼作品
This embroidered butterfly were attached.

RD-071

雛菊 Daisies

這幅描繪陽光照耀底下的白色雛菊的作品，是先運用淡彩描繪出花朵和枝葉的造形，再在其上以較厚重的筆觸點出花瓣和葉片的受光面及花蕊的部分。筆法熟練自如，構圖簡明而有秩序感，白色的菊花和橄欖綠的葉片在灰色的背景襯托之下，色彩顯得高雅宜人。

爲捕捉寫生花卉內在的生命神韻，畫者刻意經營花朵及草葉的姿態，葉片或正、或側、或翻覆，佈置得疏落有致。白色的花瓣則顯得質感鮮柔、清新宜人。花葉造形具有在微風光影間晃動的效果，展現出一種象外的韻律及端致秀雅的氣氛，猶如一首讚美自然、讚美生命的寧靜、安謐的田園曲。而停泊在花朵上採蜜的蜂兒，又給畫面增添一種生機活力的氣氛。這種寧靜的感覺和生機的氣氛交融在畫面上，形成一種特有的青春氣息。

畫中顯露出來的靜謐感受及花園角落的取景，旨在心智的啓迪而非感官的訴求，反映出作者精緻優雅的唯美要求及文人意趣。

Depicting white daisies under the sun, this piece portrays flowers, twigs and leaves shaped via light watercolor. And then, heavier strokes are employed to create petals, the lighted facets of leaves and stamens on top of them. The brush strokes are sophisticated and smooth, and the underlining simplicity of the composition creates a sense of order. The color of the white daisies and olive-green leaves against the gray background is elegant and pleasant.

The leaves stand straight up, tiltor lie overturned, and a spatial balance between tightness and looseness is attained, to capture the inherent exuberance of real flowers. The white petals evoke a sense of softness and freshness. The leaves are shaped in such a way as to create a wavering effect amid breeze and light and to demonstrate an unconventional rhythm and an aura of propriety and elegance, just like a serene and tranquil pastoral poem, which praises the beauty of nature and life. The bees resting on the flowers to collect honey add vitality to the picture. This kind of peaceful feeling and lively tenor blended together create a uniquely exhilarating atmosphere.

Rather than appealing to the senses, the serenity emanating from the painting and the choice of a garden as its setting are intended to attain mental inspiration. This reflects the artist's aesthetic objective of delicacy and elegance, and his literary pleasure.

圖中的蜜蜂爲刺繡裱貼作品
This resting bee were embroidered and attached to postcard.

RD-072

富士山 Mount Fuji

此張仿木紋的明信片是以早期浮世繪的技法製成的，也就是以墨印的輪廓線爲基礎，再以畫筆手繪上簡單的色彩。在狹長的畫面上，作者巧妙地運用了橫長的框，強調了主題景物的水平線，框外有著落日、船帆及其倒影所組成的垂直線，這種交錯組合，使構圖產生穩重感，並暗示了畫面的空間感。整幅作品的色彩極其簡練單純，係由紅、藍、白、綠四種顏色的對比構成，這些明確的色塊，又被黑色框邊的線條統一起來，猶如存在大自然中的各種音響，低沈、質樸而又和諧地奏出一首自然界特有的交響曲。

This card, which imitates the texture of wood, is produced by means of early Ukiyoe techniques. This means that simple color is hand-rendered on the basis of inked contour lines. Within this narrow picture, the artist skillfully employs a long horizontal frame. Perpendicular lines consisting of the setting sun, ship sails and their reflections are drawn outside this frame. This combination of intertwined elements adds stability to the composition of this picture and highlights its three-dimensional quality. Simple and pure colors of red, blue, white and green are applied to form contrasts. These concrete color blocks are unified by the lines around the black frame, as if playing a low, simple and harmonious symphony of nature by orchestrating all kinds of sounds from nature.

RD-073

雨景 A Rainy Scene

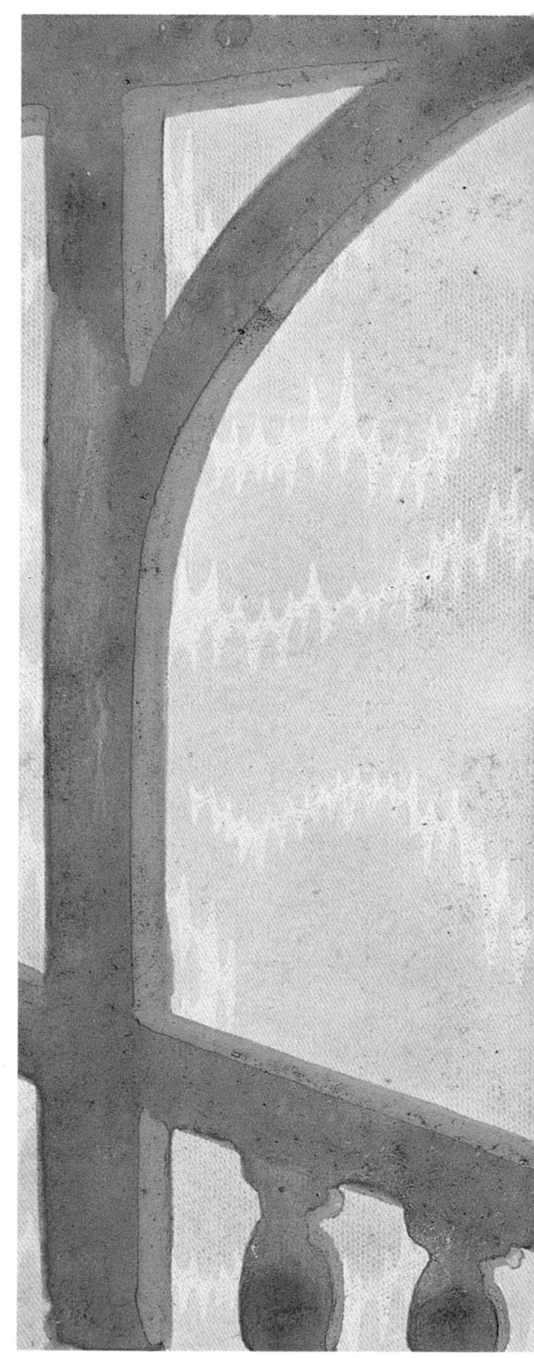

這是一件極具西方風格的作品。畫面上，淡紅淡綠的背景色和白色的上下波動紋，以及右下角的英文字母「a」，乃屬於卡片既有的印刷效果。畫面處理亦深受西洋繪畫中之透視法及遠近空氣法的影響，用以連貫整體構圖之氣氛。淡彩描繪的人物剪影，姿態優雅，穿著打扮西化，造形愈遠愈顯渺小，設色亦愈遠愈輕淡，就連人物之間的組合，也在刻意強調畫面的透視感。至於斜過畫面前方的欄杆造形，不單具備西洋風景畫中的透視原理，更以明亮與陰暗對比的立體面去突顯眼見的事物，強化遠近的深刻印象。作者還巧妙的運用了人物的剪影及雨天地面上的倒影，製造出畫面上逆光的效果及抒情的氣氛。在這件作品上，傳統水墨的筆跡及浮世繪平面的裝飾效果，早就消失得無影無踪了。

This is a Western-style piece. The rosy, greenish background and the wavery vertical white stripes, together with the English letter "a" in the lower right corner of the picture, are printing effects commonly used with cards. The painting is highly influenced by Western methods of perspective and foreshortening, which contribute to the aura of cohesion throughout the composition. The silhouettes of figures, as lightly portrayed, have elegant postures and westernized attire. The sizes of the figures appear smaller and smaller in lighter and lighter colors as they withdraw further to the background. Also, an effort was made to highlight the perspective of the picture. The rail slanting across the foreground not only conforms with the spatial concepts of Western painting, but also emphasizes objects in the foreground, through the three-dimensional effect created by the contrast between brightness and darkness, thus strengthening the illusion of three-dimensional space.

The artist also makes subtle use of the silhouettes of figures as well as the reflections on the ground in a rainy day to create an atmosphere of backlight and lyricism. Conventional ink brush strokes and the two-dimensional decorative effects characteristic of Ukiyoe can not be detected in this piece.

RD-074

RD-075

櫻花與鴿子 Cherry Blossom and Pigeon

此張看似單純的卡片其製作手法卻顯複雜，兼具實物拼貼、壓印和筆繪的過程。作者先以樹葉斜貼在畫面右方，再以版畫壓印僅具輪廓線的小鳥造形，最上方以金、白兩色描繪櫻花，淡雅的畫面透露出超現實的感覺。此張卡片乃日本手製卡片複雜、多樣化的表現手法的最佳例證之一。櫻花與鴿子均是神社的代表，因此，此卡片可能是爲某知名的神社旁的名產店所設計的。

This simple-looking card actually went through a complicated process of production, including a patchwork of real objects, presswork and drawing. The artist first attached leaves slantwise to the right of the frame and then blockprinted the contour lines of a little bird. On the top section of this frame are cherry blossoms depicted in gold and white. The light and quiet frame evokes a surrealistic feeling. This card serves as one of the best examples of the complexity and diversity of hand-made cards in Japan. Cherry blossoms and pigeons both symbolize Japanese Shinto shrines. Therefore, this card is probably designed by a gift shop of a well-known Shinto shrine in Japan.

為歷史"裱褙"
Mounting the Picture of History

明治維新以降，長期沈寂於世界史上的日本，開始活躍於歷史舞台，並逐漸掌握重要的席位，除了有賴於其適應世界形勢的能力之外，亦與其重視自身傳統文化的保存息息相關。日本政府對其「文化財」的維護所付出的心血，已是舉世有目共睹的，而一向重視文化活動的宣揚和參與的日本民間亦有其呼應的方式。此系列卡片便是以一些票據，例如公債票券、劇院入場券、節目單、特殊節日所發行的紀念票、照片、乃至於香煙包裝紙等等，重新組合裱貼，蓋上紀念戳，甚至加上插圖製作而成的，其紀念價值往往超過美學上的訴求，足見日本民間傳播文化之用心。

Japan, a nation that had lain dormant in the history of the world since the Meiji Restoration, was beginning to play an active role on the stage of world history and gradually assuming an important position. This not only was due to its ability to adapt to global situations, but was closely related to its emphasis on the preservation of its traditional culture. The efforts of the Japanese government to protect their nation's "cultural assets" were obvious to the world. The nongovernmental sectors of Japan, which had always laid stress on the promotion of and participation in cultural activities, also had their own ways of responding. This series of cards was made as collages of such articles as government bonds, theater tickets and programs, commemorative stamps issued on special holidays, photographs, even wraps of cigarette packages, etc. They were stamped with commemorative postmarks and even decorated with illustrations. Their commemorative value often exceeds their aesthetic appeal, showing the efforts of the Japanese people to disseminate their culture.

RD-076～RD-085

日本開國二千六百年紀念卡片

日本境內於紀元一世紀左右，仍屬分立為一百多個「小國」的社會形態，歷經不斷的爭戰兼併之後，方成為一統的國家，形成今日皇室的起源。至於何時及如何完成統一的局面，則無從考證，日本史書《古事紀》（西元 712 年）與《日本書紀》（西元 720 年）當中卻誇大地記載著初代神武天皇係於紀元前 660 年登基建國，日本在明治維新（西元 1868 年）成功之後，軍人逐漸得勢，在軍閥干政的情況之下，逐漸走向軍國主義，而此記載正符合軍國主義持續膨脹之後所衍生的大日本帝國心態，正所謂的日本皇紀二千六百年（昭和 15 年，西元 1940 年），便是依此推算得來的。

這一系列的卡片便是以配合紀念日本建國二千六百年所發行的宣傳圖片。東京巴士車票、在台發行的香煙包裝紙、奉祝舞蹈大會券、乃至於日本的風景小卡片，裱貼在明信片般大小的卡紙上，貼上郵票之後再蓋上日治時代日本人在台北所發行的紀念戳，日期全都是昭和 15 年 11 月 11 日。雖然這一套卡片的歷史紀念意義遠勝過其在美學上之價值，但仍足以窺見作者保存資料之用心。

東京巴士車票用以裱貼而成的紀念明信片
Bus ticket from Tokyo, mounted on postcard-sized card paper.

RD-076

RD-076〜RD-085

Postcards in Commemoration of the 2,600th Anniversary of Japan

In approximately 100 A.D., there were over 100 independent states in Japan. Due to subsequent warfare and annexation among them, a unified nation was established, giving rise to the royal system in Japan. However, the exact date and methods of national unification are unknown. The history books *Kogi Ki* ("Record of Ancient Events," 712 A.D.) and *Nihon Shoki* ("Written Record of Japan," 720 A.D.) both arrogantly claimed that Emperor Ginmu, the first emperor of Japan, was coronated in 660 B.C.

Following the success of the Meiji Restoration in 1868 A.D., the military gradually gained power, and Japan was on its way to militarism as a result of the intervention in politics. In accordance with the growing sentiment of Japanese Imperialism stirred up by increased militarism, these historical accounts were used to calculate a purported 2,600-year history of the Japanese imperial family (up through 1940, the 15 th year of the Showa era).

This series of postcards were promotional pictures issued in commemoration of the 2,600th anniversary of Japan. This series features bus tickets from Tokyo, cigarette wrappers from Taiwan, admission tickets to dance performance, and tiny scenic postcards of Japan, all mounted on postcard-sized card paper. Then the cards were pasted with postage stamps and stamped with commemorative cachets issued by the Japanese in Taipei during the Japanese Occupation of Taiwan. This series of postcards are all dated November 11 of the 15th year of the Showa Period. Although the historical significance of this series overrides its aesthetic value, the conscientious effort of the artist to preserve historical material is nevertheless discernible.

日本開國2600年紀念卡片系列之一
Postcards in Commemoration of the 2600th Anniversary of Taiwan：No. 1

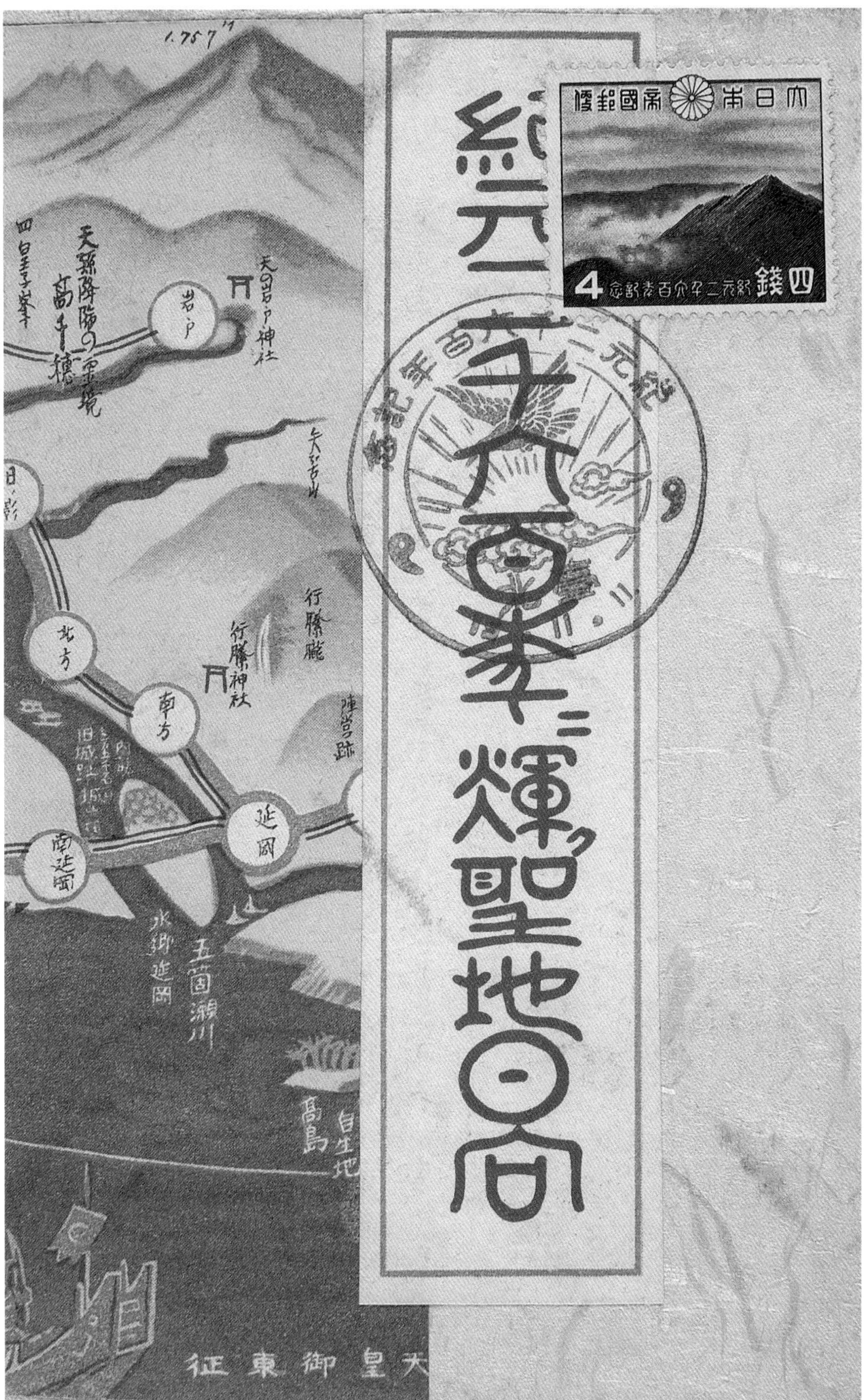

RD-077

日本皇室起源於一個分裂時代的結束

The end of spliting age, giving rise to the royal system in Japan.

RD-078

鵜戶神宮位置圖
Location of Udo Jingu

RD-079

日本初代神武天皇行跡圖

Tracing map of Emperor Ginmu (the first emperor of Japan)

RD-080

宮崎神宮之地理位置圖
Location of Miyazaki Jingu

RD-081

日本的風景小卡片用以裱貼而成的紀念明信片
Tinyscenic card mounted on postcard in commemoration of the 2600th anniversary of Japan.

RD-082

在台發售的香煙包裝紙用以裱貼而成的紀念明信片
Cigarette wrapper from Taiwan, mounted on postcard in commemoration of the 2600th anniversary of Japan.

RD-083

奉祝舞踊大會的設計圖案用以裱貼而成的紀念明信片
Designed portrait to dance performance, mounted on postcard in commemoration of the 2600th anniversary of Japan.

RD-084

奉祝舞踊大會券用以裱貼而成的紀念明信片
Admission ticket to dance performance, mounted on postcard in commemoration of the 2600th anniversary of Japan.

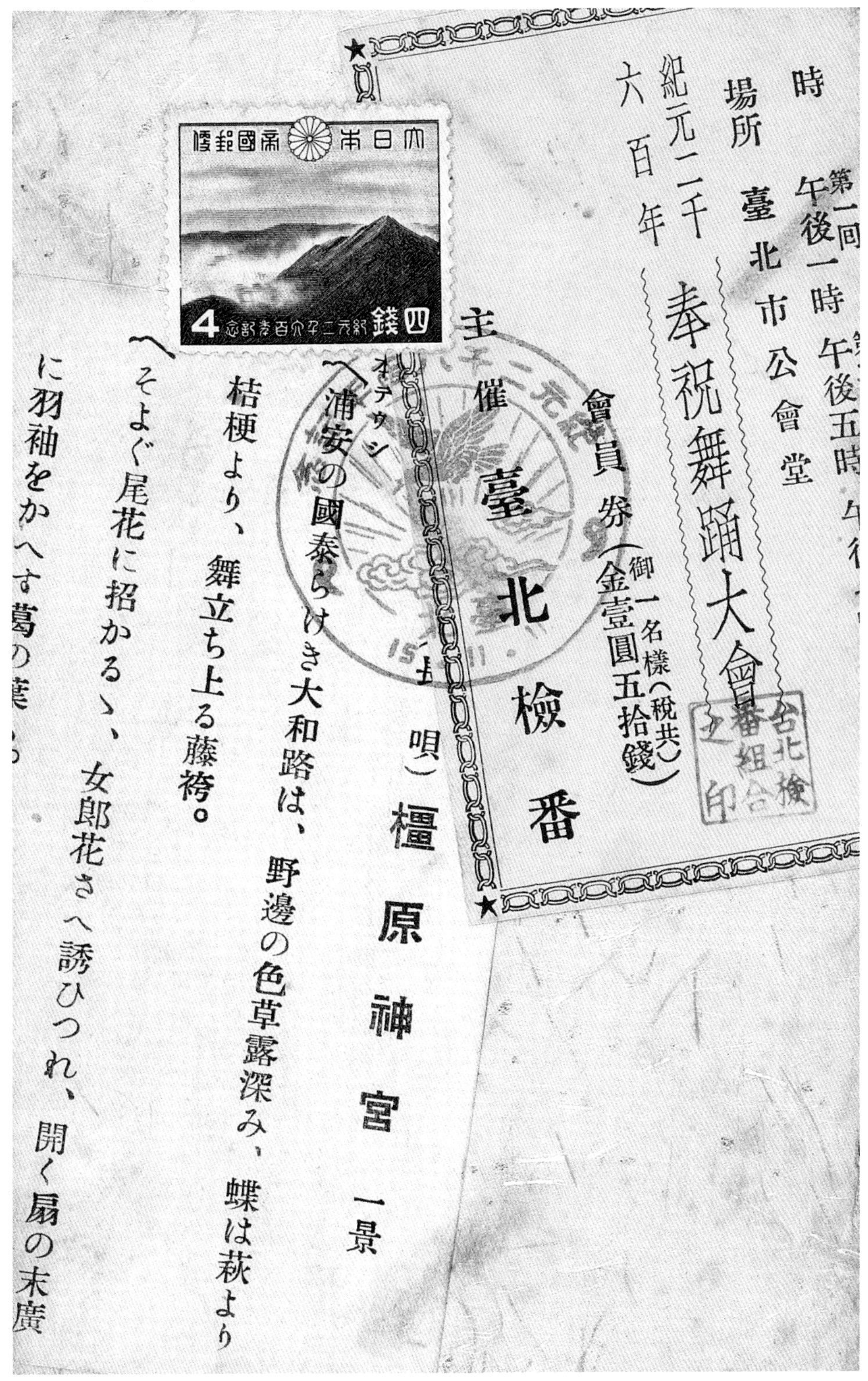

RD-085

百圓證書 100-Yen Bond

明治 28 年（西元 1895 年）中日甲午戰爭結束，訂定馬關條約（4 月 5 日），台灣於是年 6 月正式爲日本的殖民地，日本政府曾於戰爭期間及戰後爲解決經濟困境而大量發行公債。此張卡片便是以明治 28 年 12 月日本大藏省（財政部）所發行的「大日本帝國政府整理公債」的樣票做爲創作素材。灰色的卡片上有計劃性的裱貼著兩張面額百圓的公債證書，因爲是樣票所以一英一日的百圓證書有著完全相同的序號，足見巧思。作者並以筆墨抄寫前一年所發行公債的說明(明治 27 年)做爲背景。

畫面上的紅色圓印亦是以丹色手繪而成的，精緻的描繪效果足以亂眞。

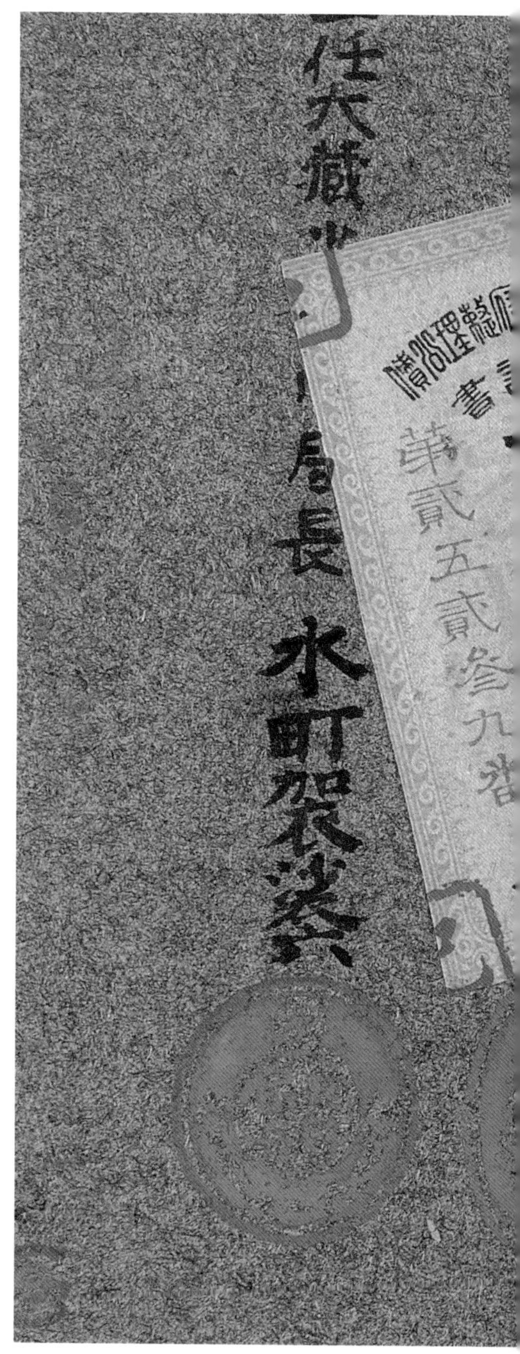

In the 28th year of the Meiji ear (1895), the Sino-Japanese War of 1894 was concluded, and the Treaty of Shimonoseki was signed (on April 5). In June of that year, Taiwan formally became a colony of Japan. During and after the war, the Japanese goverment faced an economic crisis and resorted to issuing a large number of bonds.

This piece employs as its motif the samples of the"Japanese Imperial Government Consolidated Public Loan Bond" issued by the Ministry of Finance of Japan in December of the 28th year of the Meiji Restoration. Two bond certificates with face values of ¥100, printed in Japanese and English and bearing exactly the same serial number (because they are samples), are intentionally mounted on gray card paper. The artist's originality is discernible from his use of the specifications for the bonds issued one year before (in the 27th year of the Meiji Restoration) as the background of this piece. The red round seal on the frame is hand-rendered in vermilion, and the exquisite draftsmanship gives a realistic touch to this piece.

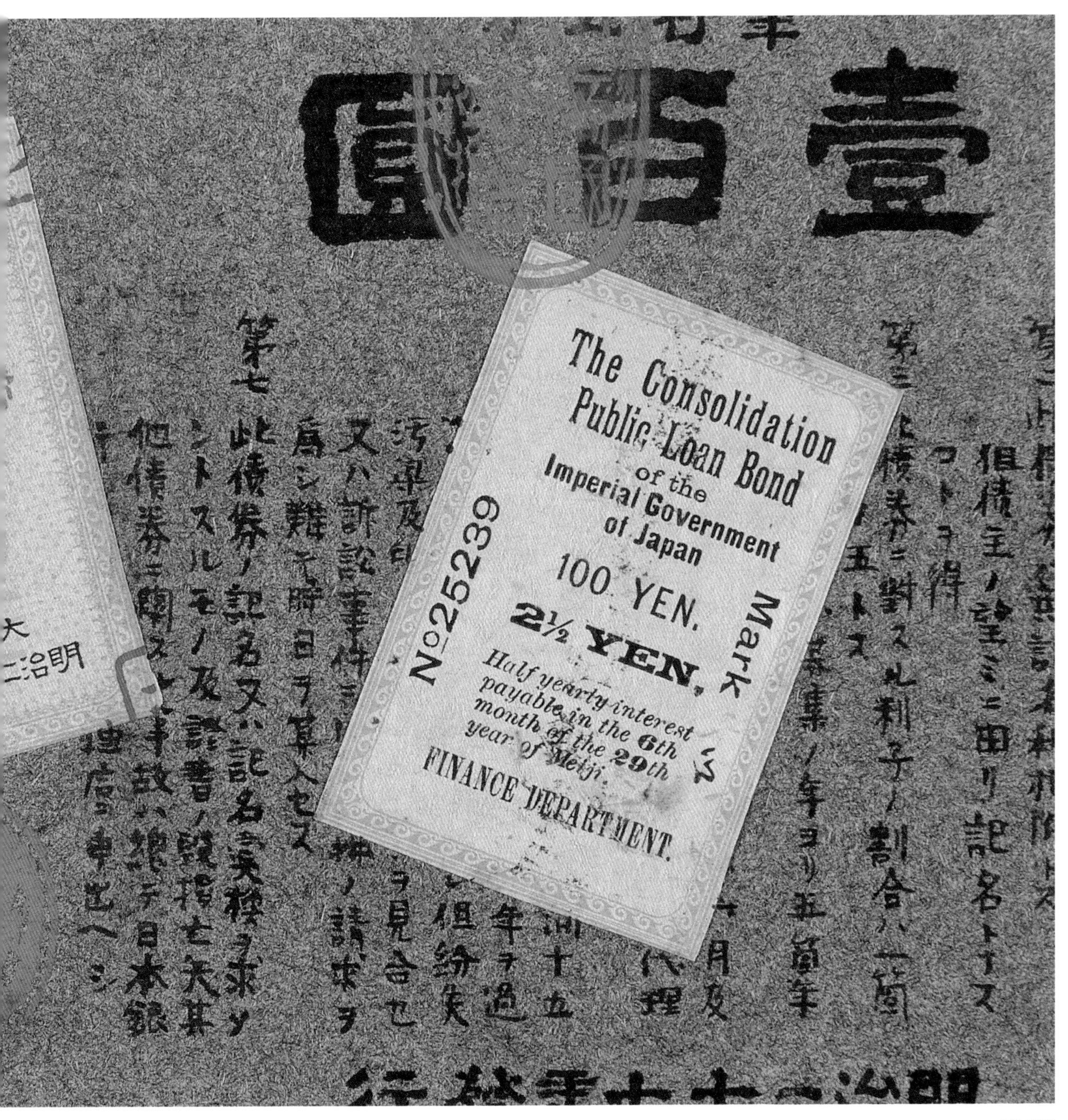
壹百圓
The Consolidation
Public Loan Bond
of the
Imperial Government
of Japan
100 YEN.
2½ YEN.
Half yearly interest
payable in the 6th
month of the 29th
year of Meiji.
FINANCE DEPARTMENT.
No 25239
Mark

RD-086

鈴個森 Suzugamori

鈴個森乃昔日東京尚未開墾之森林，傳言盜賊冥怜時而出沒，人聞喪膽。此張卡片便是以東京新橋演舞場（劇院）的入場券、「鈴個森」戲劇的演員表以及故事人物造型的版畫剪影併貼而成的。就創作手法而言，此件作品雖不及其它手繪卡片般精細、繁複、費工夫，然而，在作者重新剪貼組合之下的畫面，顯得更爲活潑、富動勢，並顯示日本人善用周遭文化資產的特質。

Suzugamori was an undeveloped forest of Tokyo in the past. Legend has it that the forest was roamed by Meirei the Bandit who terrified a lot of people. This piece is a patchwork consisting of blockprinted silhouettes of an admission ticket to the Shinbashi Theater in Tokyo, the cast list of the drama Suzugamori, and the drawings of the figures in the story. Although not as delicate, complex or troublesome as hand-rendered cards, the picture created through the artist's rearrangement of cutouts is lively or dynamic, which demonstrates that the Japanese make good use of their cultural heritage as it relates to their everyday lives.

RD-087

RD-088〜RD-090

香煙明信片

Cigarette Postcards

這三張卡片都是以日治時代，日本在台灣銷售的香煙包裝紙做爲設計的素材。畫面上一律採斜線構圖的方式裱貼，包裝紙的一角覆貼紅色的〝大日本帝國專賣局證票〞圓形圖案。巧妙的是作者還在每一張卡片上十分用心的描繪上一根根的香煙，其造形或完整、或剩下煙頭、或已半燃燒，並有片片煙灰落下。描繪的手法生動逼眞並具立體感，意趣十分巧妙。作者的癮君子友人，必會欣然等待收到這類別具巧思的明信片。

These three postcards were created during the Japanese Occupation of Taiwan through the use of wrappers for Japanese cigarettes distributed in Taiwan. With the composition of slanted lines, the wrappings mounted on the frames are each affixed on one corner with a red round pattern—the Certificate of Monopoly of Japan. What is amazing is that on each card the artist depicted individual cigarettes, either intact, burnt to the butt, or half burnt with ashes falling off. The lively and realistic depiction of these postcards and their three-dimensional feeling are remarkably fascinating. The artist's friend, presumably a heavy smoker, must have been glad to receive this unique and original type of postcard.

香煙明信片之一
No. 1 of cigarette postcard series

RD-088

香煙明信片之二
No. 2 of cigarette postcard series

RD-089

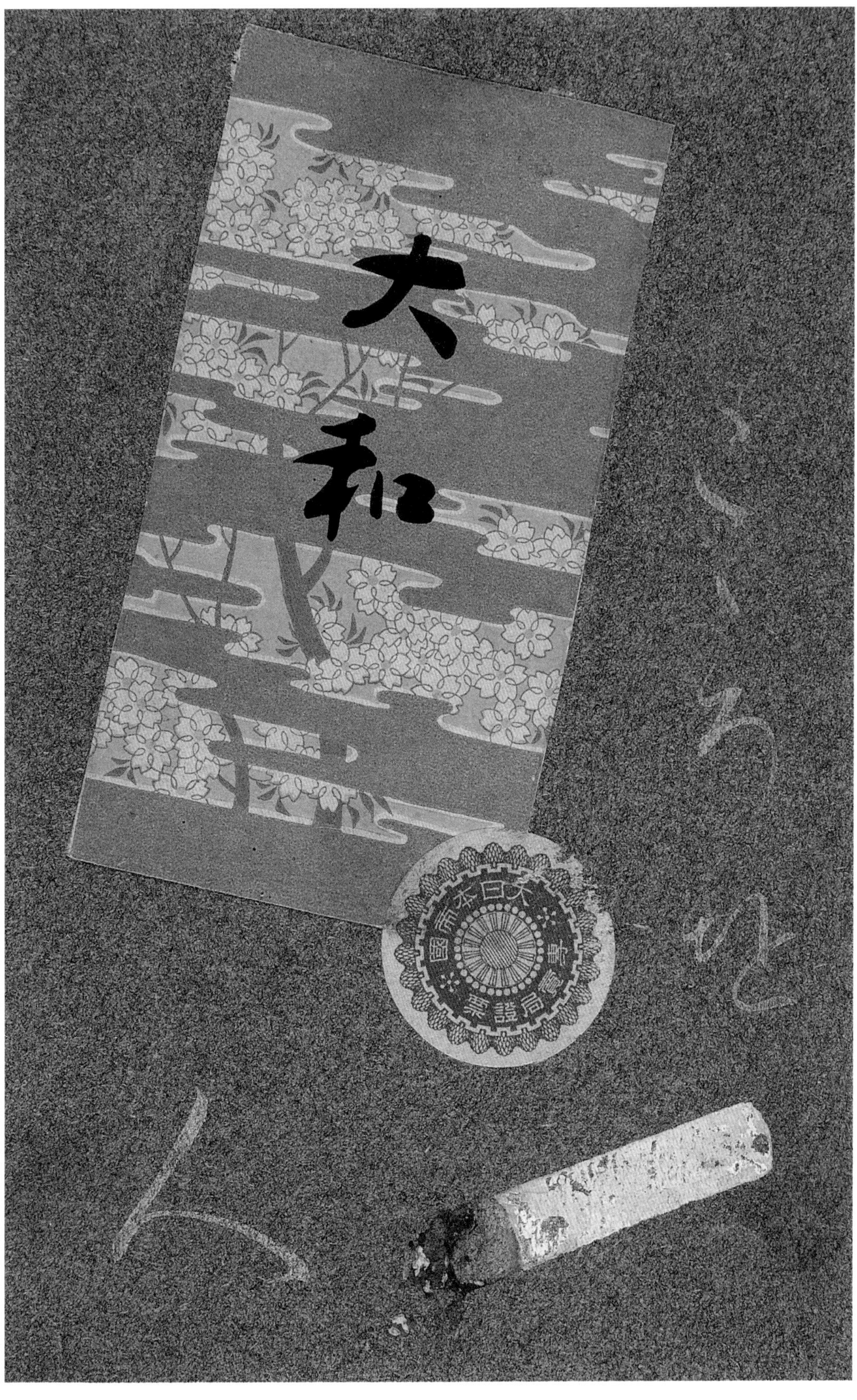

香煙明信片之三
No. 3 of cigarette postcard series

RD-090

公路車票 Highway Tickets

此圖所繪之人物爲一日本仕女，斜立而貼的車票，應屬日本當地所使用，此種公路車票，台灣自日治時期一直使用至前幾年才廢止。其上排爲停車之站名，下排爲票價，乘客上車後必須購買此票，車掌並於下車之站名及票價欄內打洞，下車時將票繳回，車掌可同時驗明乘客之下車站名與所購之車票之到站站名是否相符。

The figure depicted in this picture is apparently a Japanese lady. The slanting ticket should have been used in Japan. This sort of bus ticket had been in use since the beginning of Japanese rule, and was out of use only a couple of years ago. The upper row shows the names of bus stops, while the lower row shows the price of the ticket. Upon boarding the bus, a passenger was required to purchase a ticket, upon which the conductor punched a hole on the destination and price columns. The ticket was to be given back upon disembarking the bus, so the conductor could verify if the destination on the ticket matched the station.

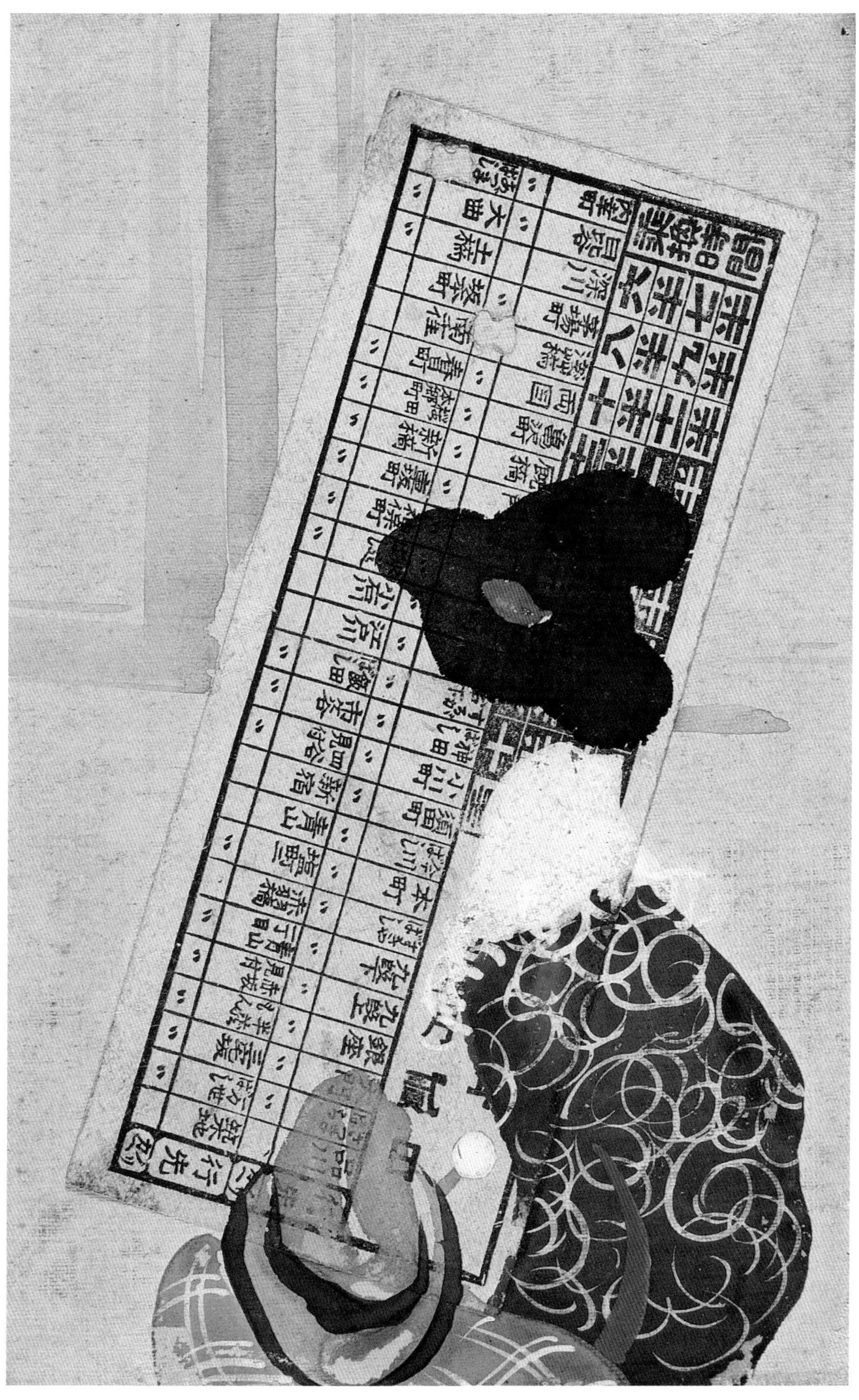

RD-091

台灣總督府第壹期彩票

此兩圖所裱貼之票券爲台灣總督府彩票局在明治 39 年（西元 1906 年）所發行之彩票，此爲彩票之正反兩面文字，載明發行單位、發行方式、發行日期及開獎日期、獎金、領獎方式。並採中、英文對照發行。

RD-092

First-Issue Lottery Tickets of the Taiwan Governor's Office

The lottery tickets affixed on the backs of these two pictures were issued by the Taiwan Governor's Office in 1906. The words on the front and back of the lottery tickets tell in both English and Chinese the date of issue, the way in which they were issued, the issuer as well as the date of announcing the winning numbers, the prize money, and the way to claim the money.

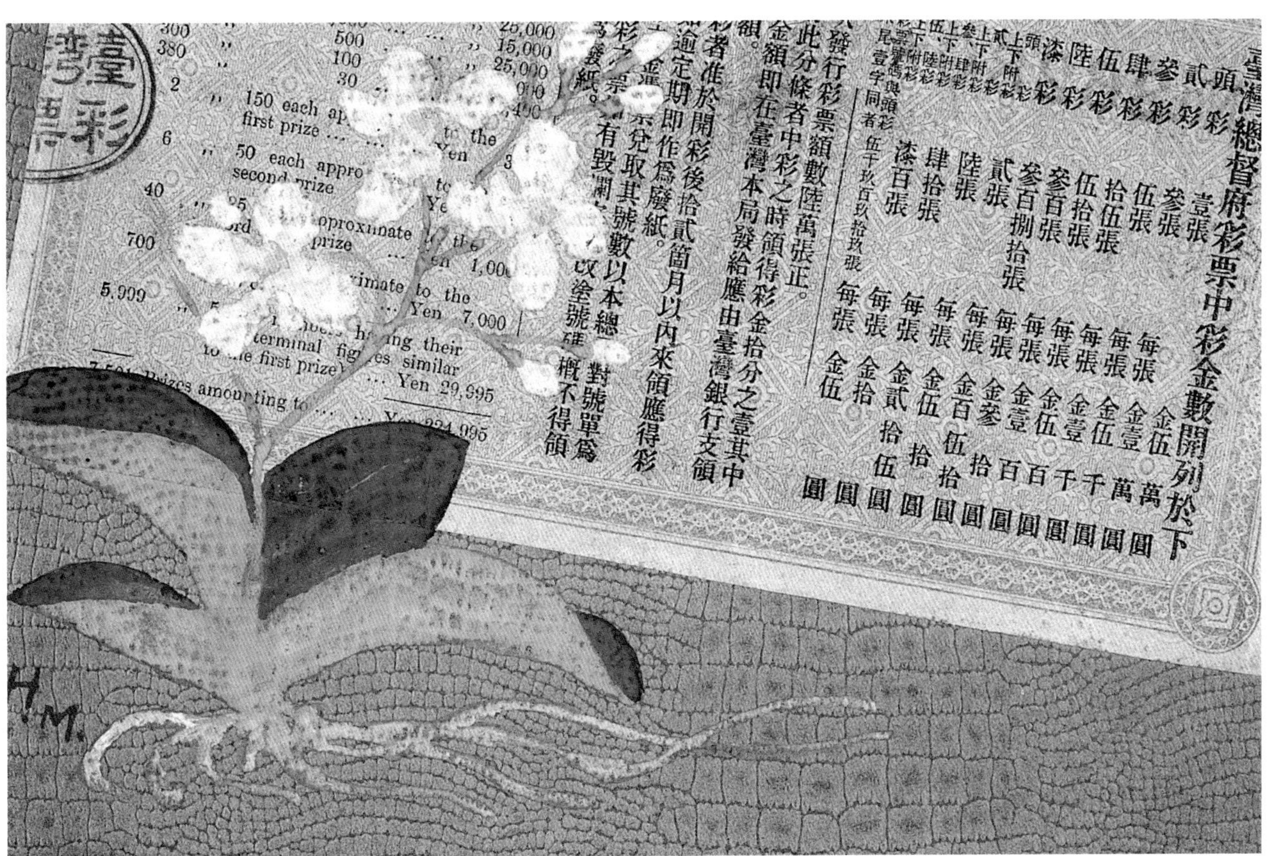

RD-093

劇場入場券

Entrance Tickets to A Theater

此票券裱貼紀念明信片是將明治42年4月時，台灣某劇場的入場券裱貼並繪上可能是該劇場的商標燈籠而成。

The ticket affixed on the commemorative postcard was an entrance ticket to a theater somewhere in Taiwan in April, 1909. The logo lantern of the theater was painted on the postcard.

RD-095

RD-094

飯店形象設計 Image Design of the Hotel

此裱貼之圖案，可能爲日治時期高雄臨海飯店的火柴盒上之設計，製作者在左下角還蓋上了該飯店的戳章以爲留念。

The pattern affixed on the picture could be a design on a match box of the Seaside Hotel in Kaohsiung during the Japanese rule. The designer left a stamp of the hotel in the lower left corner as a memento.

書法意象與情節
Imagery and Plot of Penmanship

此系列的作品是以文學、詩歌爲基礎，緊緊圍繞著文字所構成的情節，探求其內在涵義之美。作品之設計，偏重於玲瓏剔透的曲線趣味和非對稱法則，所採用之和歌紙條或詩文的扉頁，多半是傾斜裱貼在卡片上的。而文字本身，除了有補充畫面主題、統一意象的功能之外，其造型魅力，在整體畫面的視覺平衡上，亦扮演重要的角色，兼具裝飾和傳達意念之功能。配合文字及圖像的構圖繁而不亂，除了能將古老日本詩文中的文學氣息做恰如其份的表達之外，通常亦能予人一種振舞欲飛的美感享受，使人的目光能在方寸之間，悠游品味良久。

This series of pictures is based on pictures of poetry and literature. It surrounds closely the "plot" constituted by words, searching for the beauty of its inner meaning. The layout of the works lays particular stress on exquisite lines and asymmetry. Most of the notes of Japanese music or title pages of the relevant literature and poetry that were used were affixed at an angle to the postcards. In addition to the wording's functions of supplementing the subject manner of the picture and of unifying the imagery, its charming style also plays an important role in the visual equilibrium of the whole general appearance of the picture, thus having the function of both decoration and communication. With words and complicated but not disorderly composition, not only is the literary flavor of classical Japanese literature duly expressed, but also one can experience an exhilarating aesthetic treat. To our eyes' content, we may leisurely savor these small but wonderful works.

RD-096~RD-098

樂譜與圖像

Scores and Images

此三張圖係以日本淨琉璃之樂譜（有唱詞，有樂譜）裱貼，並賦以彩繪圖案而成之作品，因無曲牌名，詞亦不完整，無法判斷其圖與樂譜內容有無關係。

The three pictures are works affixed with scores of Japanese Joruri(folk songs)and colored with patterns. Owing to the lack of a title and the fact that the lyrics were only fragments, it is out of the question to determine if the pictures are related to the scores.

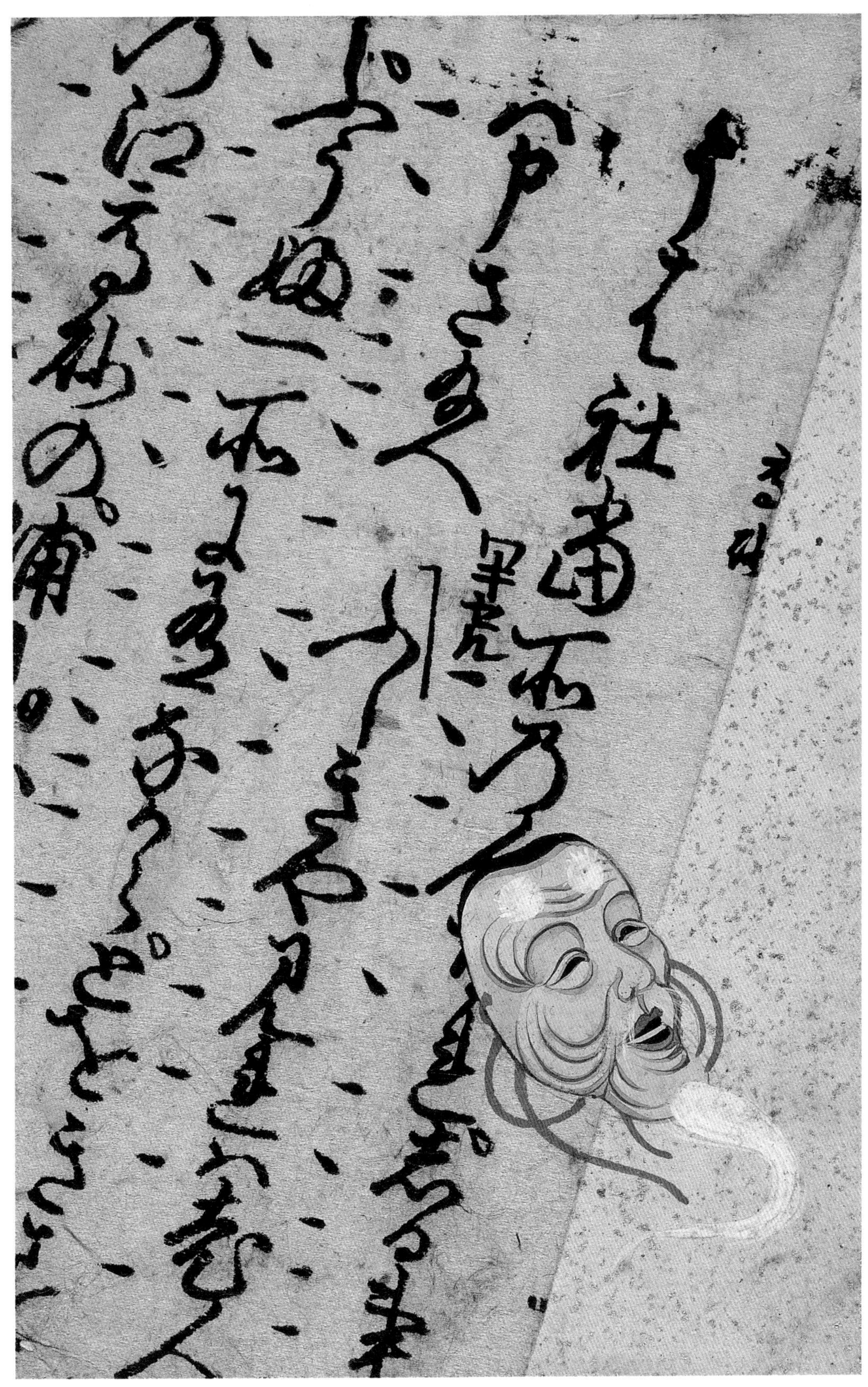

RD-096

RD-097

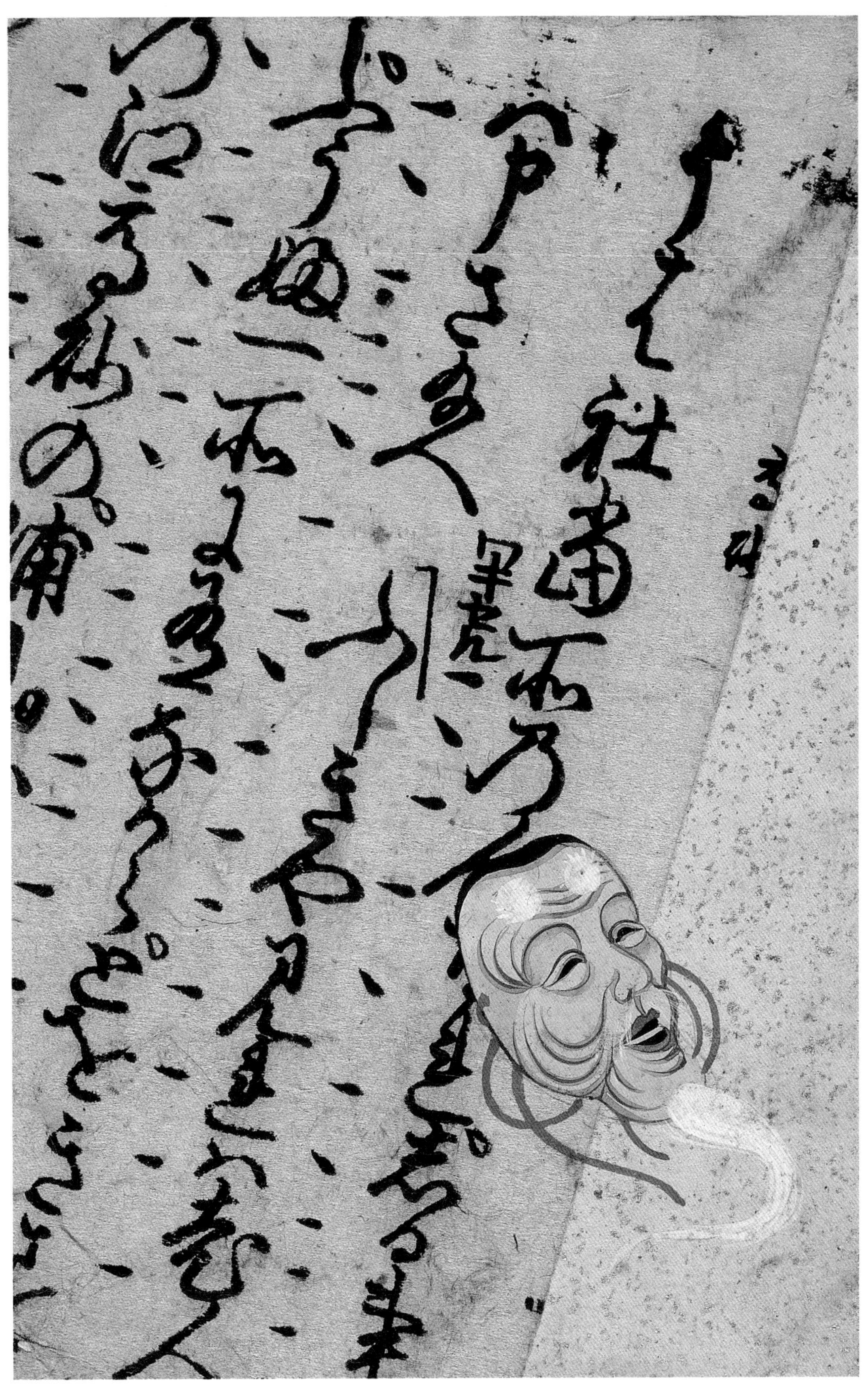

RD-096

RD-097

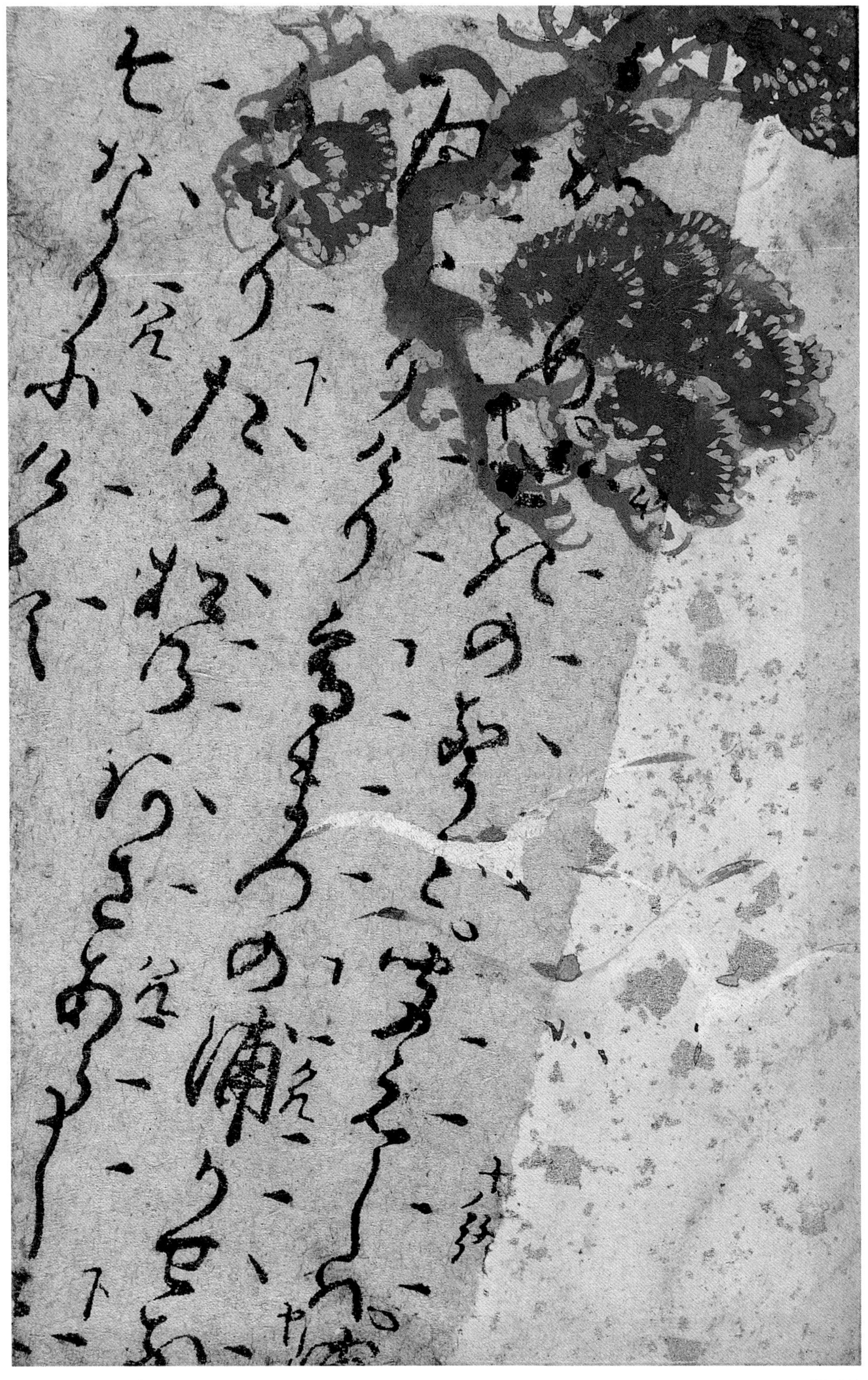

RD-098

獨木舟 Canoe

這件作品是以日本淨琉璃裱貼在灑有金蔥的卡片上做爲背景，再配合其內容作挿圖。斜裱的淨琉璃在畫面的左下方做了適當的留白，其上散落著數顆貝殼，暗示著邊的存在。一艘手繪平塗的獨木舟斜倚岸上，搖櫓和舟上垂置的繩索，爲這單純的景致增添了較細膩的變化，並與行草的淨琉璃相呼應。畫面設色質樸、氣氛幽靜，幽靜得足以令人產生哀怨的情懷。沒有風浪的岸邊，時間似乎也靜止了，所呈現出來的超現實意象，使整個畫面充滿了惆悵的詩意。

The background of this work is a piece of joruri, song lyrics with melodic annotation, mounted on a card speckled with golden dots. Then an illustration was rendered in conformity with the content of the script. The slanted script of Joruri poem creates a space in the lower left of the picture, where shells are scattered, indicating the presence of a sea shore. An even, hand-painted rendering of a canoe sits tilted on the shore. The oar and rope of the canoe lend delicate variety to the simple scene, and fit perfectly with the *xing cao* ("running" or semicursive) style in which the annotated lyrics were written. The coloring of the frame is quaint and simple, with a tranquillity that evokes a sense of melancholy. On a beach without wind or waves, time seems to stand still. As a result, the surrealistic image fills the picture with poetic sadness.

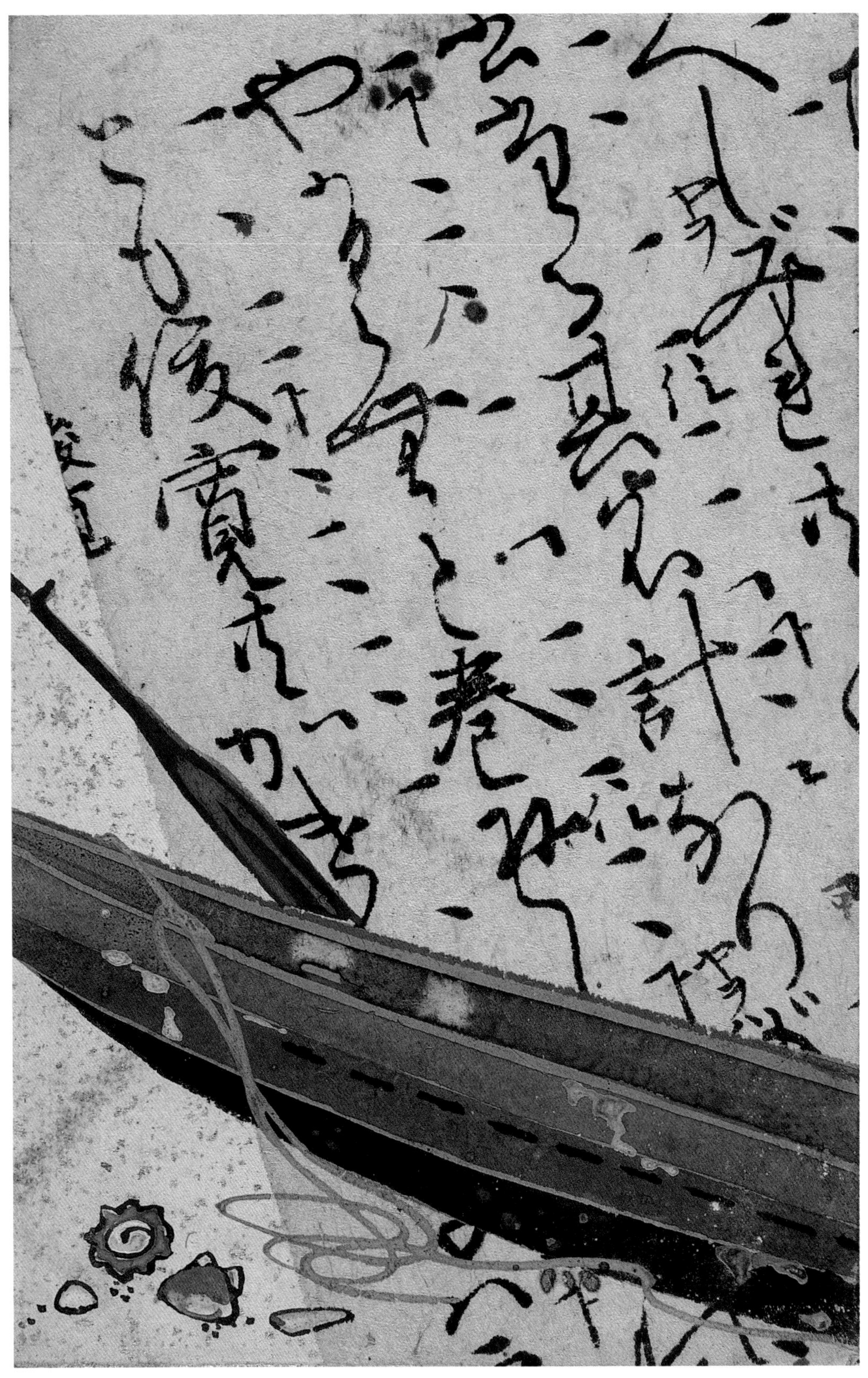

RD-099

翁千歲 Chitose

「翁千歲」是日本能劇的戲目之一。能劇是伴隨演唱謠曲的一種歌舞劇，原本是農村祭神之歌舞，在室町時代初期，因獲足利將軍賞識，而被提升推廣爲一種精緻的表演藝術；表演者需帶假面具，登場各種角色的性格，端賴以捕捉人類喜怒哀樂之刹那感情的「能面」來反映深刻入裡的人性。能劇的演出崇尚幽玄之美，規避寫實的風格，將人物夢幻化、象徵化。

此張卡片便是以能劇中的翁千歲台詞裱貼在卡紙上，再以版畫的方式印上有假鬚的翁面面具。而其下的松樹則以柔潤、稀薄的淡彩描繪，剩餘的空白背景便以鮮明的朱紅色填補，以襯托主題輕淡的設色，並反映能劇所崇尚的玄幻、清幽之美。

Chitose is a No drama from Japan. The No drama is a kind of musical incorporating the singing of folk songs. Originally singing and dancing activities as a rustic ritual to sacrifice to demons, the No drama received high regard from General Ashikaga, and was promoted to the status of a refined performance art. In a No play, the performers wear masks, and the personalities of all the characters are reflected primarily by (Momen), which capture people's spontaneous feelings of joy, anger, sorrow, and happiness, to reflect human nature in depth. The brooding and quaint beauty of the No drama avoids a realistic style and adds a dreamy and symbolic quality to the figures.

This card was created by mounting the script of the No play Chitose on the silk card, and then printing an image of Chitose's mask with a false beard using block printing. The pine trees below the mask are portrayed in light color which is soft and thin. The white background is then colored in bright vermilion to add splendor to the light coloring of the theme, and to reflect the mystic, illusory and quiet beauty of the No drama.

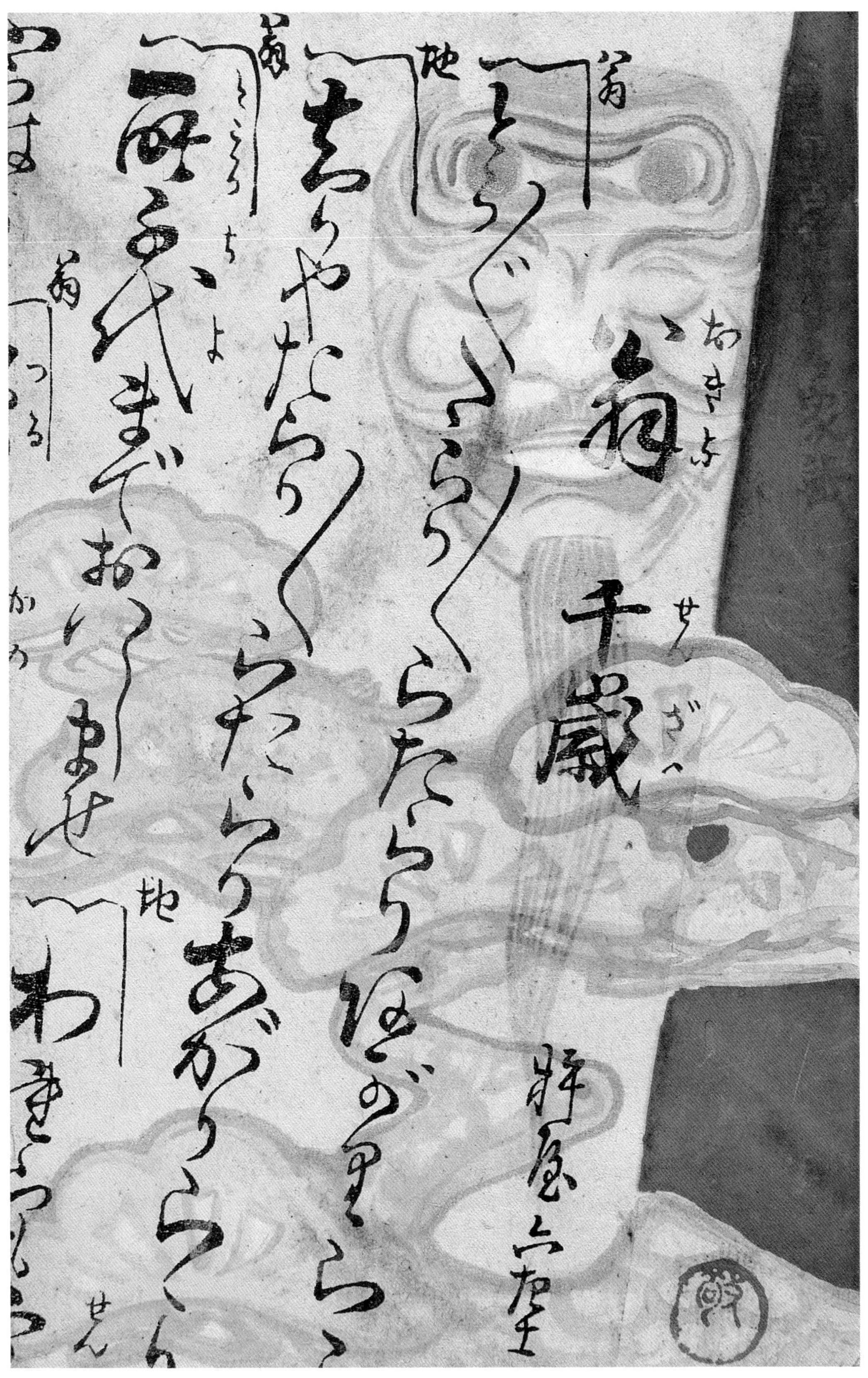

RD-100

土蜘 Trap-door Spider

天保年間，日本幕府政權已到了山窮水盡之際，水野忠邦實行節約和嚴厲的天保改革，西元 1843 年改革失敗，諷刺天保改革的浮世繪因應而生，後因涉及政治誹謗罪而告絕版。而土蜘蛛在源賴光公館之中作妖怪的作品便是當時的產物，用以隱喻因改革而備受傷害的江户（東京）町人（指的是都市中從事各行各業的族群）的怨懟。

畫中便是以描寫這段史事的謠曲「土蜘」斜裱在紙卡上，再製版繪上若隱若現的蜘蛛網，畫面右下方則有手繪的日本武士刀以及可能是代表源賴光的「花押」(形同個人的簽名或蓋章的圖案）和「源賴光」三個字。蜘蛛網高掛與兵家武器閒擱的淒涼畫面，正暗示著自源賴朝開鎌倉幕府以來的武家政權，亦將在天保改革失敗之後逐漸走向滅亡之路。

During the Tenpo Period, the shogunate of Japan was desperate to the extent that Mizuno Tatakuni instituted the Tenpo Reform, which is known for its austere measures of frugality. The reform turned out to be a failure in 1843, giving rise to Ukiyoe paintings, which often satirized it. Later, Ukiyoe paintings were forced out of print due to allegations of political slander. This piece depicting the havoc wreaked in the residence of Minamotono Yorimitsu by a trap-door spider which turned into a monster was a production of this period. It was created to indicate the antagonism of the Edo (Tokyo) chōnin people from all walks of life who suffered greatly from the reform.

This story is delineated by the lyrics mounted slantwise on card paper; cobwebs were then painted with great subtlety. In the lower right corner of the picture is a hand-rendered katana and a probable paraph (a pattern which resembles a persona signature or seal) of Minamotono Yorimitsu. The scene of desolation created by the contrast between the flourishing cobwebs and the disused weapon seems to indicate that the Kamakura Shogunate created by Minamotono Yoritomo was well on its way to its downfall following the failure of the Tenpo Reform.

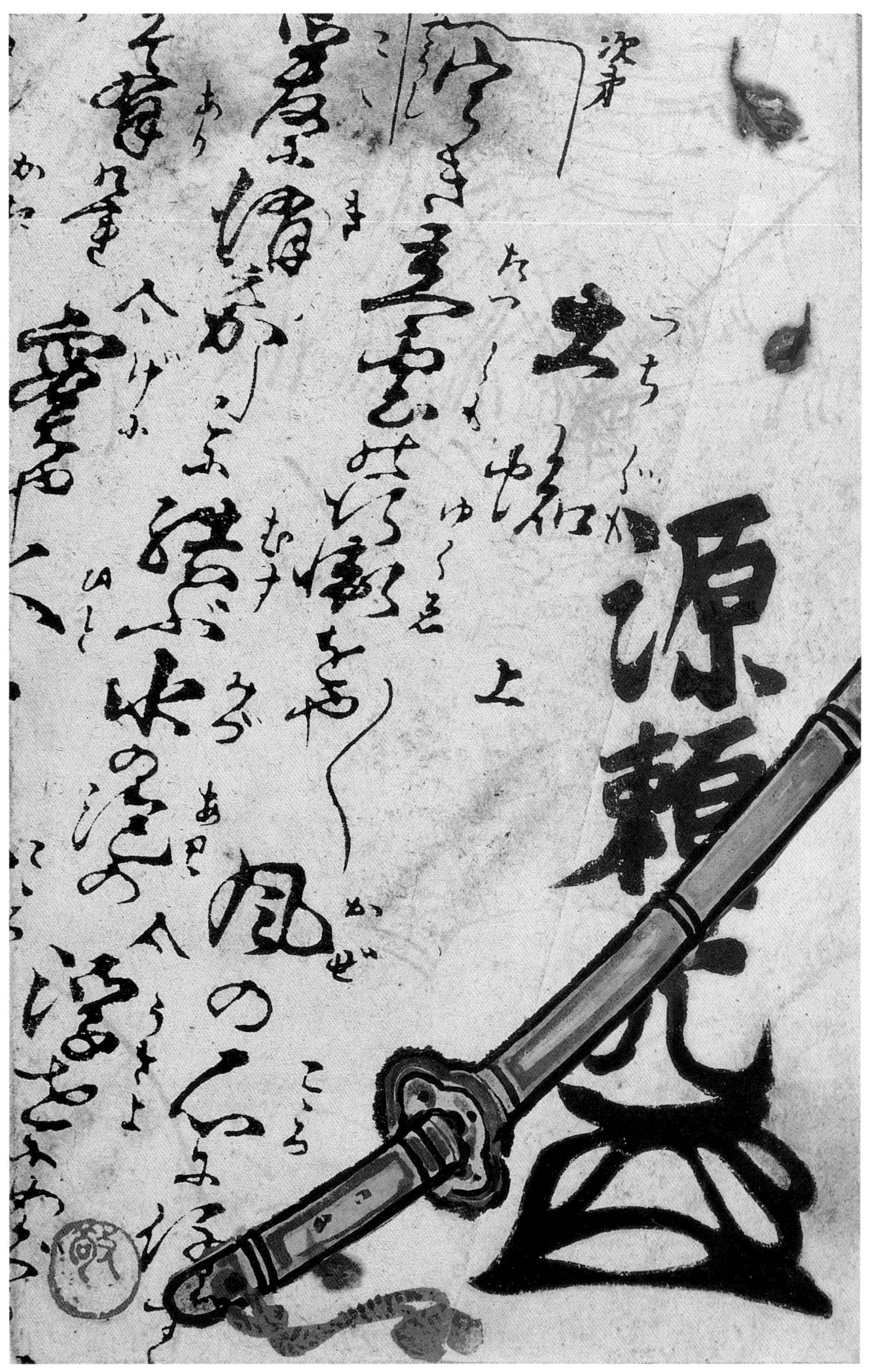

RD-101

筑磨川 Chikuma-Gawa

此張卡片題以日本謠曲的歌詞斜裱在卡紙上做爲背景，再繪上與文句相呼應的揷圖。歌詞中描寫著筑磨川的川水在大木曾山（現今長野縣木曾郡境內）南面匯集，水流拍打岸上，激起浪花。畫與文相呼應，平面化處理的山巒之間，瀉下一股清流，色調柔和的波浪流動性的線條，使水面充滿動感，加上噴灑的浪花，彷彿可聽見一波波的潮浪撞擊在山脚岩石上的聲音。波浪中，載浮載沈地飄著一頂日本武士於日常生活中，用來搭配便服所戴的帽子，帽上並有家族的徽章。作者以唯美的手段來表現加賀（現今石川縣南部）騷動的悲劇意義，畫面的右邊及下方並有淡雅的白色線條裝飾。畫中嫻熟的技巧、流暢的曲線構圖，使全幅作品有如一首優美的詠嘆詩般動人。

In this piece, a Japanese song is mounted slantwise on the cardboard as the background, with an illustration added to correspond with the lyrics. The lyrics say that the water of Chikuma-Gawa gathers in the south of Ohkiso-Yama Mountain (now located in Kiso of Nagano Prefecture). White water is created as the torrent hits the river banks. To correspond with the content of the lyrics, from the mountain treated in two-dimensional style emerges a fresh stream with soft, tender waves and fluid lines, lending forcefully to the dynamism of the water. The splashing white water seems to create the sound of water waves collapsing against the rock at the foot of the mountain. Floating amid the waves of the river is a hat carrying a clan symbol and typically worn by a samurai to go with casual costumes in daily life. The artist adopts an aesthetic approach to portray the tragic uprising in Kaga (now south of Shikawa Prefecture). In addition, on the right and lower sections of the frame are quiet and white lines created for decorative purposes. The sophisticated skills and the smooth composition of curvy lines make this piece a touching production which resembles a beautiful aria.

RD-102

鶴龜

Crane and Turtle

此張卡片是以用來祝人如鶴龜般長壽的祝賀謠曲斜裱貼在紙卡上，再以版畫刻印人物的衣著及輪廓線，最後才用彩筆平塗上色，這種以墨印線爲基礎，然後以手繪上色的技法，便是早期浮世繪的「丹繪」。畫中人物的穿著，則屬於參加正式場合時的裝扮，由此可知，這可能是一張用來表示如人親臨祝賀，祈福祝壽的生日卡片。

Intended to convey a congratulatory message, this card contains lyrics wishing the recipient longevity just like cranes and turtles. The lyrics are mounted slantwise on the cardboard where the costumes and contour lines of the figures are then blockprinted. To put a finishing touch to it, the artist used color pens to paint the color evenly. This technique from the early stage of Ukiyoe, featuring ink lines as the basis for the subsequent hand-rendered coloring is known as Tan'e. The costumes of the figures were dressing code for formal functions. Thus, this is probably a birthday card used to send a congratulatory message as if the sender were attending the birthday party in person to deliver the congratulatory message.

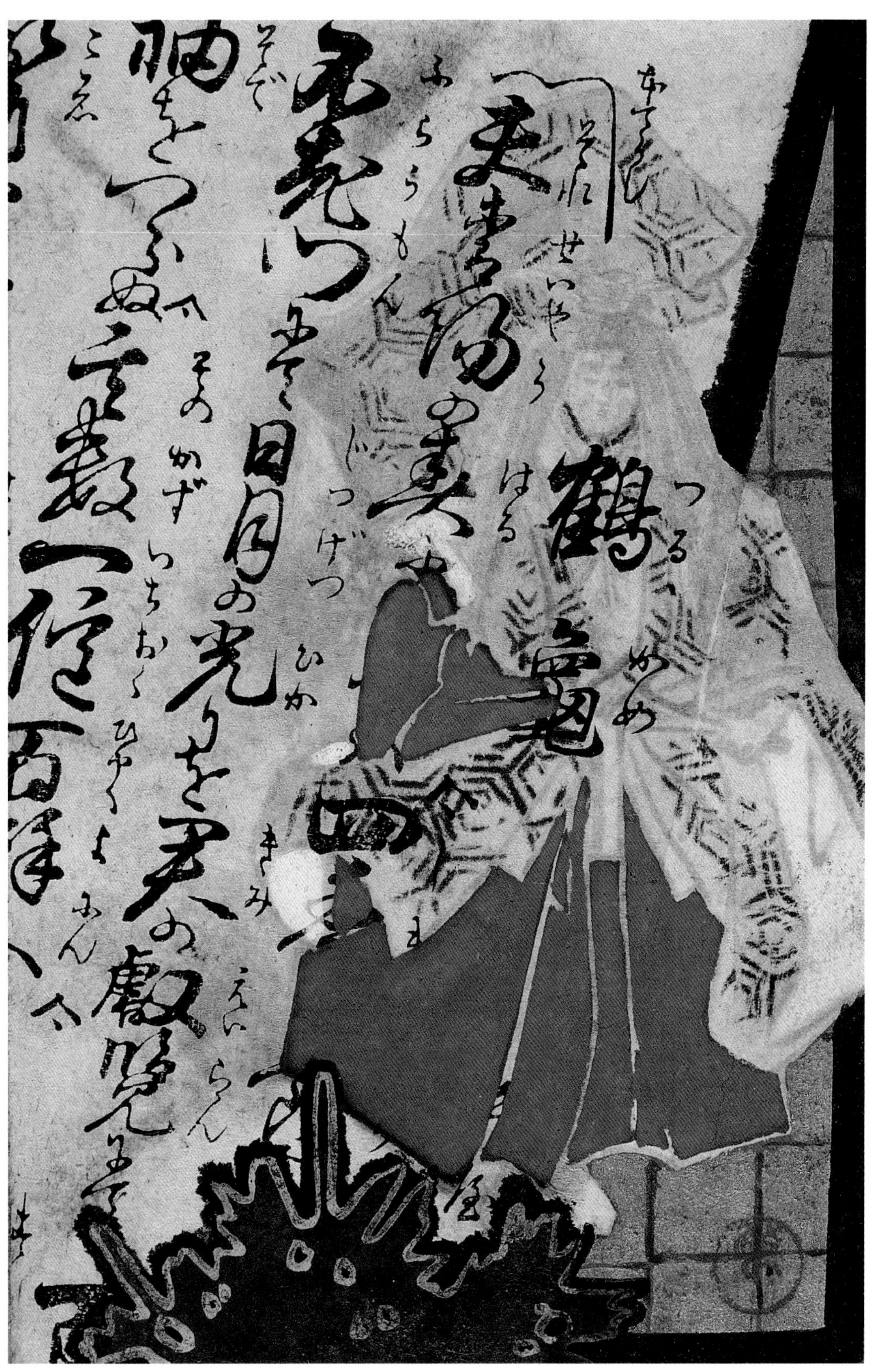

RD-103

秋色種 Autumn Flora

這件作品的製作手法較爲特殊，所使之材料也較爲奢華。作者先將以「秋色種」(秋天的花草) 爲主題的謠曲歌詞，傾斜裱貼在絹本明信片之上，再以銀灰色的顏料描繪主題。覆蓋住畫面四分之三的草書原稿，上下均不完整，其存在之目的僅在於做爲裝飾背景，並以文字點出主題。

季節原是日本文化生活中的重要部分，屋內不僅要飾以時令花卉，客廳通常更須選掛意味著季節的畫作。因而，具有裝飾的效果的四季花鳥畫，便成爲普受歡迎的題材。而其中則以秋季花草別具色彩，文人雅士便特別喜愛以這個季節的景物來抒發情懷。

作者將芒草、桔梗、野菊等秋季花草寧靜的剪影，疏落有致地安排在畫面的邊緣，畫風精緻、銀灰色的設色莊重而典雅，散發古樸優美的氣質。這種淡雅而平面化的風格情調，呈現出一種單純、古典的裝飾效果，並將秋日寧靜的氣氛表現無遺。

This piece is characterized by its unique craftsmanship as well as the extravagant material employed for its creation. The artist first mounted the lyric titled "Autumn Flora" slantwise on a silken postcard and then depicted the theme through silver-gray pigment. The script, written in *cao* (free-flowing) style characters, occupies three fourths of the entire picture, yet neither its beginning nor its end can be seen. The script is intended as a decorative background only, with a text to reflect the theme.

Seasons were an important aspect of the cultural life in Japan. Not only was the interior of a house decorated with seasonal flowers, but also the living room was often draped with paintings signifying the seasons. Therefore, highly decorative paintings depicting the four seasons, birds and flowers were especially popular, particularly those portraying autumn flora. Thus, literators and connoisseurs specially enjoyed expressing their emotion by means of autumn scenes or objects.

The artist properly spaced silhouettes of autumn flowers and plants such as reeds, bellflowers, and wild daisies on the corners of the picture. The delicate draftsmanship, together with the silver and majestic coloring, creates a quaint and aesthetic atmosphere. This elegant, quiet and two-dimensional style contribute to a simple and classic decorative effect through which the tranquillity of an autumn day is thoroughly conveyed.

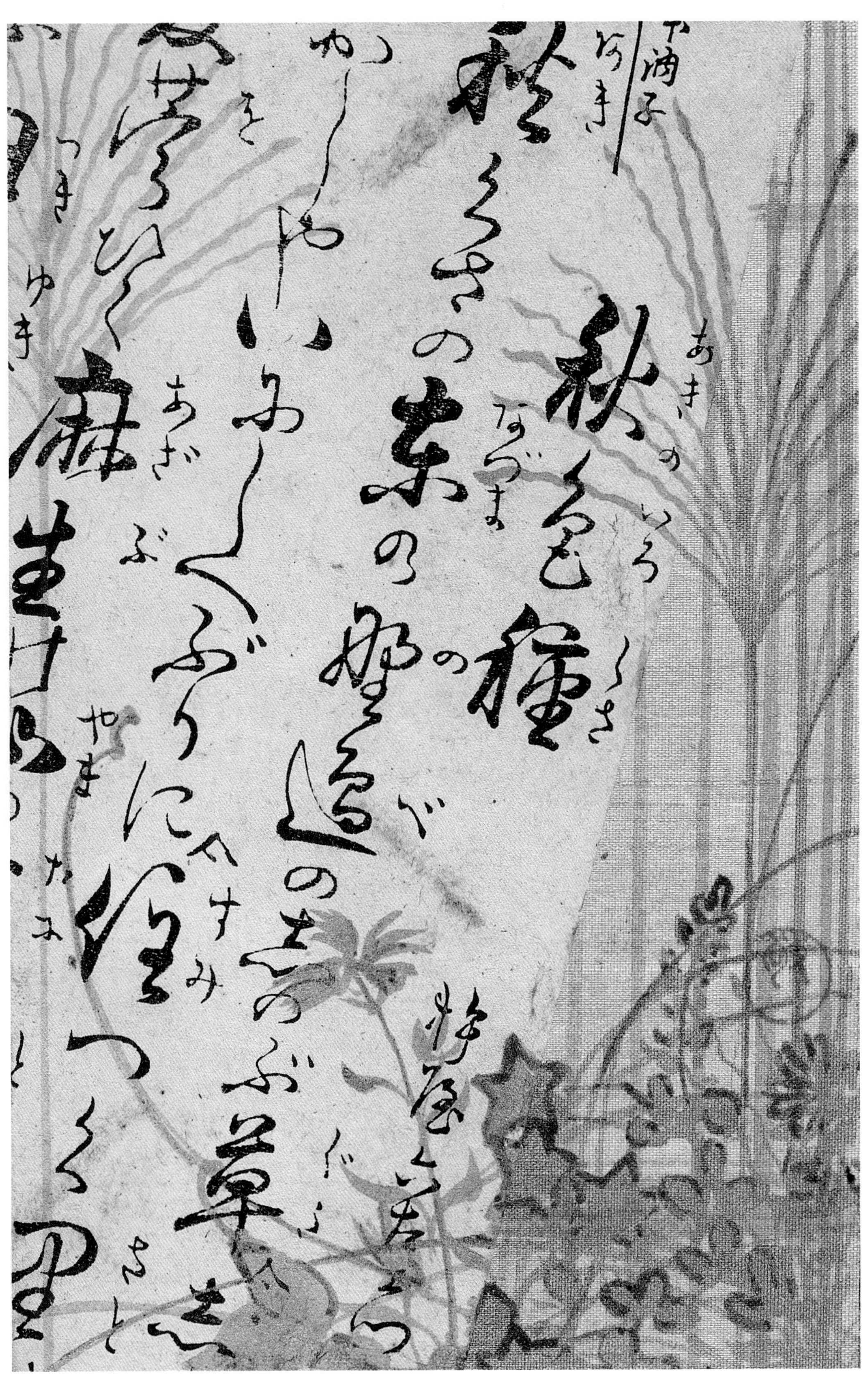

RD-104

勸進帳 Kangincho

勸進帳乃日本傳統的十八種歌舞技之一。這件作品就是以裱貼的勸進帳台詞做爲背景，至於畫面的右下角則是以橙色顏料厚塗至足以覆蓋底下的印刷台詞，再框以三條黑色線條，目的在於製造觀者視覺上的錯覺，彷彿是另一層裱貼的效果。而橙色的底色上，則有深藍色線條描繪的俳優（演員），這些線條是運用類似〝複寫紙〞刻描線條的技法，與一般用軟毛筆線描的效果迥異。用筆工整細膩逼眞，乍看之下，彷若是裱貼的印刷品。作者捕捉了歌舞伎入戲剎那的神態，將之表現在這片橙色的畫面上，並用巧妙的圓形構圖及相對的目光聯結其間的關係，每一個人物上面，都用文字標示其姓名，他們都是江户時期著名的演員。而畫面上，這種刻意模仿印刷品的作法，其目的可能是在製造類似歌舞劇的海報效果。

Kangincho is one of the 18 traditional Kabuki plays of Japan. A script of Kangincho is mounted as the background of the frame, and thick orange pigment is applied to cover the printed script on the bottom. Three black lines are added to create a visual illusion that another material has been mounted. Against the background in orange color, deep blue lines are employed to depict *haiyu* (actors). Created through a technique similar to the use of carbon paper, the lines are quite different from those created through soft hair pencils. Due to the meticulous and accurate strokes, a glance at the picture creates an illusion that printed matter is mounted on the picture. The artist captured the spirit of actors engrossed in their performance and presented it in this orange-colored picture. In addition, the artist employed a composition of round shapes and their relations to the relative visual effect, and specified the names of the figures who were all famous actors in the Edo Period. It is quite possible that printed matter is imitated intentionally to create an effect of posters for musicals.

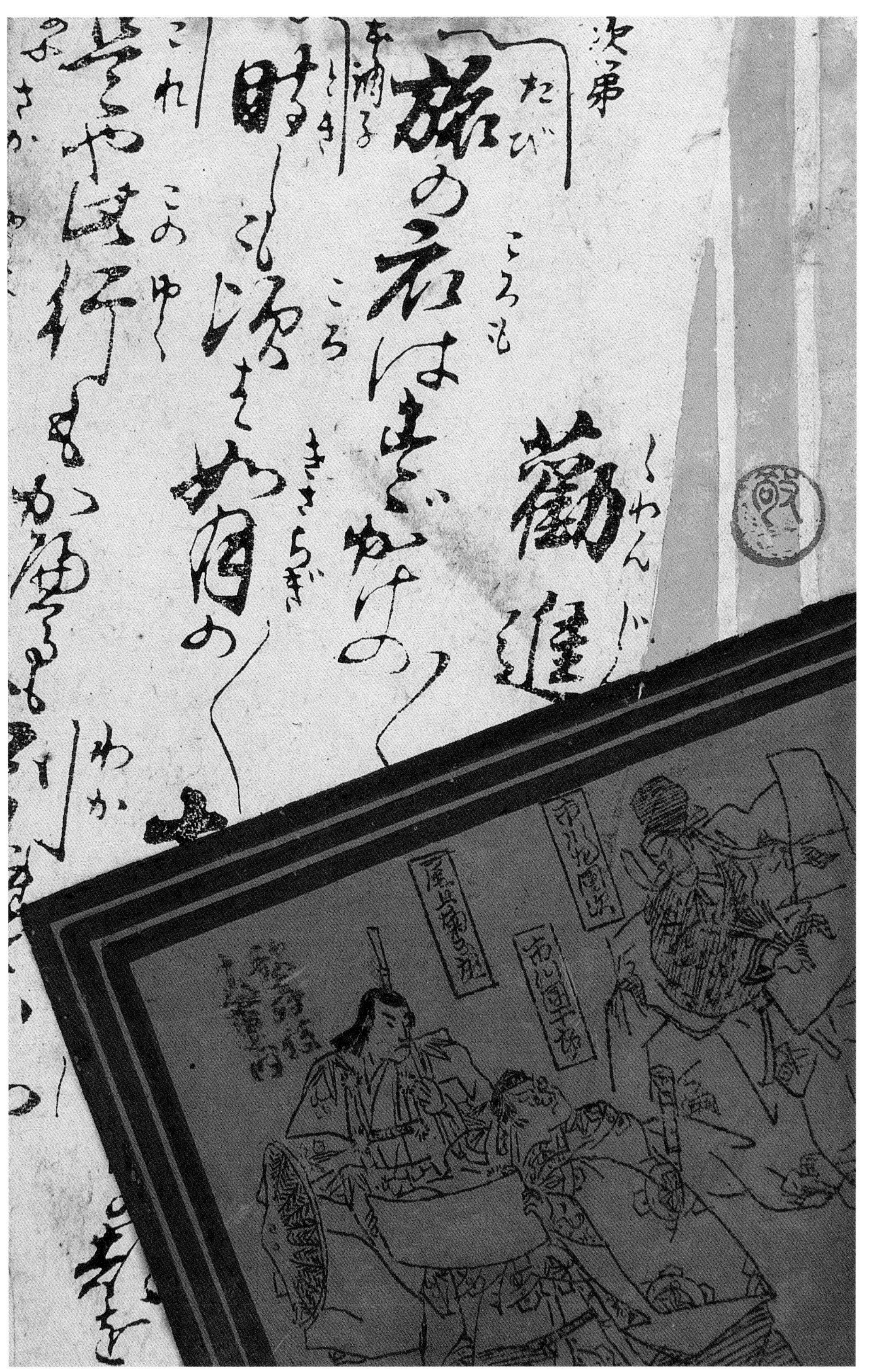

RD-105

老松 Old Pine

老松是一種代表長壽的吉祥植物。這件作品是以極薄的木板薄片裱貼在明信片上，再斜貼上以「老松」爲歌詠主題的謠曲歌譜，畫面構圖瀟灑自由，手繪部份偏重幾何平塗構成的趣味性，與草書書寫的歌詞相映成趣，是一件純粹爲鑑賞而藝術的作品。

Old pines are auspicious plants symbolizing long life. In this piece, a very thin wooden sheet is mounted on a postcard where the lyrics titled "Old Pine" are then attached at an angle. This piece is characterized by untrammeled composition. The interesting effect created by flat and geometric application of pigment corresponds with the lyrics written in the free-flowing *cao* style of calligraphy. This is indeed an artistic work created solely for the purpose of aesthetic appreciation.

RD-106

長良川 Nagara-Gawa River

這張描寫長良川鵜飼的作品，是以淡墨印刷的詩詞斜裱在灰色的卡片上做爲背景，詩詞的內容描述川上鵜飼及烹煮料理的閒適景致。主題的描繪在整個畫面的下半部，頭戴高帽的鵜匠們乘著船頭點著火把的獨木舟，正以細繩操縱著鵜以捕捉鮮魚。畫面上的人物形象和一切事物，都以簡化了的幾何，造形和平面的色塊勾以流暢的銀色輪廓線處理之。然而造形雖然簡化，卻仍栩栩如生，淡雅明亮的設色使畫面呈現出一種瀟灑、愉悅的效果，充份表現出愉快抒情的上流社會的情調。

長良川位於日本名古屋附近的岐阜縣境內，川上的鵜飼乃岐阜市最著名的觀光資源。除了水位過高或水濁之外，每晚七點至九點，鵜匠（漁夫）乘著以火把爲照明的鵜舟，巧妙地操縱著頸子被縛著細繩的鵜（**野生的鵜生性勇猛，但被捕後嘴尖被切除，並被餵食飼料及訓練，野性日失，只得甘心被鵜匠役用表演了。**），敏捷的捕捉著魚兒，在火光耀動的水面上，交織成一幅美麗的畫面，此景因而有「古典畫卷」的美譽。每到了鵜飼季節（五至十月），便吸引了數百萬慕名而來的國際觀光客，乘著靜靜泊在鵜舟旁的豪華屋形船觀賞這項表演。

This piece depicting the feeding of pelicans at the edge of Nagara-Gawa River contains a poem printed in light ink and mounted slantwise on a gray card as the background. This poem basically depicts feeding of pelicans on a river and the carefree lifestyle of officials from the imperial court who are fishing and cooking on a boat.

Nagara-Gawa River is situated in Gihu Prefecture near Nagoya of Japan. Feeding of pelicans is one of the most well-known tourist events in Gihu. Except when the water level on the river is too high or when the water becomes turbid, pelican raisers (fishermen) usually ride on a canoe illuminated by torches between seven and nine every evening and skillfully manipulate pelicans to catch fish with dexterity through the thin wires attached to their necks. A beautiful scene is thus created on the river bearing the reflection of flickering torches. It is for this reason that this scene has since earned its reputation as an image worthy of a "classical scroll." During the season when pelicans are fed (from May through October), millions of tourists are attracted from all over the world to take a deluxe house-shaped boat anchored quietly alongside the canoe where the feeding of pelicans is conducted, and to watch this performance.

The focus of the motif is on the lower half of the picture. The pelican raisers wearing high hats are canoeing in a river in spring. Riding on a canoe whose bow is illuminated by several torches, pelican raisers are manipulating pelicans to catch fish with thin wires Which they have attached to the birds. The figures, images and objects in the picture are created through simplified geometric shapes and two-dimensional color blocks, with smooth, silver contour lines. Though simplified in form, the figures nevertheless look vivid and lively. The quiet and bright coloring creates a dashing and pleasant effect, bringing out a feeling of leisure, merriment and lyricism typical of the upper class.

Note: Wild pelicans are ferocious. However, the tips of their beaks are amputated when they are caught. In the processing of feeding and training, they are gradually tamed and become manipulated by their raisers for the purpose of performances.

RD-107

樂屋 Gakuya

樂屋是指劇場的後台或化粧室，此張運用日本歌劇的歌本斜裱佔據大半個畫面的絹本卡片，便是描寫樂屋的一角。前景閒置著一串唸珠和藝妓或「女形」（男扮女裝的歌舞伎）所配戴的假髮，而斜貼的歌本則彷若一道斜掛的布簾，僅露出一角讓人得以窺見室內牆上所垂掛的捲軸及梳妝台上猶獨自飄香的杯茶。畫面設色淡雅柔和，流露出休閒、神祕的氣息。

Gakuya refers to the backstage or dressing room of a theater. On this silken card, which depicts a corner of the Gakuya, a script of Japanese opera is mounted slantwise, taking up the majority of the frame. On the foreground are a rosary and a wig worn by courtesans or Onna gata (male actors in women's costumes in the case of Kabuki). The script attached slantwise to the frame seems like a slantwise curtain which reveals a corner of the dressing room to allow a glimpse of the scrolls hung on the wall and a fragrant cup of tea on the dressing table. Quietly and softly colored, this picture evokes a sense of leisure and mystery.

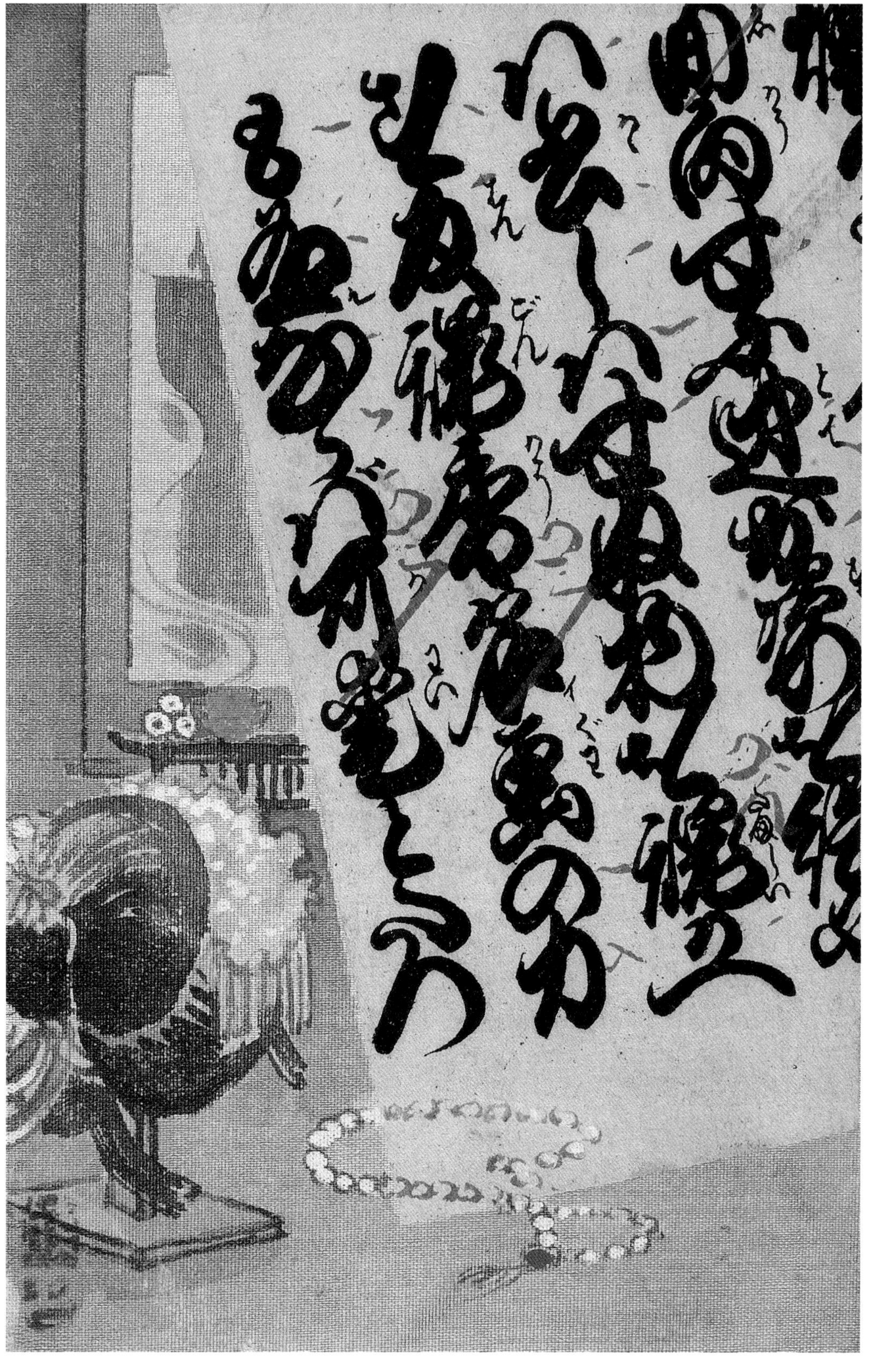

RD-108

秋的樂音 Autumn Music

此張木本明信片是以淨琉璃的扉頁加上精密的手繪而成的。作者利用未被文字遮蓋的木紋，繪上日本古琴的琴絃和角，畫面的右下方則另繪有音色淒美幽遠的「尺八」（近似中國的洞簫）以及雛菊、桔梗等秋天的花草。此外，畫面上還斜劃過幾道玲瓏惕透的曲線，予人一種振舞欲飛的感受。通幅作品流露出樂音裊裊的秋日午後般優雅、閑適的氣息。

This large-sized postcard features a flyleaf of a joruri score and exquisite hand-rendered drawings. The artist drew the cords of an antique Japanese musical instrument and a corner of the instrument on grainy texture which is not covered by the text. In the lower right of the picture, the artist also drew a Shakuhachi (resembling a Chinese flute) and autumn flowers and plants, such as daisies and balloon flowers. In addition, a few delicate and lovely curvy lines are drawn slantwise across the picture, adding inspiration and stimulation to this piece, which is permeated with an aura of grace and relaxation to the accompaniment of music.

RD-109

RD-110～RD-113

情節與戲碼 Plot and Number

此爲又一系列以書法線條與彩繪圖案結合之作品，其書寫之內容，應爲可供吟詠之詩詞歌賦，每篇皆有名稱，並於每個漢字之旁，以日本平假名拼音。其內文情節應與所繪圖案息息相關。

This is yet another series of works combining calligraphy strokes and color patterns. The content of the writing should be verses that could be sung. Each verse has a title, and Japanese Hiragana spelling can be found next to each Han character. The content of the writing should be closely related to the patterns.

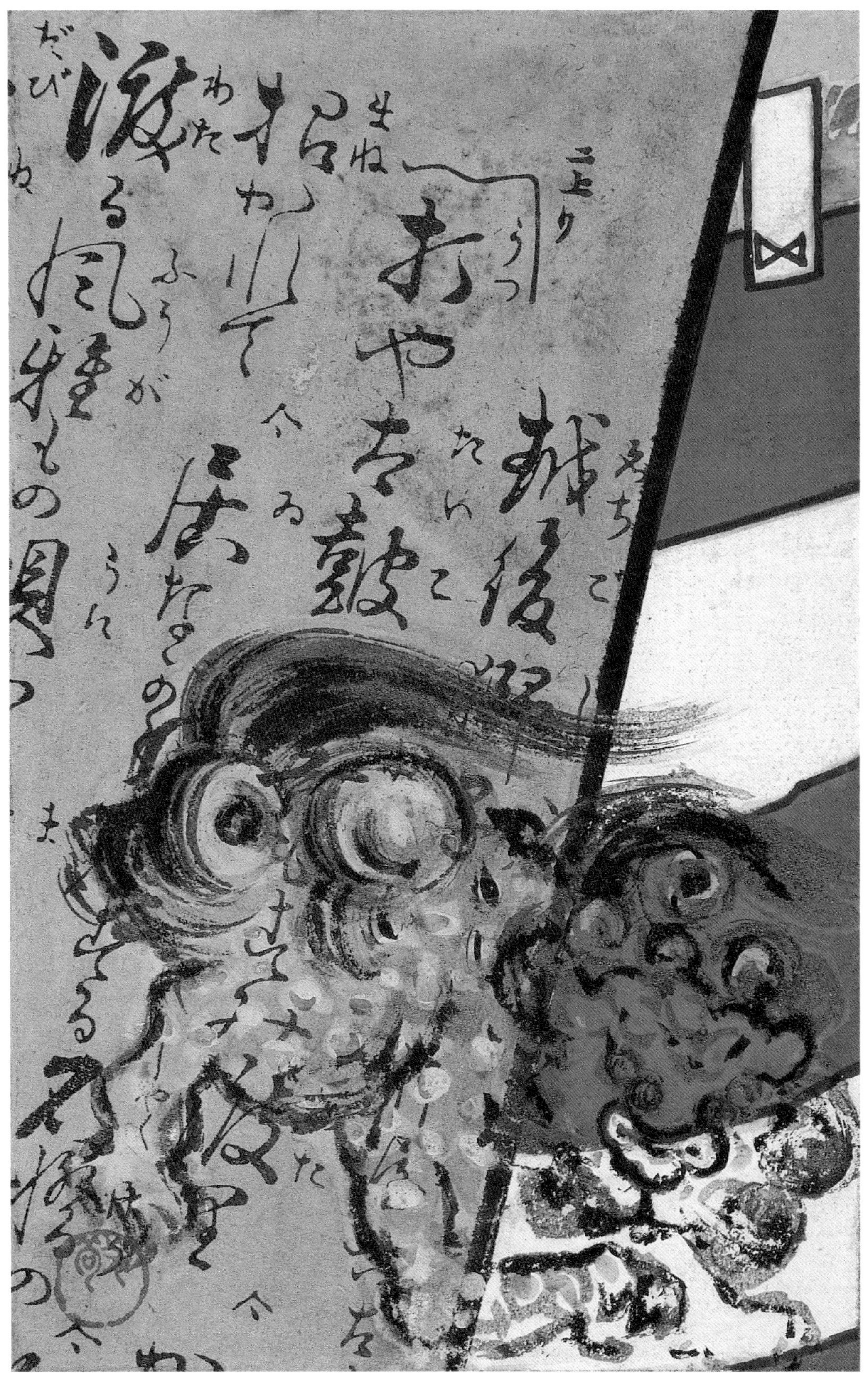

RD-110

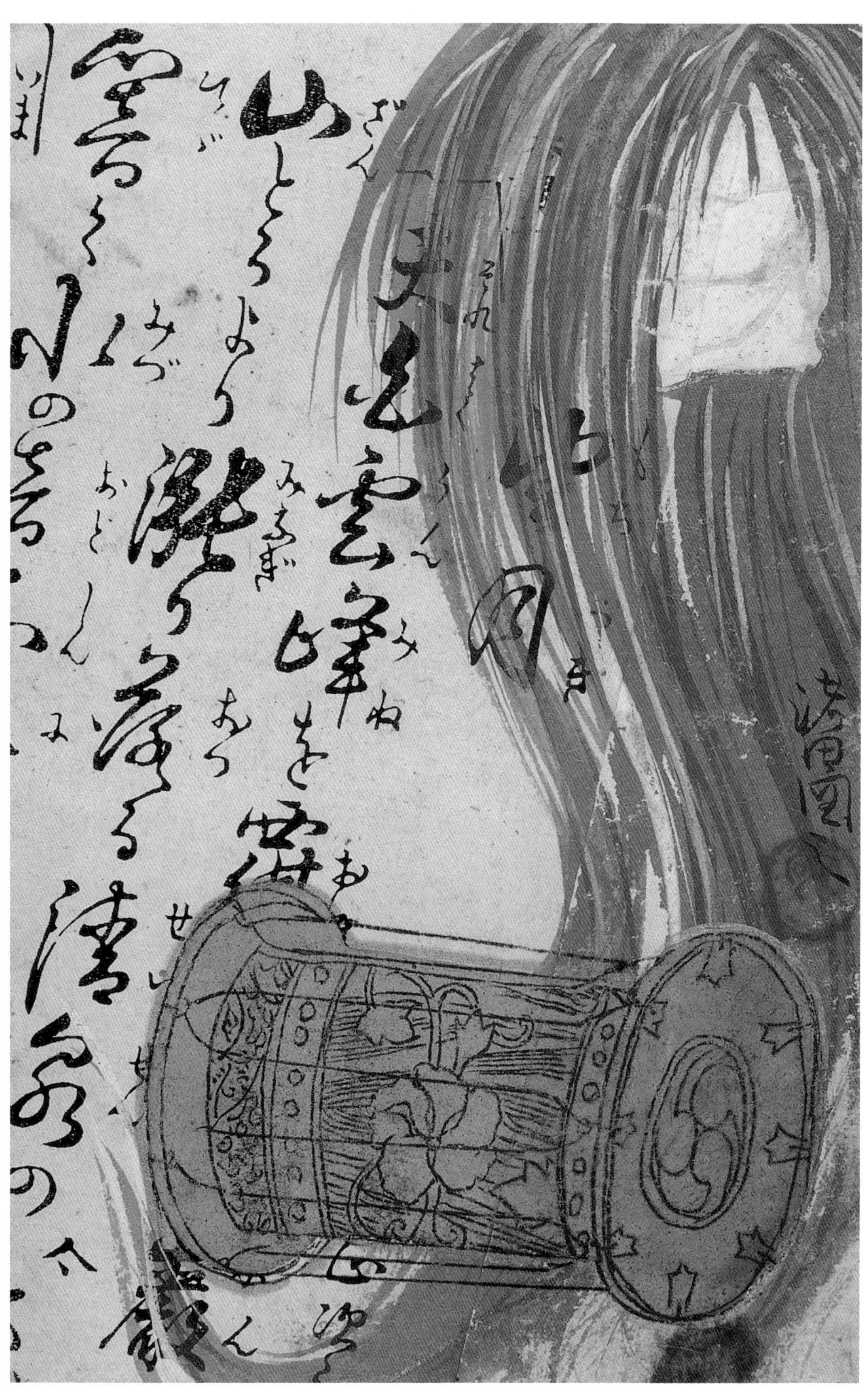

RD-111

RD-112

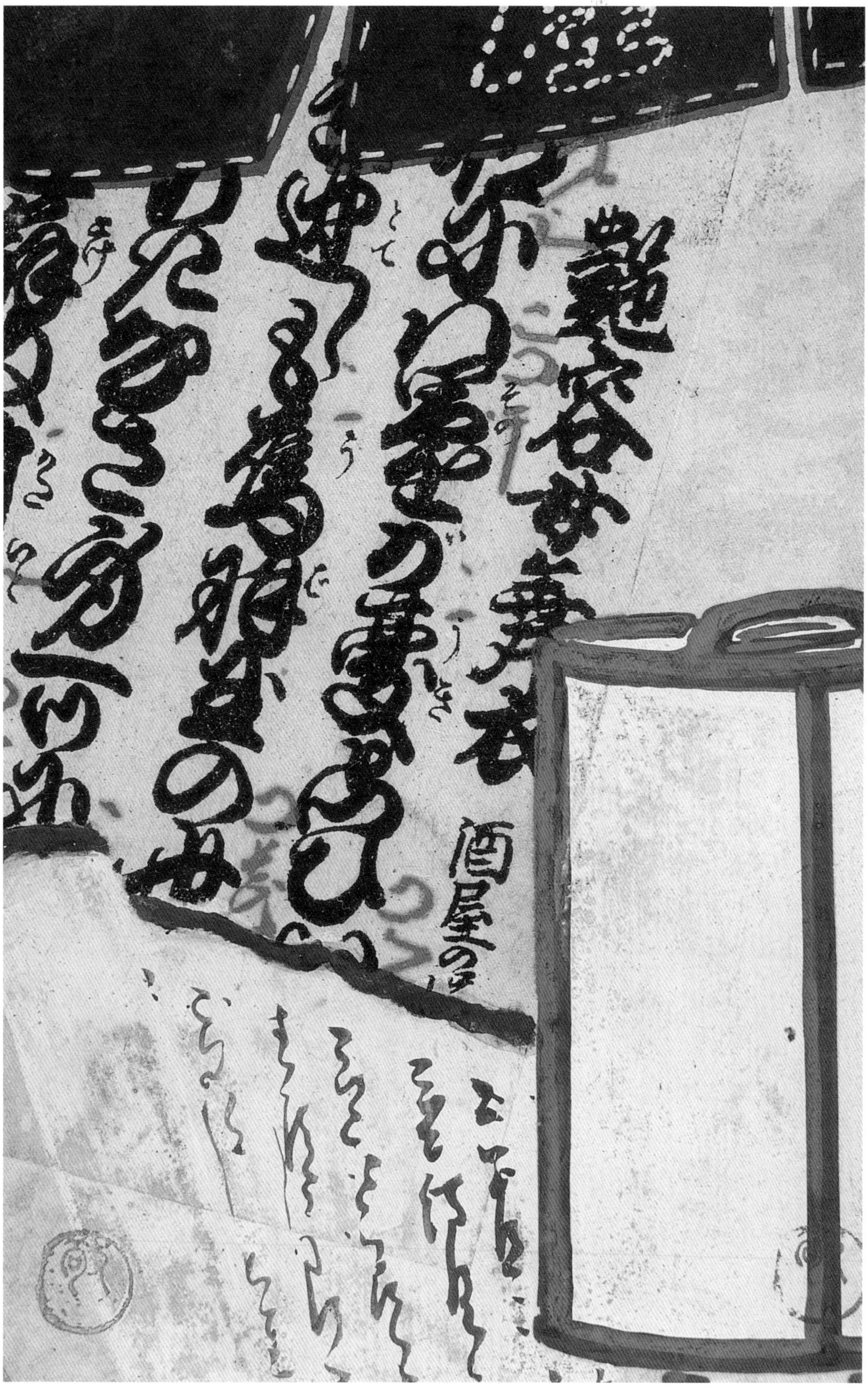

RD-113

木本勝地寫景
Wooden Scenic Postcards

這一系列十二張的日本風景明信片是運用黑白照片的技術，將影像顯現在經過特殊處理過、薄若紙張的木片上，再透過手工敷彩的過程所完成的。經過挑選的木板薄片的紋路細緻，加上其上的特殊處理，適當地提供了畫面更豐富的變化及晶瑩、剔透的光澤感。黑白照片的顯像效果則賦予每一張卡片清晰、細膩、柔和的基調，而手工舖染的淡彩，除了更加強調每一個別景象的光影色彩變化之外，同時也渾染出其特有的氣氛，顯現出各個景緻的特色。全系列的卡片均流露出一種古樸、豐潤、神祕、歷久彌新的韻味。

This series of 12 Japanese scenic postcards employed the technique of black-and-white photography to project images on thin, specially processed wooden sheets, and then colors were applied to the sheets by hand. The fine and delicate texture of the thin, specially selected wooden sheets, along with special techniques employed in processing the sheets, aptly create rich variations, and a glittery and lucid touch of brilliance. The black-and-white photographic images lends clarity, delicacy, and softness to each postcard. The light colors applied manually add variation to the lighting and coloring of each individual scene, and create a unique atmosphere to project the special characteristics of each scene. This series of postcards is permeated with a quaint, rich, mystic and enduring aura.

大阪城　Osaka Castle

大阪城位於大阪東區，是日本三大名城之一。該城於西元1583年動工興建，費時三年，勞動三萬民工，可說是豐臣秀吉統一天下的紀念品，其後，屢遭戰火摧殘，現今大阪城則是1931年所重建的，規模僅原有的五分之一。

舊大阪城外被全長12公里的石牆與濠溝所圍繞，石牆耗用了50萬塊千里迢迢自日本各地而來的石塊。城內則有許多著名的旅遊據點，例如天守閣、大手門……等。

Located in the east of Osaka, Osaka Castle is one of the three great castles in Japan. The castle was built in three years, starting in 1583, and 30,000 civilian workers were enlisted for its construction. Indeed, this is a commemoration of Toyotomi Hideyoshi's unification of Japan. Later, the castle was ravaged by wars. The Osaka Castle of today was rebuilt in 1931 and is only one-fifth the size of the original castle.

Osaka Castle is surrounded by stone walls and trenches with a total length of 12 kilometers. The stone walls consist of 500,000 rocks gathered from many places in Japan. The castle features many well-known scenic spots, such as the Tensyu Pavilion and Ōte Gate.

木本明信片
Wood shaving postcard

RD-114

奈良春日神社

Kasuga Temple, Nara

春日神社位於奈良公園之內，神社建於神護景雲2年（西元768年），乃日本最古老、最著名的神社之一，現今本殿則為江户時代末期所建。神社建築可說是日本漆器工藝運用於建築上的代表作，丹紅色的建築全部都是以精緻的漆器堆砌而成，優雅的色澤在翠綠色樹林的襯托之下極為搭調。該神社尚因其境內燈籠之多，造形之豐富而馳名，社殿檐簷高懸之吊燈與社內庭院參道兩側信徒進獻之石燈籠，共計三千餘盞，每年節分或中元時節，這些燈籠會點上火，稱為「春日萬燈籠」，景緻十分壯觀。

Located in the Nara Park, the Kasuga Temple was built in the second year of the Gingo-Keiun Era (768 A.D.), and is one of the oldest and most famous temples in Japan. Its main temple was built in the closing years of the Edo Era. Shinto temple buildings can be described as the culmination of the Japanese lacquerware craft as used in architecture. The red structures are built completely from stacks of exquisite lacquerware pieces. Set amidst the bright green of trees, their elegant thincture looks very stylish. This temple is also famous for the multitude and variations of its lanterns. The lanterns hung high from the beams and rafters of the temple's main building, and the number of lanterns contributed by worshipers and hung on both sides of the passages within the temple reach a total of 3,000 lanterns. These lanterns are lit at the beginning of each season or during the Ghost Festival. Called "the myriad lanterns of Kasuga," it makes for a most magnificent spectacle.

木本明信片
Wood shaving postcard

RD-115

日光御神橋

The Sacred Shinkyo Bridge, Nikko

傳說西元 782 年，日光的開山祖師勝道山人和弟子在此渡河，由於「大谷川」水勢湍急，擋其去路；此時突有青紅兩條巨蟒相互蟠結成橋，助大師渡川。

17 世紀中葉，營建東照宮之時，便在川上架設了一座長 28 公尺、寬 7 公尺的新月形的木造拱橋，當時名爲「山菅橋」，現今日本人稱之爲「神橋」。

該橋曾於 1907 年重建，然自永寬 13 年（西元 1636 年）便禁止行人通行，平日僅供遊客觀賞，唯有在東照宮祭典時，方允遊客過橋，並得收「過橋費」。這座木橋仍然以朱紅爲主色，在一片翠綠的杉木林的烘托之下，更顯超凡脱俗，實兼具自然與人工之美。

It is said that in 782, Katsuyama Dojin, the founding father of Nikko, crossed the river from here with his disciples. However, they could not make their crossing because of the torrents of the Ōya-Gawa River. In the meantime, two snakes, green and red, intertwined to form a bridge to help the master cross the river.

In the middle of the 17th century when the Toshogu palace was being built, a crescent-shaped wooden bridge, which was then called the Sankanbashi Bridge, 28 meters in length and seven meters wide was built over the river. Japanese nowadays refer to this bridge as the Shinkyo, or "Sacred Bridge."

Rebuilt in 1907, the bridge has been off limits to pedestrians since the 13th year of the Eikan Era (or 1636). The bridge is only for the scenic pleasure of visitors, and is not open for crossing except during festivities of the Toshogu palace, when a toll is collected. With vermilion as its basic color, this wooden bridge, set against a forest of fir trees, appears all the more sublime and unworldly, possessing beauty both natural and man-made.

木本明信片
Wood shaving postcard

RD-116

安藝宮島 Miyajima, Aki

宮島，古稱「嚴島」，位於廣島灣西岸的瀨戶內海上，自古日本人便視爲「神祇之島」。與「松島」、「天橋立」並稱「日本三景」。

搭建於島上海灣泥地上的「嚴島神社」，始創於西元593年；仁安3年（西元1168年）時，因平清盛爲其母祭祀而重修整建。其建築樣式據說是仿當時貴族寢宮而設計的，型式優雅。每當漲潮時，海水淹沒神社的支柱，僅剩朱紅色的神殿建築群，虛無飄渺地立在水中，彷若海上龍宮，令人嘆爲觀止。

神社本殿前約200公尺的海面上，豎立著華麗耀眼的朱紅色大鳥居。以楠木爲建材的大牌坊，主柱間寬約10公尺、高約16公尺，唯有在海水退潮時，方能沿沙灘步行到達，目前爲日本政府指定維護的重要藝術財產。

Miyajima, also known as Itsukushima in ancient times, is located in the Seto inland sea, and has been regarded as the Island of God by Japanese since ancient times. This island, along with Matsushima Island and the Amanohashidate sandbar, are collectively known as the "Three Great Scenes of Japan".

Built from the muds of the inland sea, the Itsukushima Temple was established in 593 AD, and was renovated by Tairano-Kiyomori in the third year of the Ninan Era (or 1168 AD) to honor the memory of his mother. It was said that its elegant architectural style was derived from the designs of the living quarters of aristocrats. During high tides, the supporting columns are flooded by sea water, leaving only the vermilion structures of the temple standing ethereally above the water, just like the palace of the sea god.

About 200 meters in front of the temple is positioned a large, resplendent vermillion *torii* (entrance gate) . Its main panel was built from nanmu cedar (Phoebe nanmu) , and its two main columns are ten meters apart and 16 meters high. This sign, which is accessible on foot along the sand beach only after the ebbing of the tides, has been protected by the Japanese goverment as a major artistic possession.

木本明信片
Wood shaving postcard

RD-117

木本明信片
Wood shaving postcard

RD-118

京都保津川 Hotsu Rapids, Kyoto

保津川是京都近畿境內的大河川，短而急的川水溪谷景觀壯麗，別具風格，兩岸及川面滿佈奇岩異石，鬼斧神工、意境絶佳。陡直的溪谷岩壁，看似險峻，卻一直是京都境內溪谷探勝，尋求變化刺激的主要據點。乘小舟溯流而下，穿梭於奇岩怪石之間，頗能予人「兩岸猿聲啼不住，輕舟已過萬重山」的感受。

The Hotsu Rapids is a major river in the vicinity of Kyoto. Fast and torrential, this river is unique for its magnificent valleys. Strange and exotic rocks scatter in the water and on the river banks, offering an excellent impressionistic theme. Steep river cliffs, which look dangerous, are a major scenic spot in Kyoto for tourists in pursuit of excitement and variations. Taking a small boat down the river and traveling amid the exotic rocks evokes a feeling of grandeur just like canoeing through magnificent and breath-taking natural wonders.

木本明信片
Wood shaving postcard

RD-119

神戸布引雌瀧 Nunohiki No Taki, Kobe

雌瀧源自六甲山的「生田川」中游，乃一自古以來便名列於許多詩歌的名瀑布，水流自山洞中傾瀉而下，有如白色布匹般美麗動人。其附近尚有許多著名的瀑布，例如雄瀧、夫妻瀧等。

Originated from the middle stream of the Ikuta-Gawa River in the Rokko Mountains, Nunohiki No Taki is one of the famous waterfalls cited in poem and song since ancient times. With water running down from a mountain cave, Nunohiki No Taki resembles an unreeled roll of immaculate cloth and is extremely beautiful. In its vicinity are other famous waterfalls, such as Otaki and Meototaki.

木本明信片
Wood shaving postcard

江之島 Enoshima

江之島位於鎌倉的西南外海，其形成係因地殼隆起，乃典型的「陸繫島」。島上面積僅0.18平方公里，爲常綠濶葉林所覆蓋，氣候溫暖、景色秀麗，故名「綠色江之島」。此島亦爲鎌倉地區的宗教中心，宗教氣息濃厚，乃人文旅遊的重要路線。

Located in the water off the southwestern part of Kamakura, Enoshima Island was formed by the upheaval of the earth's crust, and is a typical island joined to a continental land mass. With an area of just 0.18 square kilometers, this island is covered with broad-leaved trees and is blessed with a moderate climate and beautiful scenery. Therefore, this island is called "Green Enoshima." With a strong spiritual aura, this island is also a religious center for the Kamakura area, and a major site for cultural travel.

RD-120

木本明信片
Wood shaving postcard

RD-121

橫濱三溪園 Sankeiyen, Yokohama

三溪園是沿著本牧海岸丘陵地所建造的日式庭園，原爲富豪原富太郎（三溪）的庭園，1906年起方開放供民衆參觀。園内設計是利用自然的山谷間或配置了水池，並遍植梅、櫻、菖蒲……等花草，其内建築則是由關西、鎌倉各地收集而來的舍殿、寺塔、樓閣等古建築物，泰半都屬於重要文化財産。

A Japanese garden built on the hill along the Honmoku Coast, the garden was originally owned by a wealthy man, Hara Tomitaro (Sankei). The garden has been open to the public since 1906. The design of the garden makes use of pools, either formed from the natural terrain of the valley and the extensive cultivation of plum trees, cherry trees, calami and other plants. The buildings within the garden are mostly antique structures, such as temples, pagodas and towers gathered from such places as Kansei and Kamakura. Most of them count as important cultural relics.

木本明信片
Wood shaving postcard

RD-122

東京明治神宮 Meiji Shrine, Tokyo

明治神宮位於東京原宿的表參道(東京〝香榭大道〞)終點，是西元1920年，爲祭祀明治天皇與昭憲皇后而建的，二次大戰期間毀於戰火，1958年重建。神宮面積廣達七十萬平方公尺，苑内遍植自日本各地獻納而來的巨木，使人步入宮中，猶如置身山野森林，倍覺神清氣爽。

圖中所見乃通往神宮本殿道上的第二座鳥居，高12公尺，柱直徑1.2公尺，爲日本最大之木造鳥居。建構此座鳥居的檜木，係由台灣阿里山砍伐運送而來的。神社殿堂亦是全部以檜木爲建材，造型簡素而有魄力，乃日本神道建築的代表作。

Located on the end of Omotesando (the "Champs Elysees" of Japan) of Haragiku, Tokyo, the Meiji Shrine was built in 1920 to honor Emperor Meiji and Queen Shoken. The shrine was destroyed during World War II, and was rebuilt in 1958. With a total area of 700,000 square meters, the shrine is planted with giant trees collected from a lot of places in Japan. Stepping into the shrine, one feels refreshed and stimulated because it is like walking into a forest deep in a mountain.

In the frame, we see the second *torii* leading to the main building of the shrine. The columns of this *torii* are 12 meters in height and 1.2 meters in diameter. The biggest wooden *torii* in Japan, if is made up of the hinoki cypress logged and shipped from Mt. Ali in Taiwan. The structures of the shrine are all made up of hinoki cypress. With a simple and powerful design, this piece is a masterpiece representative of the Shinto architecture of Japan.

木本明信片
Wood shaving postcard

RD-123

天橋立 Amanohashidate

天橋立乃一橫隧若狹灣的細長沙洲，長 2.4 公里，最寬處約 150 公尺，最狹處僅 20 公尺。潮汐所挾帶海沙堆積而成的沙洲，沙質皎白，有如一道天橋，故名爲「天橋立」，自古以來，即爲日本的觀光勝地。

洲上廣植青松，俯觀之下，彷若巨龍盤旋海上，在日落後猶徘徊在天空的彤雲烘托之下，景緻絶美，不在話下。

The Amanohashidate is a long sandbar 2.4 kilometers in length and 20 to 150 meters in width. Its sand, built up from deposits from the sea, is bright white, giving the sandbar the appearance of a "heavenly bridge," which is the meaning of Amanohashidate. Since early times, it has been an important scenic spot in Japan.

The sandbar is planted extensively with green pine trees, and, if viewed from the air, resembles a huge dragon hovering above the sea. Naturally, the scenery of the sandbar is most engaging against the background of the lingering clouds in the sky after the sun has set.

木本明信片
Wood shaving postcard

RD-124

西湖觀富士山景 Mount Fuji Viewed from Saiko

富士山位於日本地理的中央位置，高 3776 公尺，是全日境內最高峰，也是日本民族精神的象徵與依歸；其外形輪廓皎美，自古以來便是詩歌、文學、繪畫所歌誦的對象。

山的東、北兩側橫臥著著名的富士五湖，其中以西湖面積最小，開發程度也最低，然而湖的西側卻是觀賞富士山景的最佳地點，遊客在此可以欣賞到富士山最完整的面貌。

Located in the geographic center of Japan, Mount Fuji is 3776 meters in altitude, the highest mountain in Japan. Mount Fuji has long been the emblem and spiritual sanctuary of the Japanese people, and it has become an object of poems, lyrics, literature and paintings due to its beautiful shape.

In the east and west of the mountain lie the well-known five lakes of Fuji, among which, Saiko is the smallest and least developed. However, the west side of Saiko is the best location for observing Mount Fuji. Here, tourists can catch the most complete glimpse of Mount Fuji.

木本明信片
Wood shaving postcard

箱根 Hakone

箱根位於富士山脚下，地處於山谷之中，境內多湖泊，湖水清淨，滑而不膩，是日本著名的溫泉區。全區湖光山色、景色怡人，尤其以卡片中的〝蘆之湖〞水景，最爲著名。蘆之湖乃四千多年前所形成的火山湖，背倚富士山，環湖步道遍植青松翠杉，湖山相映，隨著四季的變化而有不同的景緻和情趣，乃箱根地區的旅遊核心。

Situated at the foot of Mount Fuji, Hakone is surrounded by valleys, with a number of clean-water lakes. As a well-known hot spring, Hakone features beautiful scenery of mountains and lakes, particularly the water scene of Ashinoko depicted by this postcard. Ashinoko is a volcanic lake formed over 4,000 years ago. With Mount Fuji at its back, the lake is circled by pathways where green pines and fir are planted everywhere. The reflections of mountains in the lake, in addition to its seasonal variations, constitute the essence of tourism in Hakone.

RD-125

編後語

「手繪封」的由來

本書所命名的「手繪封」是一種以明信片爲底本的藝術作品，是集繪畫、裱褙、拼貼……等技法的綜合運用。

本書所搜羅的這百餘張手繪封，全爲終戰後日本人所遺留下來的，其中有不少是總督府官員的收藏品，此批作品乃首次公開，創作年代爲明治維新之後的作品，但它確承載了許多台灣及日本文化的縮影。

關於這批「手繪封」的內涵及其美學賞析，已見諸文字內容的闡述。論其歷史背景及日本人製作的用心非但其來有自，而且頗堪玩味……

話說19世紀，法國殖民時代即藉諸殖民地的文化素材，製作成明信片，然而此風似乎亦波及19世紀中葉之後的日本明治維新時期，而形成日本美術風格中的一環。因此，日本以殖民地的文化內涵作爲影像素材製作而成的明信片，也就順理成章；同時，藉著同樣手法，日本大量地以其文化題材創作明信片的情況也就不難想見。

職是，本社出版《台灣影像歷史系列》的第三冊《斯土繪影》承載的正是台島文化的顯影；而本書《典藏手繪封》中整批眞跡作品在台灣的發現，正可略窺日本在殖民台灣期間，一些日本文人雅士親自創作的成績，不管作品內容是以日本文化或以台灣作爲題材，這些作品的共同特色是都無郵票或章戳，足見其在台日人典藏此些眞跡作品大過宣傳日本文化的用心，然而日本人在終戰後，卻將這些作品留在台灣，如今更由本社整理付梓，對日本人來說，恐怕是始料未及的吧！而對於台灣人而言，或以爲這是日本人蓄意留下的一筆文化滲透，然而爲了讓讀者諸君理解這筆極珍貴的文化資產，才是本社出版此書的宗旨所在。

The Origin of "Postcard Drawings"

The "postal hand-paintings" which are the subject of this book are works of art originally created as picture postcards, employing a combination of techniques such as painting, mounting and collage.

The more than 100 hand-painted postcards exhibited herein were all left behing by Japanese people after the end of World War II. A number of these were works privately collected by officials of the colonial government. This is the first time for this selection of works to be publicly displayed. These are pieces of art created since the period of the Meiji Restoration, yet they indubitably comprise a reflection in miniature of much of Taiwanese and Japanese culture.

As for an exploration of the content and aesthetic value of this group of postcard drawings, the reader is sure to have already read the accompanying commentary in this volume. Yet the works' historical background and the creative dedication of the Japanese artists who made them remain a quite interesting story in itself…

During the 19 th century, the colonial-era French borrowed the cultural themes of the lands they colonized as the creative inspiration for postcards. This trend also appears to have affected Meiji-ear Japan during the latter half of the 19 th century, becoming an important element of Japanese artistic style. Therefore, it was a matter of logical progression that the Japanese would produce postcards influenced by the cultural elements of their colony. And it is not hard to imagine how the Japanese, employing similar techniques, came to produce a great number of postcards with such cultural subject matter.

The Drawings of That Land, the third volume of our series *A Collection of the Visual History of Taiwan,* examines the cultural development of the island of Taiwan. In addition, the discovery of the batch of authentic works which appears in this volume, *Postcard Drawings,* offers us a brief glimpse at the personal achievements of many refined Japanese scholars during that period when Japan governed Taiwan as its colony. Regardless of whether the subject matter of the art pieces was derived from Japanese culture or from Taiwan, the special feature which all these works share in common is that none are marked with any form of postage stamp, demonstrating the special care the Japanese people who lived in Taiwan took in collecting these authentic objects of art in order to pass on Japanese culture. However, because after the war the Japanese left these works behind on Taiwan, their appearance today as arranged and published in this volume may very well come as quite a surprise to the Japanese! As for the Taiwanese, some may consider them to be a cultural infiltration intentionally left behind by Japan. Nevertheless, our objective in publishing this volume is to help our readers appreciate these precious culture assets.

參考書目 Reference Books

- 路易斯・弗洛伊斯（葡）　**日歐比較文化，**(Louis Frois, Kulturgegensätze Europa -Japan)，1585；周田章雄譯注，日本岩波書店，1965；范勇、張思齊譯，北京，商務印書館，1992。
- 坂本太郎　**日本史概說，**日本至文堂，1978；汪向榮、武寅、韓鐵英譯，北京商務印書館，1992。
- 余又蓀　**日本史，**台北，中華大典，1966（民國 55）。
- 林明德　**日本史，**台北，三民書局，1986（民國 75）。
- 陳炎鋒　**日本「浮世繪」簡史，**台北，藝術家，1990。
- 李欽賢　**浮世繪大場景——江戶市井生活十帖，**台北，雄獅，1993。
- 李欽賢　**日本美術史話，**台北，雄獅，1993。
- 蔡英傑、蔡鄭淑子　**日本之旅，**高雄，大衆書局，1986（民國 75 再版）。
- 原榮　**浮世繪の諸派，**弘學館，1952。

- ABRAMS, L.E *Japanese prints: A bibliography of monographs in English,* Chapel Hill, University of North Carolina Press, 1977
- AKIYAMA, T. *Japanese painting,* Trans. by J. Emmons. Geneva, Skira, 1961. Reprint. London, Macmillan, 1977.
- BEARDSLEY, R. K. and SMITH, R.J. *Japanese Culture; Its Development and Characteristics,* (*Tenth Pacific Science Congress*), Aldine Publising Co., 1963.
- BORTON, H.*Japan's Modern Century,* Roland Press, 1955.
- ELISSEF, D., and ELISSEF, V. *La civilisation japonaise,* (*Collection Les Grandes Civilisations, 13*), Paris, Arthaud, 1974
- ELISSEF, D., AND ELISSEF, V. *L'art de l'ancien Japon,* Paris, 1985.
- ELISSEF, V. *Japan,* Trans. by J. Hogarth, London, Barrie & Jenkins 1974.
- FEDÉRIC, L. *Japan, art and civilization,*New York, Harry N. Abrams, 1971.
- FRENCH, C.L. *Trough closed doors: western influence on Japanese art 1639－1853,* Rochester, Mick., 1977
- GHIBBETT, D. *The history of Japanese printing and book illustration,* New York, Kodanska International, 1977.
- HALL, J.W. *Japan from prehistory to modern times,* New York, Delacorate, 1970.
- IENAGA, S. *Japanese art: a cultural appreciation,* Trans by R.L. Gage, New York, Weatherhill, 1979.
- IENAGA, S. *Japanese art,* Encyclopaedia Britannica, New York, London, 1933.
- IENAGA, S. *History of Japan,* New York ,Japan Travel Bureau, 1953.

参考書目 Reference Books

- MICHENER, J.A. *Japanese prints, from the early masters to the modern,* Tokyo, Ruttand, C.E. Tuttle Co., 1959.
- MORAOKA, K., and OKAMURA, K. *Folk arts and crafts of Japan,* Trans. by D.D. Stegmaier, New York, Weatherhill, 1973.
- MORRISON, A. *The painters of Japan,* London, Edinburgh, T.C. & E.C. Jack, 1911.
- MUNSTERBERG, H. *The arts of Japan, an illustrated history,* Tokyo, Rutland, 1957.
- MURDOGH, J. *A history of Japan,* New York, F. Ungar, 1964
- NARAZAKI, M. *The Japanese print: its evolution and essence,* Trans. by C.H. Mitchell, Tokyo, Kodansha, 1966.
- NOMA, S. *The arts of Japan,* Trans. and adapted by J. Rosenfield and G.T. Webb, Tokyo, Kodanshg 1966—67.
- REISCHAUER, E.O. *Japan, past and present,* New York, A. Knopf, 1974.
- ROSENFIELD, J.M. and SHIMADA, S. *Traditions of Japanese art,* Cambridge, Fogg Art Museum, Harvard University, 1970.
- SANSON, G.B. *Japan, a short cultural history,* New York, Appleton, Century, Crofts, 1962.
- SANSOM, G.B. *A history of Japan,* Stanford University Press, 1958—63
- SANSOM, G.B. *The western world and Japan,* New York, A. Knopf, 1950.
- SIEFFERT, R. *Le Japon et la France: image d'une découverte,* Paris, Publications orientalistes de France, 1974.
- SMITH, B. *Japan. A history in art,* New York, Doubbly & Company, 1964.
- *Sources of Japanese Tradition,* Columbia University Press, 1960.
- STERN, H.P. *Master prints of Japan: Ukiyoe hanga,* New York, Harry N. Abrams, 1969.
- STERN, H.P *Ukiyoe painting,* Washington, D.C., Smithsonia Institution, 1973.
- STORRY, R. *A History of Modern Japan,* New York, Penguin Books, 1960.
- SUGIMOTO, M., and SWAIN, D.L. *Science and culture in traditional Japan, A. D. 600—1854,* Cambridge, Massachusetts Institute of Technology Press, 1978.
- SWANN, P.C. *A concise history of Japanses art,* Tokyo, Kodanska International, 1979.
- TAKAHASHI, S. *Traditional woodblock prints of Japan,* Trans. by R. Stanley-Baker, New York, Weatherhill, 1972.
- TAMBURELLO, A. *Japan,* Paris, Frenand Nathan, 1975.
- TERADA, T. *Japanese art in world perspective,* Trans. by T. Guerin, New York, Weatherhill, 1976

參考書目 Reference Books

- TSUDA, N. *Handbook of Japanese art,* Rutland, C.E. Tuttle Co., 1976.
- TSUNODA, R., DEBARY, T., and KEENE, D. *Sources of the Japanese tradition,* New York, Columbia University Press, 1958.
- UYENO, N. *Japanese arts and crafts in the Meiji era,* Tokyo, Pan-Pacific Press, 1958.
- VARLEY, H.P. *Japanese culture: a short history,* New York, Praeger, 1973.
- VIE, M. *Histoire du Japon des origines a Meiji,* Paris, Presses Universitaires de France, 1969.
- WICHMANN, S. *Japonisme: the Japanese influence on western art since 1858,* London, Thames and Hudson
- YASHIRO, Y. *Two thousand years of Japanese art,* New York, Harry N. Abrams, 1958.
- YOSHIKAWA, I. *Major themes in Japanese art,*Trans. by A. Nikovskis New York, Weatherhill, 1976.

臺灣影像歷史系列

典藏手繪封

A Collection of the Visual History of Taiwan

POSTCARD DRAWINGS—THE RARE COLLECTION

編審委員：陳奇祿(召集人)、丘秀芷、石明江、李欽賢、吳文星
林衡道、施添福、唐　羽、夏目志郎、高橋正己
陳宏博、陳秋坤、陳景容、陳淑華、童春發、黃秀政
雷永泰、鄭淑敏、蔡中涵、龍冠軍、簡榮聰、蘇玉珍
(依姓氏筆劃排列之)

撰　　文：陳淑華

發 行 人：藍世彬
社　　長：周　鼎
副 社 長：林美欄
執 行 長：黃嘉志
總 編 輯：施淑宜
編輯顧問：陳宇佐、陳秋隆、黃子康、黃明正、黃傑閱、李歸坵
吳德勝
企劃顧問：丁博祥、周元宇、黃　新、胡超群、陳榮財、王永慶
呂代豪、鄭文郎、邵逸軒、黃政旭、陳進權
執行編輯：夏靜凝
採訪編輯：黎晉禎、潘玉芳、劉謦豪、方水源
資料編輯：蔡弘武、陶威妮
美術編輯：蔡瓔竹、楊傳芳
法律顧問：王存淦律師、John Kenehan, Esq.
攝　　影：彭延平、劉姵君、張修政、陳耀欽
印　　務：陳元慶、沈昭翰
英文翻譯：曾文忠、王志遠
英文校訂：Brent Heinrich(韓伯龍)
日文名詞校訂：李欽賢、高橋正己
封面設計：李男工作室
照相打字：美吉電腦照相排版有限公司
打字排版：正豐電腦排版有限公司
製版印刷：紅藍彩藝印刷股份有限公司
裝　　訂：精益裝訂股份有限公司
出 版 者：立虹出版社
出版日期：85年 9 月初版
出版登記字號：局版北市業字第360號
社　　址：臺北市光復南路296號8F-1
電　　話：886-2-777-2245　傳真：886-2-721-4854
郵政劃撥：帳戶：立虹出版社　帳號：18791202
海外總經銷：Rainbow Sign Trading Co., Ltd.,
1905 E. Charleston Blvd.,
Las Vegas, NV, 89104, USA
電話：(702)382-7966　傳真：(702)362-1765

■定價：新台幣3600元

■本書紙張採用特製150磅象牙雪銅

■如有缺頁、破損，請寄回本公司更換

Editing Advisor：Chen, Chi - Lu／Chiu, Hsiu - Chih／Shir, Ming - Chiang／
Lee, Chin - Hsien／Wu, Wen - Hsing／Lin, Heng - Tao／Shih, Tien-Fu／
Tang, Yu／Willing S. Natsume／Taka Hashi Masami／Chen, Hung - Po／
Chen, Chiu Kun／Chen, Ching - Jung／Chen, Shu - Hua／
Masegseg Jingror／Huang, Hsiu - Cheng／Lei, Yung - Tai／
Cheng, Shu - Min／Saflo Katsao／General Lon／Chyen, Jung - Tsong／
Gertrude Su

Author：Chen, Shu - Hwa

Publisher：Lan, Shih - Ping
President：Dean T. Chou
Vice-President：Lin, Mei - Lan
Chief Executive Officer：Huang, Chia - Chih
Chief Editor：Connie Shih Shu - Yi
Editing Consultants：Chen, Yu - Tsuo／Chen, Chiu - Lung／Richard Wong／
Huang, Ming - Chen／Huang, Chieh - Yueh／Lee, Kuei - Chou／
Wu, Teh - Sheng
Planning Consultants：Ding, Po - Hsiang／Chou, Yuen - Yu／Xin L. Wong／
Hu, Chao - Chun／Gary Chen／Wang, Yong Ching／
David Lu Tai - Hao／Cheng, Wen - Lang／Shao, Yi - Hsuen／
Huang, Cheng - Hsu／Chen, Chin - Chuen
Executive editors：Hsia, Ching - Ning
News Editors：Li, Chin - Chen／Joyce Pan／Liu, Ching - Hao／Fang, Shuei Yuen
Materials Editors：Tsai, Hung - Wu／Tao, Winy
Arts Editors：Trista Tsai／Yang, Chuan - Fang
Law Consultant：Wang, Tsuen - Kan
Copyright Attorney：John Kenehan, Esq.
Photographers：Peng, Yen - Ping／Liu, Pei - Chun／Chang, Hsiu - Cheng／
Chen, Yao - Chin
Printing Supervisor：Tony Chen／Shen, Chao - Han
English Translators：Joseph Tseng／Wang, Chin - Yuen
English Proofreader：Brent Heinrich
Japanese Terminology Proofreader：Lee, Chin - Hsien／Taka Hashi Masami
Cover Designer：Lee, Nan Studio
Photo Typing：Mikey Computer Photo Type - Setting Co., Ltd.
Typing／Type - Setting：Cheng Feng Computer Type - setting Co., Ltd.
Engraving／Printing：Red & Blue Color Printing Co., Ltd.
Binding：Ching Yi Binding Co., Ltd.
Publishing Company：Rainbow Sign Publishing Company
Date of Publication：September 1996 1st Edition
Publication Registration No.：Chu - Pan - Pei - shih - yeh - tzu No. 360
Office Address：8F - 1, No.296, Kuang Fu South Rd., Taipei, Taiwan R.O.C.
Tel No.：886-2-777-2245　**Fax No.**：886-2-721-4854
Post Box No.：P.O.Box No. 80-91, Taipei, Taiwan
Postal A／C Name：Rainbow Sign Publishing Company
Postal A／C No.：18791202
Distributor：Rainbow Sign Trading Co., Ltd.,
1905 E. Charleston Blvd.,
Las Vegas, NV, 89104, USA
Tel. No.：(702)382-7966　**Fax. No**：(702)362-1765

* Price：US$129.00
* The paper used for printing is specially mat-finish coated
* In case of skip leaf and damages, please sent the book back by mail to the publishing company for replacement.
*

台灣影像歷史系列
A Collection of the Visual History of Taiwan

■**見證——台灣總督府(1895~1945)上、下冊**
Witness—The Colonial Taiwan (1895~1945) Volume Ⅰ、Ⅱ

■**斯土繪影(1895~1945)**
The Drawings of That Land—The Interpretation of Taiwan(1895~1945)

■**典藏手繪封**
Postcard Drawings—The Rare Collection

■**海國圖索——台灣自然地理開發(1895~1945)**
The Landscape of the Island Country—The Development of the Natural Geography of Taiwan(1895~1945)

■**高砂春秋——台灣原住民之文化藝術**
The Exquisite Heritage—The Culture and Arts of Taiwan Aborigines

■**開台尋跡**
Strolling the old Trails

■**蓬萊舊庄——台灣城鄉聚落(1895~1945)**
The Abodes in the Bygone Era—Taiwan's Town and Country Settlements(1895~1945)

■**台灣古書契(1717~1895)**
Archaic Land Documents of Taiwan(1717~1895)

■**殖產方略——台灣產業開發(1895~1945)**
The Schemes of Production—Taiwan's Industrial Development(1895~1945)

■光碟、錄影、圖片、圖書製作
CD Rom / Video, Illustrations, Books Production.

典藏手繪封=Postcard drawings： the rare collection／陳淑華撰文. --初版. --臺北市 ： 立虹, 民85
面 ； 公分.--(臺灣影像歷史系列)
參考書目：面
ISBN 957-99222-4-1(精裝)

1.美術 - 臺灣 - 歷史 - 日據時期(1895-1945)

909.278 85010202